RED WHEELS TURNING

Red Wheels Turning: A Novel of The Great European War

Hugh Ashton

ISBN-13: 978-1-912605-48-4

ISBN-10: 1-91-260548-1

Published by j-views Publishing, 2018

DISCLAIMER

The events described in this book are, of course, fictitious and take place in a branch of history that never existed. However, some of the characters and places described and mentioned here have a place in our real history. As far as possible, these characters behave as they did in real life, only in different circumstances. All other characters are fictitious, and bear no intentional resemblance to real life individuals.

www.j-views.biz

publish@j-views.biz

www.HughAshtonBooks.info

j-views Publishing, 26 Lombard Street, Lichfield WS13 6DR, UK

ALSO BY HUGH ASHTON:

Tales of Old Japanese
At the Sharpe End
Beneath Gray Skies
The Untime
The Untime Revisited
Leo's Luck
Angels Unawares

SHERLOCK HOLMES TITLES:

Tales from the Deed Box of John H. Watson MD
More from the Deed Box of John H. Watson MD
Secrets from the Deed Box of John H. Watson MD
The Darlington Substitution
The Trepoff Murder
The Deed Box of John H. Watson MD
Notes from the Dispatch-Box of John H. Watson MD
Further Notes from the Dispatch-Box of John H. Watson MD
The Death of Cardinal Tosca
Without My Boswell
Last Notes from the Dispatch-Box of John H. Watson MD
1894
Some Singular Cases of Mr. Sherlock Holmes

FOR CHILDREN:

Sherlock Ferret and the Missing Necklace
Sherlock Ferret and the Multiplying Masterpieces
Sherlock Ferret and the Poisoned Pond
Sherlock Ferret and the Phantom Photographer
The Adventures of Sherlock Ferret

Hugh Ashton was born in the United Kingdom, and moved to Japan in 1988, where he lived until a return to the UK in 2016.

He is best known for his Sherlock Holmes stories, which have been hailed as some of the most authentic pastiches on the market, and have received favourable reviews from Sherlockians and non-Sherlockians alike.

He currently divides his time between the historic cities of Lichfield, and Kamakura, a little to the south of Yokohama, with his wife, Yoshiko.

More about Hugh Ashton and his books may be found at: hughashtonbooks.info

Foreword

Red Wheels Turning is set in the same timeline as *Beneath Gray Skies*, a few years before the events described there. This story introduces Brian Finch-Malloy, described by one reviewer of *Beneath Gray Skies* as "a 1920s James Bond".

The *Netopyr* actually existed much as described here. An amazing piece of Russian engineering, it never became a practical weapon put into production, for many of the reasons that Brian and Harry point out. However, it remains one of the most amazing objects in the history of warfare, seemingly more a product of the Middle Ages than the twentieth century. The *Zaamurets* armoured train also existed in real life. There seem to be remarkably few detailed descriptions of these vehicles, though, so I have been forced to invent some details, which I hope retain consistency with the sparse known facts. Of course, there may be more in Russian, which is a language I do not read with any fluency.

Since no Americans (or Confederates) appear on-stage in this novel, I have used British English throughout (my native version of the language). I hope this doesn't upset my American readers too much.

⁂

A note on units: in real life, pre-Revolutionary Russia used its own units; poods, versts, and so on, at the time that *Red Wheels Turning* is set, and only adopted the metric system in 1924. Since most readers will be unfamiliar with these units of measurement, I have given metric (or in some cases, Imperial) equivalents.

As far as I am aware, all pictures and diagrams of the *Netopyr* used here (including the cover photos) are in the public domain.

Acknowledgments in the Inknbeans edition

AS ALWAYS, THANKS ARE DUE to my wife, Yoshiko, for her patience while I churn out my books. To all my friends, the physical friends whom I know personally, as well as my e-friends on Twitter and Facebook, thanks for your comments and encouragement. Simon Varnam in particular has once again lent me his eyes and ears to discover my errors of style and fact. Any still remaining are my responsibility, not his.

And Jo at Inknbeans continues to provide invaluable support for my work, not only as an editor and publisher, but as a friend and source of energy and inspiration.

❧

Kamakura, March 2015

SINCE THIS WAS written , I am sorry to report that my editor and friend Jo, died, and Inknbeans Press ceased to be. It has been hard to make the adjustment, knowing that she is no longer there to cast a critical but friendly eye over my work.

❧

Lichfield, May 2018

RED WHEELS TURNING

A NOVEL OF THE GREAT EUROPEAN WAR

HUGH ASHTON

J-VIEWS PUBLISHING, LICHFIELD, UK

Chapter 1: The trenches, Flanders, autumn 1915

"Dash it all, he's hardly what you would call a gentleman, is he?"

L IEUTENANT BRIAN FINCH-MALLOY stood rigidly at attention as Lieutenant-Colonel Wilkins, his commanding officer, addressed him.

"I don't know what you've been up to, young Finch-Malloy, but you seem to have attracted the attention of those secret Intelligence chappies in London. I'm ordered to release you from the delights of this pleasure garden, and to return you to the hell of Blighty, where you are to report for duty to some infernal pit in London, the existence of which I became aware for the first time today. And that, Lieutenant, leaves me with a hole in my command that's going to be hard to fill. What have you to say to all this?"

The news came as a shock to Brian. He hadn't been angling for a transfer, and as far as he knew, there was no reason for London ever to have heard his name, let alone ask for him. There was nothing useful for him to say, so he remained silent.

"Humph. Well, I don't know what to say to you, either. This is the first time that anything like this has happened to me."

Not surprising, thought Brian. The Lieutenant-Colonel ("Wobbler Wilkins" to the rest of the world, when he was out of earshot, so called because of his pendulous jowls, as well as his seeming inability to come to a decision on any subject) had come straight into the muddy hell of Mons from the barracks in England, where he had been in charge of the regimental mascot and ceremonial parades, never having heard a shot fired in anger. His present elevated rank was chiefly the result of more senior officers' retirement, rather than any military skills or his own political machinations. His family connections hadn't hurt, either, mess gossip whispered, pointing to his wife, the daughter of a prominent member of the Cabinet. It would be good to be far away from the man and his constant ineptitude, thought Brian, remembering the times when he had had to argue forcefully, sometimes practically to the point of insubordination, against the older man's harebrained schemes to fight the Germans in their trenches almost as if they were dressed in red coats, re-fighting the battle of Waterloo with muskets. Brian's own battle tactics leaned towards what his superiors frowned on as "ungentlemanly"; camouflaged night raiding parties, fighting savagely and mercilessly in grimly silent battles against the German sentries and machine-gun posts. Ungentlemanly he might be, thought Brian, but he'd been effective.

"So off you go, I suppose," Wilkins said, shrugging his shoulders. "I can't really argue with these Whitehall johnnies when they start to put their feet down. Who do you suggest should take your place and lead your band of thuggees in their nocturnal rambles, then?"

"I think it's time that Sergeant Braithwaite got his commission, sir. He has an excellent tactical sense, and he has a born gift for getting the men to follow him."

As expected, this produced a snort. "I can't have a fellow called

Braithwaite as an officer in my battalion. Good God, man. He may be a clever chap and all that, but dash it all, he's hardly what you would call a gentleman, is he? I mean, can you see the fellow at the formal Mess Nights or the Regimental Ball?"

Brian silently counted to ten, slowly and deliberately. He took a deep breath. "With all due respect, sir, he has vastly more experience than anyone else in the battalion. And something tells me that he probably wouldn't enjoy the company of the officers' mess that much. It seems to me that being what you call a gentleman might be a handicap rather than an advantage where we are right now. But of course, sir, if you feel that it's more important that an officer speaks with the right accent rather than his being able to do a good job, then that's your decision." After a short pause he added a "Sir".

Wilkins flushed. He knew that Brian was baiting him, but couldn't put his finger exactly on what it was that was annoying him. "Very good, Finch-Malloy," he replied, returning tit for tat as best he could manage under the circumstances. "I will treat your thoughts on the matter with all the attention and respect that they deserve."

Brian flushed in his turn, but held his peace. He only had to put up with the pompous old fool for a day or so at the most. Just as long as it took to get away from this muddy hell-hole. He saluted as smartly as any Sandhurst cadet. "Permission to arrange the transport back to London, sir?"

"Yes, damn you. Dismissed."

Brian saluted again, did an insolently perfect about turn and marched smartly out of the room, closing the door behind him. On his way back to the trench where his platoon was billeted, he ran into Sergeant Harry Braithwaite.

"Harry," he called. "Over here." When the two were out of earshot of others, they used Christian names. In public, they used the usual addresses of rank. In the six months they had known each other and fought together, they had developed a mutual respect and friendship that cut across the usual rigid class boundaries of the British Army. The constant shared strain of the artillery bombardments, and the danger and terror of the nerve-racking raids on the enemy trenches had removed Harry Braithwaite's natural deference to his social superiors in Brian's case, especially when he discovered that the other's skill in swearing and his creative use of profanity could outclass that of even a veteran Regimental Sergeant-Major. It hadn't hurt matters, either, that Brian had saved him from serious injury, if not death, several times. Brian, for his part, had little time for the kind of snobbery that so many of his fellow-officers displayed, preferring to judge others on, as he put it, the contents of their heads, rather than that of their fathers' bank accounts. He'd long ago dropped the English public school habit of addressing his friends by their surname, and he expected them to call him by his Christian name.

"You look a bit down in the mouth, Brian," remarked Harry, accepting the cigarette that Brian offered him.

"Do I?" replied Brian. "It must be the thought of leaving this charming holiday spot and this picturesque residence we are currently inhabiting." He gestured to the bunker, and the ankle-deep mud leading to it.

"Going on leave, then?" asked the sergeant. "Seems to me you're a bit overdue for it."

"Wish that's all it was," replied Brian. "No, some bloody crowd in Whitehall has written to HQ and asked for me. Some sort of secret intelligence outfit. I'll be out of here tomorrow or the next day. It looks like they're in a hurry, but God knows why."

"Sounds exciting. Anyway, you'll be well out of this muck,"

pointing in his turn to the mud all around them. "So you'll have a cushy little desk number all lined up, then?"

"God, I hope not," replied Brian. "If that's what they have in mind for me, I'm going to demand that I come straight back here."

"So you're going to be one of those spies, you think? Going behind enemy lines and counting guns and reporting back where the next offensive's going to start? Now that sounds like something I could get into."

"Quite honestly, Harry, I don't know. I'm just more than a bit peeved at having to leave you and the blokes, though."

"Oh, don't talk daft. You know you'll have forgotten us in a week or two once you're back in Blighty. You'll be too busy having a good time."

"That's a very long way from the truth, Sergeant," said Brian. He had just spotted one of his platoon's corporals walking along the trench towards them.

"Sir?" asked Harry, taking his cue from Brian.

"Damn it, I didn't ask for this posting. I won't pretend we're living the life of Riley out here, or that this is the most comfortable I've ever been in my life, but we're a team, and I don't want to leave you chaps suddenly like this with too many loose ends flapping in the breeze. I can tell you, Harry," (the corporal was now out of sight and earshot) "I see trouble coming your way. I told old Wobbler Wilkins that you should be commissioned and take my place, and he nearly burst a blood vessel. Expect trouble from there."

"Just a thought," said Harry. "What would happen to the platoon if I was to leave at the same time as you?"

"I suppose they could promote Hawkins to sergeant, and bring in a subaltern from the rear. But you're not going anywhere."

"You're going to need an assistant in your new job, aren't you?"

Brian looked at Harry, astonished, and then started to laugh. "And why the hell not? That's a bloody good idea. You know, I'm really looking forward to seeing old Wobbler's face when we go in and tell him you're leaving with me."

"You really reckon you can make it happen?" asked Harry.

"Trust me," replied Brian.

❧

Chapter 2: The Imperial Weapons Testing ground, Kubinka, Russia

"It is a great step forward. Time for a vodka."

Nikolai Nikolaivich Lebedenko adjusted the cable connecting the clutch lever to the engine assembly, for what he hoped was the final time.

"Let her go!" he called to his nephew, Boris, standing by the controls. Obediently, Boris yanked on the clutch lever, only to have the cable snap.

"You pulled it too hard, you dumb ox!" called his uncle, turning off the engine. "Your turn to fix it this time. Oh, never mind, we'll do it together."

The two men swore as they picked up the broken ends of the cable. "If only we'd been given a decent grant from the Ministry, we could have had it all working properly by now," complained Boris. His cousin, Alexander, joined them as his uncle replied.

"Well, we weren't, and we're not getting it from the Ministry, even if we are allowed to work here at Kubinka. His Imperial Majesty is funding us, as and when he feels like it, and whenever he remembers us, which I have to admit isn't that often at the moment. We're going to have to do the best we can with what we've got here and now. We're at war, remember," said Lebedenko.

"Which is exactly why we should be given the money by the government on a regular basis," answered Alexander. "This will make sausage meat of the Germans, and strudel out of the Austrians if we can only persuade those Petrograd bureaucrats of how we're going to win the war for them while they sit on their fat arses. And we'll only do that if we get the money. There's no way we should be relying on the goodwill of an imbecile who only has money because his father was an imbecile before him. Sausage meat and strudels," he repeated. "That's what this could make of them."

"I'll make good Russian borscht out of you if you don't pass me that wrench in a minute, and stop spouting that revolutionary rubbish," his uncle retorted. "You should know better than to say things like that in public in any case." The three men worked in silence for a while, sweating as they tightened bolts and adjusted fastenings.

Eventually the clutch was fixed. "I think I'd better try it this time," said Nikolai. "You two are like a couple of drunken oxen when I let you anywhere near the controls. This may be a big machine, but it needs a delicate touch."

Boris carefully adjusted the carburettor and the Maybach engine started with a bang and a clatter. Nikolai grasped the clutch lever. "One, two, three and..." He gently pulled on the left lever, and the motor wheel lowered itself slowly onto the driving wheel, pressed against it by a powerful leaf spring. With a wheeze, the enormous wheel started to turn, spinning the massive machine in a circle. Boris started to cheer. "And now..." said Nikolai, pushing hard against the force of the spring to disengage the motor wheel. The spinning stopped. "Whew! That was hard work," said Nikolai. "We're going to have to do something to make that a bit easier for the drivers."

"But it worked, Uncle Kolya," pointed out Alexander. "You're a genius."

"Hardly," replied Lebedenko, shaking his head. "There's a lot more to do. Much, much more. But at least we know we can make the thing move and that the basic idea of the driving mechanism works at full scale. On one side, anyway." His natural Russian pessimism seemed to outweigh his nephew's triumph, but his face cheered. "You're right, Sasha. It is a great step forward. Time for a vodka."

"Or two," said Boris.

"Or two, Borya," agreed Nikolai. "But let's keep it to no more than three."

⁂

THE YOUNG ENGINEER left his uncle and his cousin drinking with their colleague, Zhukovsky, celebrating the success of the test of the drive mechanism.

When he had been living in England a few years previously, he had made contact with various Russian malcontents, including the socialist and anarchist friends of the brother of a plotter, Aleksandr Ilyich Ulyanov, who had been executed for his part in the attempted assassination of the then Tsar, Alexander III. Ulyanov's younger brother, Vladimir, had become the leader of a small group of revolutionaries, and was now living in self-imposed exile in Switzerland, waiting for the right time to light the fire to burn away the corruption and filth of the Old Russia.

When the engineer's contacts from the Swiss exile group had learned of what he was working on in Kubinka, they had eagerly demanded details. At least one of the revolutionaries had interested himself in the massive machine, and saw its potential as a way of helping the revolution to come to pass. Certainly it seemed to him that if Uncle Kolya's vision ever became a workable reality, and enough reliable machines could be constructed by the revolutionaries, it was certain that the Imperial troops would be mopped up and the revolution would succeed, wiping out the Tsar and his ministers, and ensuring the death of capitalism throughout Russia.

He reported every major development on the machine, whether the design or the actual working machine itself, to his local revolutionary cell organiser, who passed it on through the international network until it reached Switzerland. He heard little in return, but assumed that his reports were useful, as they were still requested. At least, no-one had told him to stop sending them.

He returned to his own room and pulled a pen and paper from his desk drawer. Frowning with concentration, he started to write his report of the day's doings, pointing out the strengths and the weaknesses of the design as he saw them.

He signed the report using his revolutionary pseudonym, and folded the report into an envelope. Tomorrow, on his way to the proving ground, he would leave the papers in a hollow birch tree; the agreed dead drop for the messages he exchanged with the Bolshevik leaders.

Chapter 3: Whitehall, London

*"I seem to have acquired two of the finest potential
agents I have come across in a number of years."*

"YOU APPEAR TO HAVE STRANGELY MULTIPLIED, Finch-Malloy," remarked C, the head of the British Secret Service, blinking over the top of his wire-rimmed spectacles at Brian. "There seem to be two of you, when I requested one. Sit down, for God's sake, man, and don't stand at attention like that. We're not in the bloody army now. Do you know why I asked for you?"

"No, sir," replied Brian. The enigmatically-named C was unlike anyone Brian had ever met before. A full head and a half shorter than Brian, and with a mere fringe of hair round his otherwise completely bald head, he would have seemed like yet another senior officer with no obvious talent other than boot-licking, except that he seemed to know exactly what was going on all around him and to react to it smoothly and efficiently. In the ten minutes since Brian had entered the office, waiting for his interview to begin, C must have read through thirty pages of reports, signed several other documents, and read the *Times* leading articles and agony column, making notes on the latter, almost absentmindedly, while doing all this other work. Brian decided this was not a man to be underestimated.

"Well, I'll tell you why you're here, Finch-Malloy. It's because your commanding officers complained about you to their superiors."

"I'm sorry if I caused trouble, sir."

C chuckled. "Quite the reverse, Finch-Malloy. You were marked down as a trouble-maker because you thought for yourself and refused to obey the instructions of your superiors." Brian started to protest, but C held up a hand. "Hear me out. I have standing orders that reports on people like you should arrive on my desk. Of course, most of them turn out to be nothing but the kind of idiot who can't follow orders. But a few, like you," C smiled, "turn out to be people who can think for themselves." The smile left his face. "But, Finch-Malloy, tell me how on earth you have this," glancing at a piece of paper, "Sergeant Harry Braithwaite in tow with you? I've never heard of the man, don't know him from Adam, and want to know just what the hell you think you're up to dragging him here and wasting my time. I want a good answer from you before I send him – and you – back to where you came from."

"Well, sir, we had a bit of a problem. When you sent those orders for me, there was no officer left to replace me as leader of the platoon, and Colonel Wilkins wasn't that keen on giving Sergeant Braithwaite his commission. So, thinking that two heads could be better than one in your line of work, sir, I took the liberty of persuading Colonel Wilkins to let the Sergeant travel with me." C said nothing, but cocked his head on one side, and looked at Brian curiously. "The Sergeant and I have been through a lot together and we work as a team."

"You'd describe your relationship with him as friendly, then?"

"Most certainly, sir. We've trusted each other with our lives on many different occasions and I have great respect for his intelligence and personality. Quite frankly, sir, if Sergeant Braithwaite had been to a better school, he would be commanding me, rather than the other way round."

"You're a Harrow and Brasenose man, I see. And Sergeant Braithwaite?"

"Well, he's certainly not a University man. And I believe he went to Nantwich Grammar School. He taught himself a lot about mechanical engineering and cars, and even went to Germany for a year or so after he'd left school to learn more there. After that, he became a chauffeur and mechanic. His German is pretty fluent, by the way."

"Well, I can't really see that background recommending itself to Wilkins," C commented. "I've had to meet Wilkins on a number of occasions and been slightly underwhelmed each time." Brian smiled at C's remark. "And you can keep that opinion of mine to yourself. If you join our little outfit, you're going to have to get used to keeping secrets. But the Sergeant's mechanical skills and his German could well be useful in this line of work, especially with what I have in mind for you. You're right there."

"Sir?" Brian kept his tone of voice neutral.

"So, young Finch-Malloy, apart from a set of enviable skills in underhand brawling, what do you bring to us?" He picked up a sheet of paper and perused it. "School fencing champion. Hah. Half-blue for fencing at Oxford in your first year there. Not a team player, it would seem. Hunting man, are you?"

"Afraid not, sir. Horses and I seem to disagree with each other. Never really seen the point of dressing up in a red coat and chasing foxes, either."

"Don't worry about it, Finch-Malloy. I tend to associate the hunting crowd with fools like Wilkins." He continued reading. "School chess champion. Interesting."

"I was taught as a boy by a Russian, sir. A friend of my mother's."

"That would be Vladimir Ilyich Ulyanov, I take it? At the time he was living in London, using the Reading Room of the British Museum?"

"Yes, sir. At least, I suppose so. He was living in London, anyway. At my age I'd never even heard of the Reading Room. I used to go to the Museum to frighten myself with the Egyptian mummies." Brian didn't bother to hide his surprise that C knew of Ulyanov.

"I take it that you've somewhat lost touch with Vladimir Ilyich over the past few years, then?"

"I haven't seen or heard anything of him for over ten years now, I suppose. Since I was about ten or eleven."

"Well, you may be interested to know that he is now the leader of a rather noisy group of exiled Russian socialists who call themselves 'Bolsheviks'."

"The majority party, sir? Are they that important?"

"By no means. It's just a title they gave themselves after defeating another faction in a debate. And that other faction would be..?" C paused, testing Brian's reaction.

"Mensheviks, sir?"

"Excellent. Did Ulyanov teach you your Russian, as well as teaching you chess?"

"A little, sir. But I've taught myself a bit."

"Good with languages are you? French? German? As well as Russian?"

"Pretty much fluent in all of those, sir." Brian was almost apologetic. "I do seem to have a bit of a gift that way. My Dutch can pass for native as well."

"Any others?"

"My Serbian is a bit rusty, but it will pass, and my Czech's good enough for me to be taken for a Czech-speaking Austrian. Spanish and Portuguese are a bit weaker than they should be."

C put his hands over his ears in mock horror. "That's enough.

And you've certainly distinguished yourself in battle. That VC of yours—"

Brian interrupted him. "Please, sir. I'd rather not discuss that. I didn't deserve the decoration, as I pointed out at the time. The credit belongs to Sergeant Braithwaite."

"Then I suppose that's whom I'm going to have to talk to next. Do you want to be in the room while I ask him just what the hell he thinks he's doing, following you around like this? Or is he big enough to wipe his own nose?"

Brian grinned. "He's a big boy, sir. He can take care of himself."

C grinned back. "Then you wait outside while I talk to him. I'll call you in when I want you."

BRIAN FOUND HIMSELF a seat in the anteroom as a very nervous Harry Braithwaite was shown into C's office.

"It's all right, Harry, he's on our side," he had whispered, with a confidence he didn't completely feel. He had settled down with a Portuguese dictionary and a copy of *The Lusiads*, trying to make sense of the seventeenth-century epic to improve his Portuguese. It wasn't easy going, and he was wondering if this was really the best way to improve his language skills, when C's office door opened, and C himself appeared in the doorway.

"Enter," he invited, smiling. As Brian resumed the seat that he had occupied previously, he exchanged glances with Harry, who gave him a surreptitious wink, unnoticed by C.

Seating himself behind the desk, C continued smiling. "Excellent," he told Brian. "I seem to have acquired two of the finest potential agents I have come across in a number of years. Sergeant Braithwaite has acquainted me with some of the details of the past six months that you omitted to tell me, young Finch-Malloy, and I can fill in some of the remaining gaps regarding the Sergeant for myself. So I am happy to tell you both that if you agree, and I assume you do, or you wouldn't be here, you will from now on be reporting here, rather than to your regiment. For the record, you will remain on the roster of the Guards, but you will not be required to wear uniform. Indeed, for many of the duties you will be performing, a uniform would be a positive disadvantage. However, it is only fair to warn you that if you are captured by the enemy while you are out of uniform, you will almost certainly be shot or hanged as spies. Hmm." He sat back and sucked his pen, regarding the other two for their reaction. There was none. "In due course, I will require your signatures on various pieces of paper, but for now, I just require your word that what I am about to tell you will be going no further. I have your words on this?" Both men nodded. "Good. Then I will be introducing you to Colonel Petrov." He pressed a button on his desk, and a secretary entered. "Harris, please send a message to Colonel Alex Petrov and ask him to come over here as soon as possible – say two this afternoon." He turned back to the other two. "Colonel Alexei Dimitrovich Petrov is, as you have probably guessed, a Russian. He is currently here as a liaison officer to co-operate with the Service. He has some English, but it may be easier for you to speak Russian or German with him if communication starts to break down. I must say, Sergeant, that your knowledge of German and technical matters you picked up when you lived and worked in Germany makes you an ideal candidate for this mission that we will be discussing later."

"Can you tell us more now, sir?" asked Harry.

"In very brief and sketchy terms, I am afraid, Sergeant. I don't know if you are aware, but I come from a naval rather than an army background, and my technical knowledge of dry land is limited. Let me start by asking you a question, Sergeant. What is the biggest obstacle facing you chaps in the trenches? Other than the obvious answer of the Boche, that is."

"That's an easy one, sir. It's the blooming mud. Those artillery bombardments may soften up the enemy, but they don't do a bloody thing about the wire – begging your pardon for the language, sir, and they churn up the mud like you wouldn't believe. Up to your knees or worse after the rain's come down overnight."

"That confirms my understanding of the situation. Now, suppose there was a way to get the artillery right up to the German trenches and blast away at the machine-gun nests point-blank, so that the infantry could follow?"

Harry shook his head. "Couldn't be done, sir. One, the Jerries would just blow the guns and limbers to bits as they crossed No Man's Land. Two, that is if they could cross at all. What with the mud and the wire and all, there's no bloody way a gun team could make it, even if no-one was shooting at them." In his animation, Harry seemed to have forgotten that he was addressing a high-ranking officer.

"Not afraid to speak your mind, are you, Sergeant? No, don't apologise, I like it. Shows you've got brains and spirit. Unlike some I could mention. Well, I think that Colonel Petrov may have something to tell you that will make you think again."

Chapter 4: Zurich, Switzerland

VLADIMIR ILYICH ULYANOV yawned and stretched, contorting his strangely Asiatic face, as he reached for his pen.

"If only those fools would turn their guns in the right direction," he grumbled to the notepad where he was writing the draft of an article on the revolution. "The Russian people should be struggling together with the German proletariat to throw off the capitalist yoke and seize power."

"It will only happen with us at the helm, Vladimir Ilyich," pointed out his companion, Grigory Zinoviev, reaching for his tea. "There is a lack of political consciousness there that will never be fully remedied unless we go over there ourselves and seize the initiative to lead the masses." He sipped, wincing. "When will these damned Swiss learn to make decent tea? I want to be in Russia again."

Ulyanov turned his deep-set eyes on his colleague. "Comrade Zinoviev, you seem to be forgetting that while we work tirelessly for the advancement of the Revolution here in Switzerland where, although there may not be decent tea or vodka, there is at least a modicum of peace, and a minimum of capitalist interference. Between us and Petrograd lie several thousand kilometres of hellish war between two enemies, either of which would gladly turn their guns away from the other to point at us, and would make common cause to seize any opportunity to imprison and silence us. We must continue our work here, Comrade. We must continue to work from afar for the comrades still in Russia. But when the time comes—" his eyes glittered. "When the time comes," he repeated, "we will strike. Strike mercilessly and smash them in the teeth. Never fear, Comrade, that time will come. In the meantime we must make ready." He bent again to his writing.

"Comrade," interrupted Zinoviev, before the pen had written even a couple of words more. "I had news today from one of our comrades in Russia. I truly believe that it would be in our best interests if at least one of us could make his way there soon. If the report I received today is true, then we have the Revolution as good as won as soon as we reach Russia." Ulyanov cocked his head. "This is the monstrous war machine I mentioned earlier that can annihilate all that stands in its path. One or two of these on our side, and the Tsar could send his whole army against us and fail. Or, should the Tsar have one or two of these machines, all the spirit of the Revolution would break against it like waves on a rocky shore, and with as little effect. Vladimir Ilyich, it is essential that we secure control of this machine, or at the very least, ensure that the Tsar never gets control of it."

"I would remind you, Comrade, that revolutions come through the spirit of the proletariat. Not through machines alone. Though machines may have their uses," he admitted. "Remind me again. How does this comrade know about this infernal engine?"

"He's a nephew of the inventor, who is developing the machine for the Tsar. He is devoted to our cause. Apparently he has been in contact with Dzhugashvili and his group."

"This development of the machine for the Tsarist reactionaries is being undertaken in exchange for money, I take it? That is the way that things are done in a capitalist society, after all."

"Yes, the inventor, Lebedenko, seems to be driven chiefly by a lust for gold. Which, in this particular case, seems to be provided directly from the Tsar's own pocket."

"So, Comrade Zinoviev, your suggestion on how we should proceed with this matter?"

"We send one of our – shall we say more muscular? – comrades to Moscow, armed with several thousand roubles. And a revolver."

"You would give the inventor a choice? Gold or lead?"

"Indeed I would. From what I understand, we may need the services of the inventor to perfect the machine, as it is not at a fully working stage at the moment, and it would be advisable to have at least the semblance of co-operation from him."

"Very well. And your suggestion for the choice of this muscular comrade?"

"I would strongly suggest Comrade Kolinski. He is dedicated to the cause, and he has remarkable powers of persuasion."

"And he lacks the intelligence or imagination to run away with the gold. His loyalty is not in question, I agree." Ulyanov chuckled. "Very good. How do you suggest that he makes his way to Russia, though? Even if he is not as well-known to the police forces of Europe and the Okhrana as you or I may be, is this a risk that we and the Party should be taking?"

"He speaks some German. If he travelled with a Swiss passport through Germany, crossing to Sweden and then entering Russia through Finland, I think there would be few problems there."

"That sounds as though it will fit the bill well enough." Ulyanov chuckled. Maybe the irony of the ferocious revolutionary posing as a defiantly neutral Swiss appealed to him. "Not that I believe in the power of any machine to win the Revolution – these scientists and engineers are only too willing to ascribe magical powers to their inventions. But as you say, it would be as well not to be faced with such a potential disaster if the Tsarist reactionaries start to use it against our people. Kolinski is to try to obtain the use of the machine for us and the revolutionary cause, if this Lebedenko can be persuaded by any means possible. If that proves impossible, he is to steal the machine—"

Zinoviev interrupted. "Vladimir Ilyich, from what I understand, this may not be possible. We are talking about a massive machine that requires a large trained crew. We both know of Comrade Kolinski's strength and prowess, but I think that even he would find it difficult to make off with this monster."

Ulyanov frowned. "I hear what you say. Very good. In that case, if the inventor is unwilling to go ahead, he must be stopped from making any further developments or inventions, and his machine and plans must be destroyed along with him. I want you to type out the orders to that effect and give them to Kolinski together with the money for the journey and to make things happen at the other end."

Zinoviev understood very well what Ulyanov was saying. If Kolinski were captured, no papers bearing Ulyanov's handwriting would be discovered, and the leader could disown all knowledge of the operation. "Very well. How much money, and which name shall I use?"

"Five thousand roubles should cover things, I think. Get a receipt from Kolinski when you hand them over and make sure he obtains and keeps receipts for all his expenses. He's intelligent enough to manage that, I assume. And sign the letter with my usual revolutionary name. Lenin."

KOLINSKI GRUNTED AS ZINOVIEV EXPLAINED his mission to him, sitting on the edge of the bed in Kolinski's lodgings. Kolinski himself sat on a wooden chair, which, though of normal size, appeared like a piece of schoolroom furniture beneath Kolinski's massive frame. Zinoviev wondered how long it could continue to bear Kolinski's weight as he rocked back and forth, absorbing the details that Zinoviev explained to him.

"So the Chief wants me to go back there? Does he remember that the bastards are still looking for me after that bank job?"

"That was in Tiflis," Zinoviev soothed him. "There's no way any-one's going to be looking for you in Moscow, let alone in the woodland fifty kilometres from the city."

Kolinski shrugged. "Show," he demanded, holding out his hand for the sheets of paper that were sticking out of Zinoviev's pocket. Wordlessly, Zinoviev handed them over, and Kolinski bent his huge shaggy head over the orders, mouthing the letters to himself as he read, a little slowly and painfully. "It's not the Chief's writing," he complained. "It's been done on one of those machines. Are these really the Chief's words? And that's not his signature. I know his signature. I see it when I take his cheques to the bank."

"Don't worry about it. The Chief knows all about this and this is exactly what he wants to happen. The reason he hasn't signed it is for your good, and the Chief's good," Zinoviev told him. He held out his hand for the papers.

"What?"

"I want those back," said Zinoviev. "I have your copy here."

"Here you are," passing the papers back, and receiving another set in return. Kolinski looked at what he'd just been given. "This is rub-bish! What sort of joke are you playing on me here? I may not have your brains and your education, but that's no reason to pass off this nonsense on me. I can't read a damned thing here."

Zinoviev flinched instinctively as the giant leaned forward.

"Please listen to me. This is for your safety. This is the same as what I gave you just now, but it's in code, so that if anyone picks up these papers, they're not going to see anything useful. Just nonsense, as you said."

"I told you, I don't have your brains. How do I start to make sense of it?"

"It's easy. Just add two to the letter on the paper to get the real letter."

"What do you mean?"

"All right, you know your alphabet?"

"Of course. *As, buki, vedi, glagol, dobro, yest—*"

Zinoviev interrupted him. "Fine. So you now take this first letter."

"*Buki.*"

"Right. And move on two in the alphabet."

"*Glagol?*"

Zinoviev nodded. "Carry on with the other letters."

"Got a pencil and some paper?"

Zinoviev passed over a pencil and a notebook open at a blank page. The giant man clumsily traced out his letters, sucking the tip of the pencil in concentration from time to time. After a minute or so he looked up, an enormous grin on his face. "It's magic, isn't it? The way you can hide words like this?"

Zinoviev had to smile a little at Kolinski's naivety. "It is useful, yes," he agreed. "Can I have my paper and pencil back, please? You can remember how to do this? Just in case you forget the details of what you're meant to be doing, or how to go about things."

The big man nodded. He scratched his head. "How much money should I give this man with the machine?"

"As little as you can to get him on our side. And try to leave him in one piece if the money doesn't work, if possible. He's no use to us as damaged goods. But if there's no way at all that he can be persuaded, then he must be stopped completely. Understand?"

Kolinski grinned. "I can persuade him with my little finger, and I wouldn't even leave a mark on him. I don't think anyone's going to argue with me. Don't worry about it." He looked again at the paper, and started to count on his fingers. "Are you going to give me enough to live on?" he asked. "It's not that I want the money, but I've got to eat. And when I eat, I eat a lot." He slapped his belly, which resounded like a drum.

"Don't worry about that," Zinoviev assured him. "The Chief and I have a real interest in you carrying out this mission successfully, and we know how you need to eat."

"And drink." The bearded face broke into a smile, and Zinoviev was faced with an uneven row of blackened and broken teeth.

"And drink," Zinoviev agreed. "I really wish that you would see a dentist, Comrade. Those teeth are really frightening."

"That's the way I like them," replied Kolinski. "As long as they don't hurt me, that's fine by me."

"So here's the money." Zinoviev pulled a leather bag from an inside pocket, and spilled the contents onto the table.

A few minutes later "…one hundred and eighty, one hundred and ninety, two hundred. That's two thousand roubles in gold tens. And," pulling out another bag, "three hundred gold German marks. Easily enough to buy your tickets to Moscow, to get to the site, and to pay off Lebedenko. And to buy you enough vodka to keep you happy."

The giant grinned. "It will be in good hands, believe me."

"And here are your passport and papers. You're Swiss, remember. No Russian here or in Germany or Sweden. You can start speaking Russian again when you get to Finland, but you'd better stick to German when you're talking to the guards or the police. And try to speak with a Swiss accent, if you can manage that."

"*Jawohl*," grinned Kolinski. "I think I can manage that." He looked through the papers and came to the Swiss passport and identity documents. "I'm not too good at reading this German lettering. Just tell me who I am and what I'm doing."

"You're Peter Helling. You're a farm labourer living in Liestal, outside Basel. You're unmarried."

"Why am I travelling?"

"Because you had a school-friend who went to Russia a long time ago, and you want to see him again. He's ill, and he sent you this letter." Zinoviev pointed to an envelope in the papers he had just handed over.

"Suppose they check the address on this letter to see where he lives?"

"They'll find a sewage works outside Moscow. And by the time they've discovered that, you will be far away, and using a different name. One of our comrades will meet you here in Petrograd on the 27th and give you your new papers, and any news and details of any changes to your instructions. Remember this date and time and place written here."

Kolinski took the proffered paper. "It says the 29th here, at 2 o'clock. You just told me the 27th. And why isn't this in that code you showed me just now?"

"Actually, it is in a sort of code," explained Zinoviev. "Listen carefully. Take away the hour of the time from the date."

"Oh, the 27th. I see, I think. So if the time was 3 o'clock, it would be on the 26th?"

"That's right. Well done. So if the police see this somehow, and want to meet you and the other comrade, they'll turn up two days late, and you'll have had your meeting and you'll be out of town by the time they get there."

"That's pretty clever," said Kolinski. "I like that." He scratched his head and thought. "That gives me three weeks – plenty of time if I start today or tomorrow." Zinoviev nodded.

"That's fine, then," said Kolinski. "I'll start packing my things."

He stuck out a massive paw to be shaken. It was clearly a signal for Zinoviev to leave, and Zinoviev took the hint. He wasn't about to start an argument with Kolinski. Though he was not a small man, Zinoviev's hand was lost in the great palm that enfolded his.

"I'd hate to be the man who crossed you," said Zinoviev, releasing his hand from the painful grip.

"Then you'd better make sure that you're not," replied Kolinski, grinning his terrifying smile.

As Zinoviev left, Kolinski moved swiftly with surprising silence to the door, where he listened, standing completely motionless. When he was satisfied that Zinoviev had reached the bottom of the stairs and had let himself out of the front door, he moved again, locking the door of his room. He took three paces to the window and stood to one side, observing the street below. He could see Zinoviev moving off, back towards the area where he knew Lenin was living, and watched until the other moved out of sight round the corner.

He moved back to the bed and picked up the leather bags into which Zinoviev had replaced the gold coins, tossing them lightly in his hand. He felt the weight of the coins inside with pleasure. His next move was to undo the broad leather belt holding up his shabby trousers and remove it. His large fingers felt the inside of the belt and pulled at a place where two strips of leather adjoined, to reveal a slot into which he carefully threaded about half the gold pieces. When he had done this, he picked up the belt, and hefted it in his hands. He grinned to himself as he re-fastened it round his waist. Next, sitting on the creaking bed, he removed both boots. He removed the heels from them, using a large sheath-knife, which he retrieved from its hiding-place under the pillow. The heels were hollow, and Kolinski packed the cavities with the remaining coins, distributing them between the two boots. Before hammering the heels firmly back into place, he stuffed some old newspaper, which had been acting as a tablecloth, around the coins. After he'd put the heels back on the boots, he held up each in turn and held it to his ear, shaking it. Satisfied that the noise of the coins was now completely muffled, he replaced the boots on his feet.

His next move was to the wardrobe. With his great height and long arms, it was easy for him to reach the heavy Nagant revolver, resting behind the decorative carvings on the top of the wardrobe. He grunted a little as he reached somewhat further back, and produced a box of 7.62-millimetre cartridges. Though his fingers were large, they moved with deceptive delicacy as he disassembled the unloaded pistol and wiped the parts with an oily rag from his back pocket.

He hesitated as he reassembled the gun, reaching for the cartridges, but changed his mind, and left the gun unloaded as he stuck it into the back of his waistband. The box of cartridges was wrapped in a spare set of underclothes that went into a small travelling bag, along with two pairs of socks and shirts, which enclosed the sheath knife. A few toilet articles, chiefly consisting of a bar of gritty soap and a straight razor, followed, and the bag was closed.

Wrapping a long black overcoat around him, and perching a broad-brimmed hat on his head, Kolinski picked up his travelling bag, and left the room. He didn't bother to close, let alone lock, the door behind him. At the front door of the house he looked carefully in both directions before turning left, heading in the direction of the station.

Chapter 5: Whitehall, London

*"It is the key to winning this dreadful war in
which both our nations are engaged."*

Brian and Harry arrived at the appointed room at the Foreign Office at the time they had been given by C's secretary. The room was empty, with no-one sitting in any of the chairs arranged around the long antique table.

"Never been in a place like this before," said Harry. "Blimey, that's a lovely bit of timber, that is." He ran his hands appreciatively over the polished surface of the table, and bent down to look underneath. "Someone did a great job of work on the underpinnings there, I can tell you. Beautiful bit of timber, that is," he repeated.

"I'm sure Mr Sheraton would be pleased to hear your judgement on the matter," replied Brian, amused.

"And these paintings on the wall," continued Harry, standing up. "Who are these people?"

"Politicians we don't care about any more."

"Then why put their pictures up there? Gloomy load of buggers, if you ask me. All look bloody constipated."

These last words were spoken just as a Foreign Office official, immaculately dressed in a formal frock coat, entered the room. He looked quizzically at Brian, who was dressed in a somewhat disreputable civilian tweed suit, more suited to the racecourse than Whitehall, and Harry, who was also in shabby, albeit clean, civilian clothes.

"Excuse me, my men, but I hardly think you are meant to be here. Weren't you chaps told that tradesmen are required to be accompanied by one of the porters at all times while working within the building? What the devil are you doing here anyway?" He flapped a hand at them as if shooing away flies.

Brian drew himself up to his full height of six foot three, and stared down in silence at the pompous flunkey for a few seconds. The civil servant appeared to wilt a little, even before Brian started speaking, with his upper-class Harrow drawl somewhat exaggerated. "Oh, I rather thought we actually were in the right room, don't y'know? I'm bally positive that C told us to wait for Colonel Petrov in Room 46. If this isn't Room 46, I'm dreadfully sorry and all that, and perhaps you wouldn't mind showing us to where we are meant to be?"

The clerk started to stammer. "Well, yes, this is Room 46. And yes, there is a meeting with Colonel Petrov scheduled here with Lieutenant Finch-Malloy and his sergeant. I'm most dreadfully sorry. You must be Lieutenant Finch-Malloy, and this here is your sergeant, then."

"Indeed so. This is Harry Braithwaite, and I am, as you so acutely deduce, Brian Finch-Malloy."

"Well, please, both of you, won't you take a seat while I bring Colonel Petrov here to meet you?"

"Thank you, my man," replied Brian, loftily.

As the official left the room, Harry turned to Brian and grinned. "That was bloody wonderful, Brian. I wish I could pull off stunts like that."

"You have your own social skills, Harry, never fear."

The door re-opened and a rather corpulent bearded figure in morning dress of an indefinably foreign cut entered, followed by another man, who appeared to be English, but was obviously not the social equal of the first.

Brian held out his hand to the first man. "Colonel Alexei Dimitrovich Petrov, I take it?" he asked in Russian. The other man's eyes lit up with pleasure at hearing his own language spoken, and he returned Brian's handshake. "And this is?" continued Brian, in English, gesturing to the other man.

"Detective-Inspector Hankey of the Special Branch, sir," in a slight East Anglian accent. "My job is to see that the Colonel comes to no harm around London. We have reason to believe that there are several people in town right at this very minute who would be happy to see him out of the way. Begging your pardon, sir," to Petrov.

"And this gentleman here?" Petrov asked Brian in Russian, gesturing towards Harry.

"My friend and colleague, formerly my sergeant in Flanders, Harry Braithwaite."

"I am sorry that I don't speak Russian, sir," said Harry in German. "However, I do speak some German."

Hankey appeared impressed at this display of linguistic fireworks, but said nothing. Petrov broke into a wide grin. "At last!" he exclaimed in German. "I find not just one, but two Englishmen who do not seem to believe that English is the only language in the world. Do you speak German, Lieutenant?" he asked Brian in Russian.

"Indeed so, Colonel," replied Brian in German. "And I will be more than happy to conduct our conversation in that language, if that is agreeable to you."

"Well," said Petrov, when the three were seated at one end of the table. Hankey stood, his back to the wall, watching the door.

"Has your strangely named superior told you anything about this meeting?"

"He mentioned that there was a technical development about which you wished to inform us."

"Absolutely correct. Lieutenant, do you know the meaning of the Russian word *Netopyr*?"

Brian thought for a few seconds. "Not a word with which I am familiar, I am afraid."

"Never mind. It means a kind of bat – *Fledermaus* – and it is the key to winning this dreadful war in which both our nations are engaged."

Harry spoke. "I'm guessing here, but it seems to me that you're describing some kind of aircraft."

Petrov looked at Brian. "Lieutenant, do you usually allow the Sergeant to speak without permission?"

Harry flushed, but Brian spoke up firmly. "If Harry here hadn't spoken up without permission on a number of occasions in the past, I would be dead by now. I am very happy for him to say what he wants whenever he wants without waiting for my approval."

Petrov took the implied rebuke well. "Very good, Lieutenant. Your attitude seems a trifle unusual, but I will overlook this, given that we are all out of uniform." He turned back to Harry. "In answer to your question, Sergeant, it is not a flying machine, though that is a reasonable assumption, I grant you. We call it *Netopyr* because when we first saw the model of the full-sized machine being carried into the room, it reminded us of a nesting bat. It is, however, very much a land-based engine. Its aim, put simply, is to assist the infantry as they advance and to carry the battle into the enemy's camp." Harry frowned. "Yes, I know the difficulties you are going to mention. Maybe a drawing will help." He reached inside his coat and brought out a bundle of papers, which he unfolded and spread out on the table before them.

Brian and Harry bent over the table.

"Ah, I begin to understand," said Brian.

"As you say, sir, the drawing makes it a lot clearer. I begin to understand what you mean when you say this takes the battle to the enemy," said Harry.

"Ingeniously simple," agreed Brian, adding hurriedly, "I mean that as a compliment." He and Harry resumed their study of the plans.

"Sorry, sir, but I can't read Russian. What does that say?" asked Harry, pointing to a label on one of the drawings.

"Gun turret," replied Petrov.

"What sort of guns?" asked Brian.

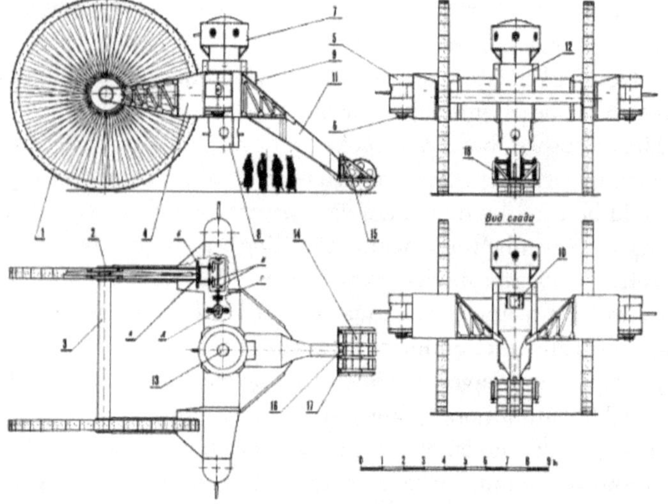

"That has yet to be finalised, and indeed, that is one of the areas where I believe you may be of help to us. The current thinking is to mount two 47-millimetre guns there – I think you British would call them three-pounders – together with a number of machine-guns.

But, as I say, we require expertise from those who have been out there fighting on the Western Front in order to make these decisions."

Harry had been poring over the drawings. "Engines here, sir? What type?"

"Maybachs are fitted to the prototype, but obviously we have no supply of such engines for future production. I am hoping to arrange that we can use some of the new Rolls-Royce Eagles. Quite frankly, our Russian industry would not be capable of producing such engines in the quantity we anticipate. The French have their own problems, the Swedes aren't interested in helping us, the Americans seem to have no wish to assist us, and the Confederates have no such industry. So that leaves the British alone as a possible source of engines."

Harry was still bent over the drawings, examining them closely and running his finger over the paper. "Sir? My guess is that this is a fuel line?"

"Yes, Sergeant, I believe that it is."

"Then it shouldn't be there." Petrov frowned at him. Unabashed, Harry went on, "If you don't mind me saying so, sir, that's a damn' stupid place to put it. A rifle bullet, or even a shell splinter, would cut that fuel line. And it's feeding both engines? Stupid again, sir. You need at least two fuel lines to each engine, each needs to be armoured, and they should take separate routes. And you can let gravity feed the engines. You don't need those fuel pumps – at least not ones that size."

Petrov was looking at him in astonishment. "In the Imperial Russian Army, if a sergeant spoke like that to a colonel, he'd be reduced to the ranks or shot for insubordination. If an officer spoke like that to a superior, he'd be reprimanded severely. But in this case, I have to admit that what you are saying makes a lot of sense. And this is really why I feel you may both be needed in Russia. One of the reasons, anyway."

"So how many reasons are there, Colonel?" asked Brian.

"A number," counting off on his fingers. "First, as I mentioned, we need people like you and the sergeant with experience of the Western Front and the conditions there to advise us on how to perfect this machine for use in battle. Next, we need technical expertise, such as the sergeant here seems to possess, to point out possible problems with the current design. Also, he can help with the installation of the Rolls-Royce engines when they arrive. Lebedenko has very little English, so would be unable to follow any written instructions coming from the factory. He will need help. And another, maybe the most important of all, we need to prevent this design, and more importantly, the prototype, from falling into the hands of the socialist revolutionaries. Especially the Bolsheviks. We think you may be of use there."

"That's the second time today that I've heard about the Bolsheviks," said Brian. "I'd never heard of them before."

"What do you now know of them?"

"Very little, except that it seems I know their leader, Vladimir Ulyanov. He used to visit our house in London sometimes when I was a boy. He taught me how to play chess."

Petrov shot him a look. "I hope you have nothing to do with him now?" His tone was anxious.

"Believe me, sir, I'd almost completely forgotten about his existence until C reminded me of it yesterday."

"Be that as it may, we are concerned that this invention may fall into the wrong hands, and we need your help to organise some sort of defence against such a possibility. And there is yet another reason why I want you to visit Russia. Once the plans are perfected, it will be your job to bring a copy of the plans back here, so that Britain can start the manufacture of its own *Netopyrs*."

"It sounds like fun," said Brian. "When do we start?"

"You're serious? Fun?" said Petrov, startled into Russian. "It might be dangerous."

"That's what I said, fun," switching back to German. Harry nodded agreement at Brian's words.

"You English are all mad," said Petrov.

"I'm half-Irish," Brian pointed out.

"English, Irish, British, whatever. Crazy. We can start for Moscow in two or three days' time, then."

It was Brian's turn to stare. " 'We,' you say? You would be coming with us?"

"Naturally. Now," pulling out his watch, "I must return to the Embassy. I will inform you of arrangements through your chief, C. And you may pass questions and enquiries to me through the same channel. A pleasure to have met you both."

He bowed in their general direction as he left, followed by his Special Branch protector. Brian and Harry returned the compliment.

"WELL, IT REALLY DOES SOUND LIKE FUN, eh, Harry?" said Brian.

"All right for you. You speak Russian. I can't even read the bloody language."

"You'll manage all right. I bet most of the technical words are English with -ski stuck on the end." Brian grinned.

"Do you reckon that contraption's going to work, then? Seems like a right pig's ear to me, looking at the plans."

Brian sighed. "God knows. It's crazy, I grant you. But then look at aeroplanes. Who'd ever have believed that they'd come to anything? Anyway, your hands are going to get oily and greasy again. Why you ever joined the Guards when you could have been in the Engineers, I still don't know. Anyway, what do you make of our future travelling companion? I wonder who he is."

"We know that. C told us, and he told us himself. His name is Colonel Petrov."

"Oh, no it's not. Believe me. I've seen that face before somewhere. I can't put a name to it, but I'm sure the name I saw when I saw that face somewhere in a magazine or somewhere wasn't Petrov. And he's certainly more than just another Colonel. I wonder just who it is that's going to be making the trip to Moscow with us."

Chapter 6: Germany

"Just a mistake," he said. "They had the wrong person."

KOLINSKI SAT IN THE THIRD-CLASS COMPARTMENT of the train, chewing a piece of Swiss sausage and taking swigs from a bottle of schnapps, ignoring the looks the German civilian passengers were shooting in his direction. Some of the men on the seat facing him looked as though they would snatch the sausage out of his hands and devour it, if only he didn't look so intimidating.

The pistol dug uncomfortably into his back as he leaned against the hard wooden seat, but he welcomed it. It would keep him awake through this, probably the most risky and dangerous part of the whole journey. He had decided to travel to Sweden from Travemunde, rather than Kiel, on the grounds that there would be more police and guards surrounding the naval base at Kiel, and he would be arriving in Malmö, which was not only safer, being some distance from the capital, Stockholm, but was also a much shorter sea voyage. Kolinski, born and brought up on the steppes, was a poor sailor, and tended to feel queasy even when in a small boat on a pond. The sea voyage was the part of his journey that he was most dreading. Water scared him.

"Tickets!" came the shout from the end of the carriage, and the uniformed conductor entered, followed by two *Feldgendarmerie* – military police – on the lookout for deserters and soldiers who had overstayed their leave. As Kolinski was approached by the three, he held out his ticket, keeping his face turned away.

"Why are you going to Travemunde?" asked one of the MPs.

"Going to Sweden," mumbled Kolinski.

"Speak up when you talk to us!" ordered the *Feldgendarmerie* corporal. "What regiment are you from?"

"I'm not with a regiment," said Kolinski, a little more clearly than before.

"You're not German, are you?" asked the conductor. "I can tell from your accent."

"Swiss," said Kolinski, still looking away.

"Papers."

Kolinski handed over his forged Swiss passport.

"Full name?" asked the corporal.

"It's written there," said Kolinski. "Right there, in the passport." He was sweating. Dear Mother of God, he'd managed to forget the name he was travelling under. What the devil was he going to do?

"I asked you for your name, you chocolate-guzzling mountain goat," replied the German.

"Peter," choked out Kolinski. It was all he could remember.

"Peter what?" demanded the other.

Holy Mother of Jesus. No, as a good Communist, he must stop using those terms. Holy whatever. Kolinski's mind, never the sharpest of instruments when it came to a crisis, had slowed to a paralysed halt. The schnapps hadn't helped him, either. "Peter Hellmann," he burst out.

The corporal smiled. "And your date of birth?"

Oh, Mother of— He'd completely forgotten. They watched

his confusion chase itself through his mind and over his face, and
grinned at him.

"Well, Peter Hell*ing*," said the corporal, emphasising the last syl-
lable of the name written in the passport, "you'd better come along
with us." He reached for one arm, and his colleague took the other.
"On your feet."

The other passengers said nothing. Kolinski had the impression
that they had seen similar scenes many times before. He stood up.
"This way, deserter scum," said the corporal, dragging him to the end
of the carriage, where the conductor's compartment was located.
Kolinski heaved a mental sigh of relief. At least he wasn't being ac-
cused of being a spy right now. But then, when he thought about it,
deserters, as well as spies, were shot by the Germans. He wished that
he'd never drunk the schnapps. Too late, he thought.

He allowed himself to be led to the conductor's compartment,
which also served as a guardroom for the two *Feldgendarmerie*.

"Hands behind your back," ordered the corporal, producing a pair
of handcuffs. Kolinski complied. One cuff was snapped tightly round
his left wrist. Now was the time. Kolinski made his move, sweeping
his left arm, with the free cuff dangling, in front of his body. The
free cuff swung from the chain, and the heavy metal hit the corporal
hard on the side of the head. He went down instantly, moaning, and
bleeding from his scalp. The other soldier, surprised, went for his
rifle, propped up in the corner of the room. Kolinski brought himself beside the guard with one enormous stride, reached behind his
back, and brought the butt of the Nagant revolver onto the back of
the man's neck with a dull crunch. The soldier slumped noiselessly to
the ground. Kolinski reached for the rifle, and grasping the stock in
one hand and the muzzle in the other, flexed his shoulder muscles.
The sweat beaded on his grinning face as the barrel slowly bent into
a shallow curve before the fascinated and horrified gaze of the railway conductor, who stood there watching, apparently powerless to

do anything to stop him. Kolinski threw the now useless weapon on the floor beside the first guard, who stirred slightly as he received a vicious kick to his ribs.

"Don't even think about following me," said Kolinski as he removed a bunch of keys from the belt of the seemingly paralysed conductor, and stepped through the door of the compartment. There was no movement behind him as he closed the door, and locked it after a brief search for the train key. Immediately he heard a hammering from inside the compartment as the conductor appeared to realise fully what had happened.

Kolinski thrust his left hand with the handcuffs into his pocket, and walked back to where he had been sitting. The other passengers looked at him curiously as he passed.

"Just a mistake," he said. "They had the wrong person." Inwardly, he chuckled. That was nothing but the truth. They really had picked on the wrong person. He reached his travelling bag down from the overhead luggage rack, and walked towards the carriage door, keeping his cuffed left hand in his pocket the whole time. The train was now travelling quite slowly, and Kolinski started looking for a place where he could jump off and land without being seen, while being relatively close to a town or village, or at least a road from where he could continue his journey.

He was in luck. He stuck his head out of the window, and saw a small town a few hundred meters ahead. A road ran parallel to the railway tracks, with a grassy bank beside it. He debated with himself whether to pull the emergency handle, allowing him to jump safely, but draw attention to himself, or to take the risk of jumping from the moving train. He had just decided to risk the moving jump, when the engine whistled and the train started to shudder to a halt. Quickly, he opened the carriage door and leaped onto the bank.

T HE DROP WAS A LITTLE LONGER than he had expected, and he fell awkwardly, with the breath knocked out of him. His bag had flown out of his hand and spilled open, and he spent the next few seconds collecting his scattered belongings and stuffing them back in. The train finally came to a halt, with the sound of whistles, followed by banging and crashing noises, all coming from the carriage where he had trapped the conductor and the soldiers.

After a final massive crash, he heard unintelligible shouted orders, and what looked like a platoon of armed infantry jumped out of the train onto the bank. Keeping as low as he dared, while still keeping an eye on the soldiers, who had started to beat the undergrowth and were obviously now searching for him, he started to crawl towards the road.

The ditch by the side of the road seemed deep enough to hide in, but Kolinski guessed that this would be one of the first places that they would look. Still, he reasoned, he could still use it as his route to somewhere more suitable. He slipped into the ditch, where he was hidden by the long grass and reeds growing at the edge. Thankfully it was relatively dry, and he could crawl along the bottom without too much difficulty.

A breath of wind blew over him, assaulting his nostrils with an unpleasant acrid smell that he recognised after a few seconds as that of pig dung. He raised his head slightly and saw what looked like a pigsty attached to a farmhouse, only about ten metres from the ditch. The soldiers behind him were looking in the wrong direction, and it was the work of a moment to make his way out of the ditch and vault over the low wall of the pigsty, where he found himself face to face with a large, but seemingly under-nourished and hungry-looking pig.

"Excuse me, your Ladyship," he said to her in German, and moved towards the shelter at the back of the pen. He crawled through the narrow doorway and, after taking up a cramped position on the straw of the sty, tried to peer through the door. All he could see was a narrow strip of sky, but he consoled himself with the fact that if that was all he could see from inside, it was extremely unlikely that anyone outside could see him. More worrying was the fact that the pig, which he had already mentally named "Hilda", after his landlady in Switzerland, had started a squealing and a snorting that made it almost impossible for him to hear anything that was going on outside the sty.

The squealing grew louder and more excited, and Kolinski could now hear the sound of approaching footsteps – seemingly those of military boots. He felt in his coat pocket for his revolver, where he remembered he'd stuffed it after his assault on the *Feldgendarmerie* corporal, but there was nothing in the pocket. Panic-stricken, he searched in all his other pockets, and in his bag, but all he could discover was the knife he'd wrapped in his clothes. It would have to do. He braced himself, gripping the hilt of the knife in his right fist.

The boots stopped, and he could hear a clatter of metal. It didn't sound like any kind of weapon that Kolinski recognised, but he didn't relax until he heard the words, "Here you are, old girl. Not as much as you want, I know, but we've all got to make sacrifices with the war on." The boots moved away, and Kolinski relaxed, listening to Hilda slurping her way through her mash.

KOLINSKI REMAINED IN THE PIGSTY for a few hours, waiting for dusk to fall and the searching troops to go away. Just before the time when he judged the farmer would come to shut Hilda up for the night, he crept out of the sty, and set off down the road. The loss of the pistol troubled him a little – it was obviously Russian, and if anyone discovered it, it would point to a Russian being in the vicinity – but worse, as far as he was concerned, was the handcuff that was still around his left wrist. Though he was moderately skilled at picking simple locks, such as the ones to be found on handcuffs, he lacked any suitable implement to exercise his talent.

He had to find a way to get rid of the handcuffs. At least he could hide them, he thought, as he passed a house where there was still some laundry on the line in the back garden, even at this time of evening.

He looked carefully at the house and listened, but could detect no signs of anyone's being inside. Keeping his left hand in his pocket, gripping the knife hilt, he marched to the front door and knocked. He could hear the sound of footsteps from inside the house, and cursed to himself. Obviously he hadn't listened carefully enough. He moved to the side of the house quickly, going round to the back, as he heard the front door open. He had just reached the laundry drying on the line when he heard a furious yapping from a small dog that stood outside its kennel, straining at its chain. Almost as a reflex action, his left hand left his pocket, and the knife he had been holding blurred through the air to bury itself in the dog's neck. The dog gave a whine of pain and astonishment, and collapsed, whimpering. Kolinski bounded to the laundry line, and picked out a pillowcase and a white towel, together with a man's white shirt. Carrying his booty, he strode back to the dog's semi-conscious twitching body, and pulled out the knife. He wondered briefly whether he should finish the job by cutting the dog's throat, and decided against this. The beast was going to die anyway. He wiped the knife on the dog's fur and put it back in the sheath as a woman's voice came from the front of the house asking if anyone was there. At least it wasn't a farmer with a gun, he thought to himself. He climbed over the fence into the next garden, and crept, keeping low, back towards the road.

He found a place where the bushes and shrubs hid him from view and ducked down. First he changed his rather grubby shirt for the clean one he had taken from the line, and put the old shirt into his bag. Taking out the knife again, he cut the towel into strips, and used his right hand to wrap the cloth around his left hand and wrist, completely covering the handcuffs. His fingers protruded from the "bandage", where he noticed a couple of smears of the dog's blood from the knife when he cut up the towel. So much the better, he thought, and smiled grimly to himself. He cut the pillowcase with the knife, and folded it into a triangular sling for his left arm. Pretty good, he told himself, rearranging the contents of his pockets so that they were now all accessible with his right hand. He brushed some of the straw, mud and leaves off himself, wishing that he'd had the foresight to do this before he'd wrapped his left arm in the bandage.

He looked around carefully, and could see no-one. The remaining strips of cloth went into his bag, and he stood up. As casually as he could manage, he walked towards the road, moving towards the village that he had seen earlier from the train, praying there was a railway station where he could buy a ticket to continue his journey.

He passed a few people on his way into the village, some using the fading light to tend their vegetable gardens, and others walking slowly along the street. There were few men of his age to be seen. All at the front, he assumed. He pulled his cap over his eyes and walked with his head down, and his bandaged arm slightly hidden, so that it wouldn't be the first thing that people remembered about him.

To his relief, the village possessed a small station, with a light in the ticket office. Otherwise, the station was deserted. "To Travemunde," he said. "By the next train."

"That's tomorrow morning at 6:30," said the clerk, after consulting his timetables. "In a hurry, are you? What did you do to your hand?"

"None of your business," replied Kolinski. "Just give me the ticket."

"What class?"

"First." He'd been travelling third class before, and if anyone was looking for him there, he would now be in first, with a nice clean shirt.

The clerk looked at him. "First?"

"Yes, damn it, I can pay." He reached for one of the gold German coins and rang it on the counter. The clerk's eyes lit up. "Haven't seen one of those for a time," he said. "Since they started printing that damned paper money last year."

"Got good eyes, then, have you?" asked Kolinski. "See things and remember them, do you?"

"I suppose so," replied the clerk. "No better or worse than most, I suppose."

"Well, how about if I refresh your memory of old times with another one of these?" producing another twenty-mark gold piece. "This one's not for the railway company, it's for you. And it's all for you, if those eyes and that memory of yours manage to forget that I've ever been here or bought a ticket. Understand?" His dark eyes glittered, and the clerk nodded.

"Never seen you in my life," he agreed, moving his hand to cover the coin, where it was immediately covered in its turn by Kolinski's enormous paw, pressing it painfully hard against the counter.

"Make sure that it stays that way," growled Kolinski. "Otherwise..." He shook his head. "You alone here?"

"Yes," the other squeaked. Kolinski's hand was exerting an uncomfortable pressure. "I'm the stationmaster. There's only a porter besides me, and he's off duty now that the last train's gone through for the day."

"Good. Now, my ticket, if you would, please." He released his grip on the other's hand.

"First class will be twenty-five marks and thirty pfennigs. That's only twenty there," pointing to the first coin.

Kolinski reluctantly fished out another twenty-mark piece. "Keep the change from that."

"Really? I mean, that's fourteen marks in change." He slid the ticket over towards Kolinski.

"Yes, keep it all. I just want you to do one more thing for me in exchange. Consider that money as payment for my lodging tonight."

"What are you talking about?"

"When do you go out of here tonight and lock up?"

"I should have done that five minutes ago."

"So leave me here. I won't take anything. Trust me," Kolinski grinned. "Just turn off the lights, don't bother putting out the fire in the stove, leave the door unlocked so I can catch that train in the morning, and no-one will be any the wiser. I get a nice warm place to sleep for the night, and you get a free night watchman and more than fifteen marks, plus the extra twenty I just gave you. Deal?"

"I don't think I have a choice," grinned the stationmaster.

"Thought you'd see it like that. Good man."

⁂

Chapter 7: Off the coast of Germany

"This is what makes all of this being cooped up
in a stinking metal box worthwhile."

THE AIR WAS FOUL; an unholy mix of machinery, diesel fuel, cabbage and some indefinable chemical smell, overlaid with the stench of wet wool and unwashed bodies, and all mixed with the stink from the chemical toilets.

The ceilings were far too low for Brian, who kept hitting his head on the pipes and valves that seemed to protrude from every surface, and he had to bend double to get through every hatchway. He'd started wearing a thick knitted woollen cap all the time to cushion the knocks he suffered every time he moved. It was uncomfortably hot, but it was preferable to continually banging his head on things.

The captain of Royal Navy submarine HMS *E9*, Lieutenant-Commander Max Horton, watched his passenger with some amusement as Brian stumbled from the tiny compartments serving as the officers' mess to the conning tower, hitting his head yet again on a pipe connected to the depth gauge.

"Careful with that pipe," grinned Horton. "It's the only one we've got on board. We can pick up new passengers any time, but those pipes are hard to get hold of, you know."

If Brian, who had hit his head quite hard, was amused by this, he hid it well. In the three days since *E9* had left Harwich, his head, shins and elbows had suffered many times – bits of submarine seemed to lie in wait for him and leap out each time he passed them. Each time it happened, he wished the party of three could have travelled to Russia by any method other than this. Life in the submarine didn't seem to bother Harry, who had found kindred spirits in the engineers tending *E9*'s machinery, and he was usually to be found sitting happily among piles of oily cotton waste in the engine room, discussing clutch mechanisms, diesel-electric drives and other technical matters.

Colonel Petrov (as Brian continued to call him, since he still couldn't place Petrov's real identity) spent most of his time on his bunk reading thick Russian novels, emerging only for meals. Brian wished he could emulate this state of semi-hibernation, but his metabolism was too active to permit such a lifestyle. Hence his constant roaming from end to end of the boat.

"Don't worry, Lieutenant," said Horton, looking at his watch. "Another hour or so and it will be really dark, and then we'll be on the surface. Fresh air, and then you can stretch your legs properly."

"Don't know how you stand it all the time," said Brian.

Horton chuckled. "It's a strange life, isn't it?" he admitted. "Just wish we had more of a chance to sink Jerry's warships for him."

"You do seem to have the merchant ships on edge, though. I was told that a lot of war matériel and iron ore is failing to get through to Germany, thanks to you."

Horton turned serious. "That's true. But I don't like the fact that food's not getting through to the German civilians, and they're going hungry, poor beggars. It's not the kiddies or the women who started this war. I'm not happy that they're suffering, and that's a fact."

"Tell that to the Belgian civilians who had their homes burned and saw their menfolk shot out of hand as the Boche tramped through their country," replied Brian. "War is hell, and this war is more hellish than any other."

The two men stood in silence for a while, eventually broken by Horton. "Your Lieutenant Braithwaite's a queer bird to be an officer, isn't he? I mean, I'm not trying to pry and all that, but how long have you known him?"

"He used to be my platoon sergeant," explained Brian, "and when this caper came up, he insisted on coming with me. He's a damned good chap, and there's no-one I'd sooner have beside me in a tight spot, to be frank with you. He got his commission just before we came down to Harwich from London. The head of the Service thought it would be best if we ate in the same mess, and so on. Not to mention that he deserves it many times over. If my CO in Flanders hadn't been such a damned stuck-up fool, he'd have been leading the platoon instead of me."

"And what about our Russian friend?" asked Horton.

Brian lowered his voice. Petrov's bunk was less than ten feet away from where they were standing. "For a start, I don't think his name is Petrov."

"What is it, then? That's the name I have on my manifest here. Finch-Malloy, B. de Q., Lieutenant; Braithwaite, G. T. , 2nd Lieutenant, both of the Coldstream Guards; and Petrov, A. D., Colonel, Russian Imperial Staff."

"That may be the name on your manifest, Commander, but it's not the name on his birth certificate, I can promise you that. I can't tell you his real name, because I don't know it, but his face looks familiar. Not that I've ever met the blighter before we started this little game, but I've seen his face in photographs, I am sure."

"Do you spend your spend time looking at pictures of Russian officers? I can think of more interesting subjects."

"No, not at all. He's famous, though, believe me. Famous enough, anyway, for his picture to have appeared in a magazine or a newspaper, and for me to remember it. That's my point."

"You're imagining things, Lieutenant. I really do think so. It must be those knocks on the noggin that have done it. Either that, or joining that gang of funnies in the basement of the Admiralty has turned your brain." Brian shook his head. "Trust me, I'm right about this, sir."

"All right, have it your own way. Now, if you'll excuse me, Lieutenant, I'm going to check that we're clear to surface. If you will be so kind as to leave the bridge?"

It was phrased as a question, but it was an order, and Brian obeyed.

ABOUT TWENTY MINUTES LATER, *E9*'s conning tower broke the surface of the Baltic Sea, followed by the sleek hull, shedding water as it rose up. Riding low in the slight swell, the black hull was nearly invisible in the moonless night, with only the conning tower visible from a distance, and a faint wake astern to alert a keen observer that there was a submarine in the vicinity. The conning tower hatch popped open, and several figures emerged.

"Bit chilly tonight," commented Brian, who had been the fifth man up. He and Commander Horton were standing a little away from the three lookouts keeping watch, scanning the horizon through their binoculars. "Smells good, though."

"Agreed," said Horton. "We haven't got the air supply in these tin cans properly sorted out yet. One day, though, we'll have proper submarines that can stay underwater all the time, without needing to come up and breathe every night." He pointed. "Just think, about fifteen miles away, the ships of the German High Seas Fleet are just sitting there, waiting for me to come along and wreak havoc. I'd be in there like a fox in a henhouse." He grinned, and his teeth shone white in the darkness. He clapped Brian on the shoulder. "Don't stay up here too long and catch cold. I've got a log to write up. There'll be hot cocoa in the mess when you decide to come down." He turned and started to descend the ladder.

Brian stared out into the darkness, unsure of how he was going to carry out the many different, and almost contradictory, tasks that Petrov had asked him to carry out when he reached Russia. Before he had left London, he had naturally reported the conversation with Petrov to C, who had told him not to worry so much about Petrov's agenda.

"Quite frankly, lad, we want you and Braithwaite to go over there and spy out what's going over there for us. Get a feel for things, get the lie of the land, that sort of thing" he had said. "From what Petrov tells us, this thing is like one of Mr Wells's wonder weapons in those fantastic stories of his, which drives all before it. What we need from you both is a report which gives us the answer to two questions. First, is this thing of any value to us militarily? Second, if it is, how simple is it to produce in quantity and reliably? I'm guessing that you will be chiefly responsible for the answer to the first question, and Braithwaite will take care of the second. But that's up to you. And if you have any time to help Petrov with his problems and keep him happily on our side, that's a bonus."

Turning these problems over in his mind, he became aware, without his having noticed the fact, that his eyes had become fixed on what appeared to be a dim speck of light immediately ahead of the submarine. He turned to one of the petty officers keeping watch.

"May I borrow those field-glasses?"

"Sir." The binoculars were unlooped and passed over. Brian focussed on the light he had seen earlier. It appeared that it was actually two white lights, one above the other, with a red and a green light underneath them. He passed the binoculars back, pointing to the light.

"Thank you, sir. Don't know why we didn't spot her before. I'd sooner you didn't tell the skipper we missed seeing her, if you don't mind, sir." He bent down to the speaking tube and uncapped it before calling down to the bridge. Horton reappeared in less than a minute, clutching his own pair of binoculars.

"There, sir," said the petty officer, pointing. Horton focussed his glasses. "Yes, there she is," he said. He turned to Brian. "I'm going to have to ask you to go below," he said. "And I can't order you, but I am going to make a very strong suggestion, that you go to your bunk and stay there. I have a feeling that we're going to get rather busy in the next hour or so and I want you out of the crew's way. No offence meant."

"None taken," said Brian. He slipped down the ladder and made his way to his bunk, the top of a rack of three that he shared with Harry and Petrov. Petrov was propped up in bed, peering along the length of the submarine.

"The engines have stopped," said Petrov. "Any idea why?" It was true – the thump of the diesels had died away. In the relative silence, Brian could hear the noise of crewmen coming down the ladder, followed by the clang of the hatch closing.

"We spotted a ship on the surface just ahead," said Brian. "I suppose we're going to dive again so they don't see us." As he said the words, the whistle signalling "Prepare for dive" sounded. "Here we go," as the bow pitched down.

The Baltic isn't a very deep sea, but the mixture of fresh and salt water makes for tricky underwater manoeuvring and station-keeping, so Brian wasn't surprised that Commander Horton had asked him to keep out of the way while the submarine dived. He wondered about Harry's empty bunk, but realised that Harry, unlike Brian himself, was probably a good deal more use than ornament when it came to submarines and was probably actually working his passage.

The quiet throb of the electric motors started, and Brian realised that they were under way, though whether towards or away from the mystery ship he had spotted, he had no idea. He lay back and closed his eyes.

After about twenty minutes, Horton poked his head round the curtain. "Thank you both for your co-operation," he said. "Lieutenant, you may care to step to the bridge for a minute. You too, Colonel, if you care to join us." When they were assembled on the bridge, he bent to the periscope, and then motioned to Petrov to take his place. Petrov shook his head, and Horton beckoned Brian to the periscope.

Brian focussed the eyepiece and saw the magnified silhouette of a ship, apparently moving towards them. There was another brightly lit shape behind it. Moving away from the periscope, he shrugged and turned to Horton quizzically.

"As far as we can tell, she's a German destroyer," said Horton excitedly. "Just what we wanted to see. We're going in closer for a better look."

"As long as she doesn't see us," said Brian.

"We're submerged, remember. They're not going to see our periscope at this time of night, believe me."

"And what is the other ship behind the German?" asked Petrov, in his accented English. He was now looking through the periscope.

"We're pretty sure that's the Travemunde ferry, headed for Malmö. She's Swedish and neutral, which is why she's all lit up. Bit of luck for us, really. Means there's someone to pick up the poor beggars on the destroyer when we sink her and we're not going to have to poke our snouts up above the water. Now if you'll excuse me, gentlemen, I have more work to do. If you'll be so kind as to return to your bunks."

Brian translated Horton's words into Russian, and he and Petrov returned, in Brian's case with some reluctance.

"They should not be taking these risks," complained Petrov when they were once more ensconced, lying listening to the noises as the submarine prepared for battle. "They are meant to be delivering you and me to Kronstadt, or to Reval if they cannot reach Kronstadt. This is madness."

"I am sure Commander Horton knows what he is doing," Brian assured him. "He is, after all, a professional in the operation of this strange machine, and we are not. Time enough to criticise him when we find ourselves clinging to a life raft in the middle of the Baltic."

"I do not find your words amusing, Lieutenant," replied Petrov, and a deafening silence ensued.

Please yourself, sighed Brian silently, and continued listening to the strange noises coming from the bow of the boat. There were clanks and muffled thumps, and a hissing noise, which Brian guessed were the torpedo tubes being prepared for firing. Unlike the Army, there was no shouting of orders, and the sailors appeared to be working in near-silence. Only a low murmur of voices told him that there were human beings and not machines carrying out the work.

A cryptic series of numbers and commands came from the bridge, presumably settings to be made on the torpedo warhead. A few seconds of silence, and then the single word "Shoot".

There was a loud hissing sound, and a whoosh as the torpedo left the tube. The sequence was repeated. And then there was silence. E9's electric motors had stopped, and there was a hush throughout the whole ship. Horton's head appeared around the curtain again.

"Stay where you are," he said. "Just letting you know that by my reckoning, if we hear anything, it will be in," looking at the stopwatch he was holding, "another two and a half minutes." He smiled. "This is what makes all of this being cooped up in a stinking metal box worthwhile," and his head disappeared behind the curtain.

The silence became almost oppressive. Brian was aware that he had been holding his breath, and he started counting slowly. A little after he reached one hundred, there was the sound of a muffled explosion, and the boat shook a little in the water. Five seconds later, the process was repeated. A low cheer could be heard from *E9*'s crew, and Horton came bounding in yet again.

"How do you like that?" he exclaimed happily. "A left and a right. Both barrels. And my guess is that the ferry will stop to pick them up." He seemed as happy about this last as he did about the sinking of the destroyer.

Brian shook his hand enthusiastically in congratulation, and Petrov stirred himself. "The risk was big," he said in English. "But you won. Well done," and extended his own hand.

When Horton had departed, Petrov spoke to Brian. "I do not know whether to be happy or not at this. Of course, it is always good to see the Germans defeated. But now they know we are here, I fear for our safety. Surely they will now be searching for us all the way to Russia?"

"I think not," said Brian. "From what Commander Horton was telling me, the effect of these attacks has been to make the German fleet more afraid to show its face. They have no weapons against submarines, and we are actually in a stronger position now than we were before."

"I hope you are right," said Petrov. "I would like to smell good Russian air once more before I die like a sardine in a tin."

KOLINSKI SAT MISERABLY on the deck of the ferry. His train journey to the port had been uneventful – presumably the money he had given the village stationmaster had been enough to keep the man's mouth shut. While he'd been left overnight in the station office, he'd found paperclips to bend and use as picklocks to remove the handcuffs, but he had decided to keep wearing the bandage and sling as a disguise.

Buying the ferry ticket had been no problem, but even the slight swell in the harbour had upset his stomach and made him feel queasy. When the ferry had put to sea, he had been forced out of the saloon onto the deck, where he slumped into a seat conveniently near (but not too close) to the lee rail. He decided it was now safe for him to remove the bandage and sling. After all, he was now on a Swedish ship, where the German authorities had no jurisdiction. It was a clear, cool, moonless night, with what would have been excellent visibility if there had been anything more than starlight to see by.

He looked towards the bow, where he could just make out a few lights of what seemed to be an otherwise darkened ship ahead of them. Without any warning, there was a flash of brilliant light, followed a few seconds later by another flash. The rumbling sound of the two explosions followed a few seconds after that.

Immediately there was a shout from the ferry's lookout to the bridge. "Mines ahead!" Almost immediately, the ferry turned hard to port, away from the stricken ship in front, from which flames now appeared to be leaping.

In a minute or so, the deck beside Kolinski was filled with passengers who had heard the noise of the explosions and felt the ship turning, and had made their way on deck to see what was happening.

One woman close to Kolinski seemed convinced that it was the ferry that was sinking, and kept hysterically asking her husband when the lifeboats were going to be launched. Though no-one else seemed to believe this, there were many anxious faces, and there was an almost palpable feeling of unease among the passengers.

Half a dozen sailors came through the crowd, headed by one of the ship's officers.

"We've received an SOS from the ship ahead. They believe it was not a minefield, but torpedoes from a British submarine," he told the passengers in Swedish-accented German. "We are perfectly safe," he reminded them, pointing to the large Swedish flag, picked out by searchlights, floating from the main mast. "The British do not attack Swedish ships. We are perfectly safe," he repeated.

"So why did the British fire their torpedoes? What is that ship?" came a voice from the crowd.

"She's a German Imperial Navy destroyer. We're going to launch our boats and take off some of her men. Most of her boats were destroyed in the blast. So I'm looking for some strong able-bodied volunteers to man the lifeboats and help save the lives of those men."

Several passengers stepped forward, but Kolinski stayed where he was.

"Excellent," said the officer. His eyes met Kolinski's, and he looked Kolinski up and down. "We need a big strapping fellow like you," he said. "Come on."

"Can't swim," mumbled Kolinski.

"Doesn't matter. You'll have a life jacket, and even if you do fall in, we'll have you out of there in no time at all."

Kolinski still hung back. A woman's voice cut through the crowd. "It could be you out there on that boat. Shame on you for refusing to help those poor men."

"Shame, shame," came the murmur from the crowd. Kolinski flushed. "Oh, very well," he muttered, and stepped forward.

"Good man," said the officer. "We'll get you fitted up with a life jacket. Come with me." He led his party, including Kolinski, to one of the ferry's lifeboats, and instructed them where to sit, giving basic instructions on how to row the boat. A sailor passed out life jackets.

"Lower away," called out the officer, when they were all seated in their places and wearing their life jackets. The davits creaked, and the boat was slowly lowered towards the water. Even before the keel of the lifeboat touched the surface of the water, Kolinski started to feel miserably sick.

"Cast off," called the officer in the stern, "and then all of you good fellows pull at my command." Kolinski's lifeboat and the others from the ferry, all crewed by a mixture of professional and amateur sailors, slowly splashed their way clumsily towards the burning ship. "Well done, men. Any of you want to sign on as permanent crew?" joked the officer in Kolinski's boat.

⚜

KOLINSKI FELT EVEN MORE QUEASY than he had done on the ship. The motion of the small lifeboat made him feel sick, and only the fear of the probably infinitely deep water beneath him stopped him from leaning over the side and throwing up. The burning destroyer grew slowly closer as the men laboured at the oars.

"We're there, ship oars," ordered the officer after what seemed like an eternity. "Stop rowing and pull your oars inboard," he explained. With some clattering and confusion, his orders were obeyed. "Ahoy!" he called to the destroyer. "We can take twenty men here."

"Thank you," came the reply. A searchlight shone from the bridge of the damaged destroyer, and the beam played over the surface of the sea before coming to rest on one of the other lifeboats. There was a splashing sound, and several men wearing life jackets swam into the circle of light surrounding the boat. The lifeboat's crew hauled them, dripping, out of the water and into the boat.

The searchlight's flickering beam illuminated Kolinski's boat. "Not sure how long this light will last," came the shout from the bridge. "The generator is damaged." With those last words, the light went out, but came on again after a few seconds, again pointing at Kolinski's boat. More life-jacketed figures swam into the circle, and the men in the boat reached out to them.

Even Kolinski, terrified as he was, felt some sympathy towards these wet and oil-soaked sailors, and he reached out to one of them, whose pale face somehow reminded him of his younger brother.

Just as his hand made contact with the outstretched hand of the

German sailor, the searchlight went out again. This time, it failed to re-illuminate, and the sailor, obviously surprised by the sudden darkness, grabbed hold of Kolinski's arm and jerked hard. Kolinski was caught off balance and fell into the water.

At that moment, there was a rumble and a grinding sound, followed by several loud explosions from within the hull of the stricken destroyer, and all her lights went out.

Damn it to hell, thought Kolinski, who had lost contact with the German sailor when he fell into the water. Don't they know that I'm here? His irritation was replaced by panic. The gold in the heels of his boots and in his belt was dragging him down, and the life jacket was incapable of supporting his weight. There was no way he could remove his boots, or even his belt, which was inaccessible under the life jacket.

He struck out in an untrained doggy-paddle, and soon found himself next to a German sailor, who seemed to be swimming easily and calmly.

"Give me your life jacket," he growled in German.

"Go and fornicate with a goat," replied the other. "You have a jacket already. Why do you need mine?"

For answer, Kolinski reached out to the other with one hand, desperately paddling with the other and kicking with his legs to stay afloat. Grasping a handful of the man's hair, he pushed his face under the water. The German was in no state to fight back, obviously chilled by the Baltic water, and in a state of shock following the torpedoing of his vessel, and his struggling soon stopped. With some difficulty, Kolinski undid the tapes fastening the corpse's life jacket, and stripped it from the body.

Wrapping his arms around the extra life jacket, Kolinski was able to relax his frantic paddling a little, and start looking for help. The destroyer was obviously sinking, and the men on her decks had started to jump into the sea, heedless of whether there was a lifeboat to receive them or not.

In any case, there were no lifeboats near Kolinski that he could see. He started to panic, calling out for help, but his voice sounded strangled, and came out as a weak bleat. Still, he thought, at least he wasn't sinking. If he could only hang on until daylight, surely someone would see him? Mother of God, but it was cold. He wriggled his arms and legs to keep the circulation going, but the chill continued to seep through him. His teeth started to chatter, and a wave splashed against his face, filling his nose and mouth with salty water, making him cough and splutter. He could hear no noise from any of the boats that he was sure were still near him. A light wind started to blow, and a slight swell arose, intermittently hiding the ferry from him, where it had been constantly in his sight before. This increased his panic. If he couldn't see them, they couldn't see him, and they wouldn't know that he was struggling in the water.

A loud sound behind him made him turn his head. The destroyer slipped beneath the waves with terrifying speed, wrapped in a ferociously hissing cloud of steam as the water met the boilers and furnaces. He felt himself being inexorably pulled towards the place where she had gone down. But it was so cold. So damned cold. Prayers he'd learned as a boy floated up into his mind. Never mind being a good Communist, he needed something to pray to. Despite moving his arms and legs frantically to keep warm, counting the strokes as he did so, he found it hard to keep concentrating, and when he reached three hundred and fifty, he lost count. There was still no sign of any of the lifeboats, and when he could see the ferry again, it seemed to be stationary – no further away than it had been, but no nearer either.

He had started to wonder seriously whether he should let go of the looted life jacket and untie his own, allowing the gold in his boots and his belt to drag him to a quick and merciful death, when he saw a strange sight. A stick or something like that, sticking vertically out of the water. Not that unusual, since there was all manner of floating debris from the destroyer surrounding him, but this stick appeared to be moving under its own power, leaving a wake behind it. In fact, it was that slight wake that had made him notice the stick in the first place. It was definitely moving towards him. Some sort of sea monster come to gobble him up? he wondered. He didn't want to be too close to it, whatever it was, and he turned away from the stick, splashing with his arms and kicking his legs as hard as he could to get away from it.

❧

LIEUTENANT-COMMANDER HORTON CONTINUED TO GAZE through the periscope.

"Just the one that I can see," he remarked to his First Lieutenant. "And he's swimming away from us like billy-oh."

"Where's he heading, sir? For one of the boats?"

"I think they've all returned to the ferry. No, he's just swimming away from us, as far as I can tell."

"Should I give the order to surface, sir? We can't leave the poor bastard to drown or freeze to death."

"Very good, Number One. There appear to be no enemy in sight, and the ferry isn't going to do anything about us. Go ahead."

The order to surface was passed down the boat, and *E9* slowly raised herself out of the water.

"Two men on deck!" called the First Lieutenant. "Lifelines and boat-hooks and life-buoys. Man in the water."

Two seamen sprinted up the ladder to the conning tower, and dropped to the deck, where they clipped their lines to the safety rail. From the top of the conning tower, Horton directed the helmsman below to steer *E9* to a point where the drowning man could be picked out of the water. Indeed, he seemed to have given up his struggles some time ago, and it was unclear as to whether *E9* would be in time to save his life.

By dint of skilful seamanship, the submarine was brought close to the floating body, and the two seamen used boat-hooks to pull the dripping weight onto the deck.

"He's a right big 'un, sir," one of them called up to Horton. Bloody great weight is this bugger, begging your pardon for the language, sir."

"I'll send another man down to help you bring him in," called back Horton.

As the three men manoeuvred the limp body up the ladder to the conning tower, Horton looked at the face.

"That's no German face, I'd swear to it," he said, half to himself.

The seaman carrying the head end of the apparently drowned man heard him as he climbed over the lip of the conning tower. "Begging your pardon, sir, but he was hanging onto a German Navy life jacket."

"But that's not a German life jacket that he's wearing," pointed out Horton. "That's Swedish writing on there, or I miss my mark."

"Dunno about that," replied the AB. "All them funny languages ain't English, and that's all I know."

Curiouser and curiouser, thought Horton. As the three men wrestled their load down the ladder, he decided to go below and see for himself. He whistled down the tube for the First Lieutenant to relieve him, and slid down the ladder.

"Where do you want us to put him, sir? Officers' quarters?"

"No, put him in the sick bay." In the case of *E9*, as with most submarines, the term "sick bay" was a euphemism for a foldaway cot with a small medicine chest mounted above it.

"Aye, aye, sir."

Horton made his way to Brian's berth. "You gentlemen may be

interested to know that we've picked up a survivor from the destroyer. Except that he probably isn't from the destroyer."

"What does this mean?" asked Petrov. "He is or he is not from the destroyer, surely?"

Horton explained about the life jackets.

"Fascinating," commented Brian. "It sounds like an interesting sort of riddle-me-ree. Mind if I – if we, rather – come along and have a look at the blighter?"

"I was going to ask you to do just that."

"Good." Brian swung his legs over the edge of the bunk and dropped to the floor. Petrov likewise stood up, and followed Horton, Brian bringing up the rear.

"He's alive, sir," said the boatswain. "Just about. He coughed up a lot of water just now. I think that's all that was in him. He's breathing easy now, but he's dead to the world."

"Good," said Horton. "Let's get those wet clothes off him and get him wrapped up in a warm blanket or something. My God," looking at the recumbent figure, whose feet overhung the end of the cot, "he really is a monster, isn't he?"

"I'll start by taking off those boots," said Brian. "His feet will hurt like the dickens if they dry on him like that." He fumbled with the fastening and drew off one boot. "Got a bucket, bosun? This is full of water, judging by the weight." A bucket was bought, and Brian turned the boot upside-down over it. A few drops of water dribbled out. "Odd. This boot's much heavier than I'd expect. All at the heel end, as well." He removed the other boot, and repeated the process. "Just the same."

"Just a well-made pair of boots, that's all," said Horton. "Good leather and all that."

"Afraid not, sir. They're not well-made at all. See for yourself." He passed one of the boots to Horton.

"You're right about that. They're pretty shoddy, and they *are* heavy." Horton frowned. "Don't worry about it just now. Let's get the rest of his clothes off him and get him warm. Can you run some hot water off the engines and fill a bottle or something for him, bosun?" The boatswain left, with the three officers now the only ones near their mystery passenger.

Horton bent to unfasten the belt and spoke in a low voice. "There's something really funny about this one. He's not German, for sure, and something tells me he's not Swedish, either."

"I agree," said Petrov, who had been straining to follow the conversation. "In my opinion, he's a Russian."

"What papers does he have on him?" asked Brian, searching through an inside pocket. "Ha!" He riffled through them. "Looks like a Swiss passport here, but the ink seems to have run. Can't read any details. Ticket to Malmö from Travemunde. Ink's run on that, too, so there's no name to read there, either. Piece of paper with some writing on it in pencil. That's lucky. Maybe there's something for us there. Oh, in Russian, I think. Colonel, you may be right." He passed the sodden scrap of paper to Petrov.

"Meet at the south end of Truda Bridge, 2 pm on the 29th. Password is 'Hammer', countersign is 'Rock'. That's in St. Petersburg – Petrograd, as we have to call it now."

"And the 29th is over two weeks away," said Horton.

"So we have a Russian, travelling through Germany with a Swiss passport and some very heavy boots," remarked Brian. "Oh, and there's a Russian passport too, in a hidden inner pocket. Paper's so wet I daren't open it, but I'm willing to bet that the ink's run in that, too. And a couple of sheets of Russian letters, but I can't make head or tail of what it's all about. Typewritten. I'll give those to you to look at, Colonel."

"And he has a very heavy belt as well as heavy boots," added Horton, who had unthreaded the article in question from around the waist of the sleeping giant. He passed it to Brian.

"You're right," said Brian. "There's something in that belt. Look, it doesn't bend as easily as you'd expect." He examined it closely. "The stitching's weak here." He looked more closely, and suddenly said, "Look, Commander. You should take these boots and this belt and store them in your cabin away from public view. For God's sake, sir, no-one else must know about these things, believe me." He thrust the boots and belt into Horton's hands. "Sir," he continued, as Horton hesitated. "I have no authority to order you to do anything, you know that. Please, just trust me on this."

Mystified, Horton meekly did as Brian had suggested, while Brian continued to strip and dry the mysterious passenger. "Some ugly scars," he commented, as he towelled the massive torso.

"The marks of the knout, if I'm not mistaken," said Petrov softly in Russian. "We have a very interesting passenger indeed, Lieutenant."

"I think we do," agreed Brian, as the boatswain returned with a rum bottle, filled with hot water, and re-corked. "Right-oh, bosun, thank you very much indeed." He wrapped the bottle in a towel and placed it against the man's abdomen. "Should be the blighter's feet, but they stick out a bit. Better get another blanket. My, he is big, isn't he?"

Horton returned. "I assume you have your reasons for asking me to do that just now? Hiding the boots and belt?" he said to Brian.

"Indeed I do, sir," said Brian. "But now is not the time or place to talk about them. I'll have him all tucked up and ready for dreamland in a minute or so. The three of us, and Lieutenant Braithwaite, should talk in your cabin. Bosun, if you would be so good as to pass the word for Lieutenant Braithwaite and ask him to meet us in the Captain's cabin?"

"Aye, aye, sir," replied the boatswain, after a puzzled glance at Horton, mutely asking if he should be taking orders from this Army lieutenant. Horton nodded, and the boatswain departed.

"I'll meet you in a few minutes," Brian said to Horton and Petrov. "Just let me make the Sleeping Beauty comfortable."

He quickly tucked the blankets round the unconscious man, and resumed the search of his pockets. Nothing of interest, other than a few scraps of white cloth and some small German coins, and what had presumably been paper money. He was just turning to meet the others in Horton's cabin, when he noticed what he at first took to be a fly on the side of the sleeper's neck. Surprised to see such a thing in a submarine, he moved to brush it off, and then realised it was a small tattoo in the shape of a star. Yet another oddity. As he turned away, he bumped into Harry, who was on his way to the captain's cabin.

"Good," said Brian. "I hope you've been enjoying yourself while we've been busy sinking German destroyers."

"I've been learning a lot about diesels and about electrical propulsion systems. Good bunch of blokes in that engine-room. Don't half know their stuff," he said.

"Well, we have a problem of a different kind. See him?" pointing to the castaway.

"Can't hardly miss him, can you?" Harry grinned. "Who is he?"

"That's what we don't know. He's a bit of a mystery man, but I have my ideas."

They entered Horton's tiny cabin, and drew the curtain for privacy. There was one chair, occupied by Petrov, as the most senior officer present. The rest squeezed side by side to sit on the bunk.

"So, what's all this about, Finch-Malloy?" asked Horton. "I'm a busy man, trying to skipper a temperamental piece of machinery through enemy waters, if you hadn't noticed."

"Sorry, sir," said Brian. "A few rather interesting things about our guest. Colonel Petrov has made the guess that he is a Russian, and this seems to be borne out by the note in his pocket that indicates a meeting in Petrograd soon. A clandestine meeting, by the look of it, with signs and countersigns. Very hush-hush. And, again according to Colonel Petrov, the man has the marks of the knout on his back, which means, Colonel?"

"Almost certainly he has been in a Siberian prison camp, where the knout is used as a means of punishing those who step out of line."

"I noticed just now that he has a small five-pointed star tattooed here." Brian touched the side of his own neck.

"Ah," said Petrov. "One of the Oupinski gang, I would guess." The others looked at him quizzically. "A criminal gang – highway robbers – but with very strong links to the socialists. There have been rumours that the proceeds of their robberies largely went to fund revolutionary activity."

"So we have a Russian bandit on board," said Horton. "Wonderful. And what's all the mystery about the boots and belt?"

For answer, Brian picked up the belt, which was resting on the floor under the chair, and worked at the seam on the inside of the belt. A gold piece fell out, followed by another, and another. Working his fingers along the belt, Brian extracted over a dozen gold coins.

Horton whistled and picked up one of the pieces. "Russian roubles."

"This one's a German coin, I think, sir," said Harry, holding it up to Petrov.

"Quite right."

"And I'd lay odds that the heels of his boots are hollow and hold more gold coins. The plot thickens," said Brian.

"Indeed it does," agreed Horton. "Any suggestions?"

"He's committed no crime," said Brian. "I really don't see how you could arrest him and keep him under confinement."

"I wouldn't like to do it in any case," said Horton. "The brute could do a lot of damage to the boat if he put his mind to it, without even trying too hard. And as you say, he's committed no crime."

"So we dry out his papers and put them back, as well as putting the gold back in his belt, and we pretend we know nothing," suggested Brian. "We aim for Reval, rather than Kronstadt, and put him ashore at the first opportunity."

"And I pass orders to the Okhrana to follow him and arrest him as soon as he spits on the pavement," said Petrov. Brian nodded agreement.

"I think it would be a good idea if he didn't know that Colonel Petrov was on board," said Harry, suddenly. "It seems to me that we shouldn't let him know there's anyone on board who can read Russian or knows what that tattoo means."

"I agree," said Brian.

"That is a good thought, Lieutenant," said Petrov approvingly to Harry. "No hardship for me to keep to my bunk out of his way for another day or so."

"And we can always keep him in the sick bay until we dock," said Horton.

"Agreed, then," said Brian.

⁂

AFTER THE CONVERSATION in Horton's cabin, the three visiting officers retired to their bunks. Since dawn was about to break, and Horton had no wish to be spotted on the surface, he ordered the submarine to dive.

None of the three had any wish to speak for the time being, and each lay on his bunk, thinking his own thoughts, as the hum of the machinery filled the hull.

The day and night it took for *E9* to arrive at Reval passed relatively uneventfully. Brian spent a large part of the time sitting by the castaway's bed, listening to the noises and words that he spoke in his semi-delirious state. All was in Russian, confirming their suspicions, and Brian wrote it down as he listened. "Chief," "Lenin," "the cause", and, somewhat unusually, "Hilda", were names and words that came up relatively often. When he reported them to Petrov, the latter frowned.

"He's definitely one of the revolutionaries. Lenin is what the leader of those Bolsheviks calls himself. You said you used to know him as Ulyanov. Well, now he's called Lenin."

"Which means what?"

Petrov shrugged. "Someone told me it was derived from the Lena River in Russia, but I really don't know and it doesn't matter. What does matter is that we have a rather dangerous revolutionary on our hands here. For the sake of us all, I hope we reach port soon. Commander Horton is quite right when he says it is dangerous to have such a man aboard a vessel like this. And I will certainly make sure that the police will follow him and detain him if necessary."

"I'm sure he has a criminal record," said Brian. "My knowledge of Russian law is limited, but I would have thought you could do something there."

"If we knew who he was, you are right. But I know this type of scum. They take a stubborn pride in not telling the authorities anything. You could flay the skin off that man's back, and he would make it a point of honour to keep his mouth shut, even to tell us his name. It would be better for the police to follow him and find out what he's up to. Maybe he can lead us to the rest of the gang."

"Well, you know where and when you can find him in Petrograd, thanks to that note."

"We do. I just hope that he doesn't have any plans for destruction and mayhem before that."

At last *E9* surfaced again, and fresh air swept away the stink that had been accumulating over the past day.

"Nearly into Reval," said Horton to Brian. "We should be docked in an hour or so. How's the patient?"

"We're going to have to stretcher him out, I think, sir," said Brian.

He's not in any state to walk or do anything under his own steam. Petrov thinks that he should be allowed to go free and lead the police to whatever terrorists he's planning to hook up with. So we'll get him to a naval hospital, where the security will be tight enough, and your people will know where he is until he is discharged. And I'll make sure it's me who carries his boots and his belt with the rest of his things. I don't want anyone else to suspect anything about them."

Horton shook his head. "That's all out of my class," he said. "My job is this lady here," patting the side of the hull, "and looking after the men who sail in her. Coming up to the conning tower to watch us berth, or are you still going to continue playing Florence Nightingale with our friend?"

"I want to keep an eye on him."

As Horton had predicted, *E9* was safely berthed within a couple of hours. Petrov was the first to leave the submarine, hurrying ashore to arrange for an ambulance for the castaway, and to advise the police and other authorities as to what had happened.

The ambulance drew up on the quayside a little more than an hour after Petrov had left, and two burly Russian stretcher-bearers made their way down *E9*'s ladder.

"We can't take a monster like that up the ladder on the stretcher," one of them said in Russian.

"Bones breaked, you know?" the other asked Brian in accented English.

"Not that we have discovered," replied Brian in Russian. The orderlies seemed impressed by Brian's ability to speak the language, and Brian went on, "He seems to have suffered quite a lot from the cold, and he swallowed quite a lot of water, which all came up when we brought him on board. As far as getting him off this boat, I'm sure that we'll find a way with some of these sailors helping you."

"Where are his clothes?" asked the other Russian.

"In the Captain's cabin, where they've been drying. I'll bring them with him to the hospital."

Somehow the Russians and some of the *E9*'s sailors managed to push, shove and haul the comatose body up the ladder, and onto the waiting stretcher on deck, from where it was carried into the ambulance. Brian followed with the man's clothes, now dried and made into a bundle, and climbed into the back of the ambulance with the patient.

A minute or so after the ambulance set off, the man lying on the stretcher opened his eyes with a start. His eyes roved around the ambulance, without his head moving or his neck turning, and came to rest on Brian, who had been watching him.

"Where am I?" he asked Brian in German.

"In Russia. Reval," answered Brian in Russian.

The man showed no surprise at being addressed in Russian, but replied in the same language. "What happened?" he asked. "I fell out of the lifeboat and it was cold, and then..?"

"We were on a British submarine travelling here to Reval, and we picked you up out of the water."

The man appeared to think about this, and then suddenly realised what he was wearing, or, to be more precise, what he was not wearing. "My clothes and my boots. Where are they?" He sounded a little panic-stricken.

"Right here," Brian reassured him, holding up the bundle of clothes.

"Is my passport in there, and all my papers?" was the next question.

"Your Swiss passport's there. And your Russian one," added Brian, a little maliciously.

A look of panic spread over the man's face. "Where am I? Why am I strapped down like this?"

"Easy, easy. You nearly died out there. You're not a well man at all, and you're going to the hospital in an ambulance. And you're strapped down because that's what they always do when people travel in an ambulance."

"Which hospital?"

"The naval hospital. It's the best, and it's closest."

The panic that had overtaken the man seemed to leave his face, and he relaxed a little. He continued to look at Brian, and eventually came out with, "You're not Russian, are you? You're not from Moscow or Petersburg, I can tell. Polish? Ukrainian? Czech? Estonian? Latvian?" Brian continued to shake his head.

"I'm British," he said at last.

The man seemed surprised by this. "Where did you learn your Russian?" he asked.

Brian thought of teasing him by answering "from Lenin", but held his tongue. The ambulance drew to a halt, and the rear doors were opened. Brian followed the stretcher down the grimy halls to a room with just one bed in it, where the castaway was laid.

"I'll just put your things here," said Brian to the man, putting the bundle down on the wooden chair by the bed. "Everything's there. And I'll be off, and I probably won't see you again, so goodbye."

There was silence from the bed. Brian thought the man must have lost consciousness again, but when he looked, the eyes were open, watching him with the kind of malevolence that reminded Brian of a wolf or some other savage animal.

Brian turned and walked out of the room. He looked back as he went through the doorway. The yellow eyes were still watching him. He walked back along the corridor, trying to ignore the noises and smells that came from the rooms on either side, until he came to the entrance where the ambulance was still parked. He waited until the two ambulance-men returned, and offered each of them a cigarette, which they accepted gratefully.

"Where's Colonel Petrov?" he asked them.

"Who?"

"The man who asked for you to come to the docks to pick up that man."

The older Russian shrugged. "No idea who you're talking about. Talk to our section chief. He'll know."

Brian dragged the directions for the ambulance office slowly and painfully from the two men, and set off across the yard. Behind the desk sat a uniformed petty officer, obviously the man in charge.

"Who?" he said, when Brian asked for Petrov.

"The man who came here and asked for an ambulance for the British submarine."

The petty officer's face cleared. "Oh, yes. Colonel Petrov," he said, with heavy emphasis. "Of course that's his name. Stupid of me. You'll find him at the Catherinethal."

"And where and what is that?" asked Brian.

"You don't know?" said the petty officer suspiciously. "Everyone knows where the Catherinethal is."

"Well, I don't know," said Brian. "I arrived here," he looked at his watch, "about ninety minutes ago, on the British submarine that carried Colonel Petrov and me here from England."

"You're a friend of the Colonel?" The petty officer seemed nervous.

"I work with him. He is my colleague, I suppose you could say."

The petty officer leaped to his feet and snapped to attention. "My apologies, sir. This way, Your Honour. I'll fetch a car to take you there immediately, Your Excellency."

Now what hornet's nest had he disturbed? Brian thought to himself.

Chapter 8: Reval to Petrograd to Moscow, Imperial Russia

Brian couldn't help noticing that she had a pair of the most beautiful dark eyes he had ever seen, set in a heart-shaped face that almost knocked the breath out of him.

A N OLD DAIMLER ARRIVED NOISILY outside the office a few minutes later. "This way, Your Excellency," said the petty officer, who had returned with the car. He rushed forward and held the back door open for Brian.

"Thank you," said Brian, returning the man's salute as the car moved off and drove out of the dock area through the streets of Reval. Catherinethal turned out to be a beautiful building in Baroque style, set in some of the most elegant formal gardens that Brian had ever seen. The chauffeur drew up in front of the mansion's front door, leaped out of the driver's seat and had the door open for him before Brian had fully realised that the car had stopped. As Brian walked up the steps to the front door, it swung upon, and a gorgeously liveried flunkey bowed and asked him his name and business.

"Brian Finch-Malloy, of His Britannic Majesty's Coldstream

Guards. I'm here to see Colonel Petrov." The servant extended a silver tray in Brian's direction. "I regret that I seem to have left my cards at home."

"Sir?" enquired the footman. "May I ask once more whom it is that you wish to meet?"

"Colonel Petrov," repeated Brian. "I was told he was here."

"If you would be kind enough to wait here, sir, I will make enquiries as to whether the gentleman with whom you wish to converse is in residence. May I trouble you to repeat your name, sir?"

After Brian had repeated his name, the footman strode off down the hall, leaving Brian under the watchful eye of another servant. Brian looked around at the furniture and decorations of the place. Fit for a king, he thought. Craftsmanship and artistry that for some reason he had never associated with Russia. He wondered what Harry Braithwaite, with his appreciation of the Sheraton table in the Foreign Office, would make of all this.

The flunkey returned. "His Highness awaits you," he said, with a low bow. "Please follow me."

Brian obeyed, somewhat confused. "His Highness?" The servant led him down a long corridor past what looked like priceless works of art, to a large set of double doors, opened them and bowed.

"Ah, Lieutenant," came Petrov's voice from the end of the long room. "Do come in and make yourself at home."

"Home was never like this, sir," said Brian, gazing at the decorated ceiling and magnificent furniture in admiration.

Petrov chuckled. "To be perfectly honest with you, it's not my home, either. But his Imperial Majesty allows members of the family to use it sometimes." Brian looked at him curiously. "Forgive the little deception," said Petrov. "But I think you will remember what that policeman told us in London. There are any number of anarchists and terrorists in London, even with your excellent police service looking out for them, who would like nothing so much as to see a dead Grand Duke. We felt it would be better when I went to Britain that I remained incognito."

"I'm very sorry, sir," said Brian. "I had no idea..." Though Brian usually had little respect for inherited rank and titles, he had some kind of confused idea that insulting one of the Russian Imperial family could result in a diplomatic incident of some kind between Britain and Russia. "May I ask how I should address you properly, sir?"

The other laughed. "I think that you may continue to address me and think of me as 'Colonel.' It is, after all, one of the honorary ranks that I hold, and I can think of worse titles. Please continue to think of me as Colonel Petrov. I've got rather attached to the fellow, myself, and I will be happy to answer to the name."

"And what exactly do you do, sir, if you're not the humble military attaché whom we knew in London? And if I might mention it, sir, you have been remarkably humble. I mean, you never had a single servant on the submarine to look after you."

Petrov laughed. "So many people seem to think that those of us in our position are helpless babies, unable to lift a finger to look after themselves. I'd have you know, young man, that in the war against the Japanese, I served in the trenches at Port Arthur, without benefit of servants or any luxuries."

"Sorry, sir. No offence meant."

"Never mind. I'm sure I have some similarly strange ideas about you where you would be happy to put me right. So, to answer your first question, I hold a rather senior position in our military organisation while not actually being part of the military," explained Petrov. "Similar in rank, I suppose, to your superior, C, but with a much more purely military function. My specialisation is the development of new weapons and the like. But also, for obvious reasons, I work with people such as your C, and our Russian equivalents from time to time."

There was a knock on the door, and in answer to Petrov's

command, a young lady entered, carrying some papers in a cardboard folder. From the fond smile on Petrov's face, it was obvious that she was not a servant or a clerk.

"May I introduce my daughter, Maria?" smiled Petrov. "Maria, this is Lieutenant Finch-Malloy from England."

Brian, who had instinctively stood up when Maria entered, bowed. Hovering between shaking Maria's extended hand and kissing it, he settled on the latter.

"That's not a very English habit," smiled Maria. Brian couldn't help noticing that she had a pair of the most beautiful dark eyes he had ever seen, set in a heart-shaped face that almost knocked the breath out of him. Her English was almost unaccented. She noticed Brian's surprise. "I was sent to school in Cheltenham. A little unusual, perhaps, but it taught me English, which, as you see, Father doesn't speak very well," (Petrov grinned a little self-deprecatingly at this) "and it gave me a taste for English things. So as well as bringing in this file which Father asked for, I came to ask if you would like some English tea."

"That would be most welcome."

"I'll arrange for some. By the way, your name is Finch-Malloy? I heard correctly?"

"That's right."

"I was at school with a girl who had a cousin called Brian Finch-Malloy, I think. Charlotte Cripps was her name."

"Yes, my cousin. She was married two years ago to a charming fellow, but I'm sorry to have to tell you that her husband was killed in action. It happened in France a few months ago,."

"Oh, that is sad news. Please convey my condolences to her when you return to England."

Petrov coughed discreetly.

"Oh, sorry, Father. I beg your pardon. I'll see about the tea. If I may join you gentlemen at tea after you've finished your business?"

Petrov nodded, and Maria handed the folder to her father, and walked out, Brian staring after her.

"Congratulations on your most charming and beautiful daughter," said Brian, when the door had closed behind Maria, and he was finally able to tear his eyes away.

"She is rather an exceptional lady," agreed Petrov. "I have to confess that I work her rather harder than I might work any other assistant, but she says that she enjoys the work, and who am I to deny a daughter her pleasures, especially when she continues to be so useful? Bismarck promoted his son in his service, and though Russia is not ready for a woman to take high office, I dearly wish that Maria could serve her country as well as Hubert von Bismarck served his country in the service of his father. Maria will be travelling with us, at least as far as Petrograd, and then probably to Moscow. I must allow her some time to herself. Like all women, she is continually complaining that she has nothing to wear, and needs to go shopping. You're not married, Lieutenant?"

"No, sir," said Brian. He nearly added "Not yet," but decided to hold his tongue.

"So, let us look at what Maria has brought me. This is the police dossier on the man we picked up out of the water. At least, it's the dossier of someone who matches what we know of our friend."

"So you've been able to alert the police as to his whereabouts?"

"Indeed so. You went to the hospital with him to take his clothes there?" Brian nodded. "You noticed that his room was for him and him alone? Maybe you failed to notice the bars on the windows and the strong doors. I described the man to one of my colleagues before I decided whether to send an ambulance for him and, at least partly due to your observation of the tattoo on his neck, we almost certainly have the man positively identified. I am very happy that he is out of that submarine and behind firmly locked doors. As soon as he is in a condition to realise where he is, he will soon recognise that his days are numbered."

"Who is he, then, sir?"

"He usually goes by the name of Kolinski. He is a vicious man. We are almost certain that he is responsible for many of the so-called 'expropriations' – that is to say, bank robberies – carried out by these Bolshevik scum seven or eight years ago. In many of these, people were killed, innocent bystanders, as well as police, and almost indisputably, Kolinski was responsible for many of these murders. In addition to this, his name has been linked, admittedly without much in the way of firm evidence, to murders and killings abroad, in Switzerland and elsewhere."

"Whose murders?"

"Typically those of members of rival parties to the Bolsheviks. As far as we are able to tell, Kolinski is devoted to your old friend Ulyanov and his cause – or at any rate, the money he receives from them – it's somewhat doubtful whether he understands the finer points of Karl Marx's economic theories. We are very glad indeed to have him in our power. It's lucky that Commander Horton picked him out of the water."

"How is that, sir?"

"We know where he is now, and we have him in our grip. If he had perished in the water, we would have been none the wiser, and we would have continued to waste time and effort continuing to search Europe for a man whose bones were at the bottom of the Baltic Sea. And, furthermore, thanks to the note that you found, we know exactly when and where he is to meet his confederate, and we can wait there and pick up the confederate, who may lead us to others of the gang. I think, Lieutenant, we are in a very good position to cut off the Russian head of this hydra, thanks to our luck in finding this man."

KOLINSKI OPENED HIS EYES and stared up at the ceiling, where the whitewash was cracking and flaking away. A spider's web stretched across one corner of the room, and the spider was sitting in the middle of it.

He shifted his gaze to the window, and cursed the bars over it. Even if he had all his strength back, he doubted very much whether he would be able to remove those solid-looking obstacles without making a noise that would bring the guards running.

For Kolinski had no illusions where he was. They might call it a hospital, and he might be lying in a comfortable bed with clean sheets, but hospitals didn't usually have reinforced and barred doors and thick bars over the windows. Nor did nurses (male, to Kolinski's disappointment) usually enter patients' rooms accompanied by marines carrying slung carbines. Kolinski was a prisoner, and he knew it.

His immediate question was whether he still had the gold with him. If he did, there was a very good chance he could bribe his way out of where he was being held, and still make his rendezvous. He looked carefully to see if he was being watched through the spyhole in the door, and decided it was safe to check. He slipped out of bed, still feeling a little weak and dizzy, and picked up one of his boots. Praise be to the saints, it still felt heavy, and so did the other one. He reminded himself yet again that as a good Communist, he should not be addressing God or the saints, but he felt happy enough about not having drowned in the sea not to care. The belt also still felt heavy. He extracted three gold coins from it, and pushed them carefully under the pillow before he slipped under the blankets again.

Patience, he told himself. He was surprised that no-one had asked him who he was, or what he had been doing in the sea, since he guessed that the strange Russian-speaking Englishman with the cold green eyes would have told the Russian authorities something about how he had been picked up. But the longer they delayed questioning him, the more time he had to plan his escape. He would have to use the gold, as he could no longer rely on his strength alone to force his way out of this guarded military institution, in his current relatively weakened state. He doubted whether he could ever have made his way through the armed guards with little more than his powerful muscles, even when he had been feeling at his strongest. He lay back and daydreamed, eventually dozing off.

He was woken by the nurse arriving with the midday meal, the two marines following him as usual. The food here wasn't that bad, Kolinski thought to himself. There was even a little bit of pork fat in the cabbage soup, and the bread wasn't too hard. Nothing like what he'd become used to in Switzerland, of course, but better than most meals he remembered eating in Russia. The wooden bowl and spoon were left beside his bed, with the hunk of bread beside them, and the nurse left the room, the door being locked behind him. Kolinski finished off the soup, and broke the bread into three parts before feeling under his pillow for the gold coins, one of which he stuffed into each of the hunks of bread.

He lay back and waited for the bowl to be collected. One thing about being in a Navy hospital; they did keep things relatively clean and tidy, and all the chores were carried out efficiently and punctually. At last the footsteps outside the door returned, the door was unlocked, and the nurse entered.

"What's the matter?" he asked Kolinski, looking at the uneaten bread. "Not hungry today?"

"There's something strange in the bread. Something hard," replied Kolinski.

The nurse picked up one of the pieces of bread, and sniffed at it. "Smells all right. Seems a bit heavy, though."

"Try it for yourself," suggested Kolinski.

"Not a chance," retorted the nurse. "You've probably pissed on it or something."

"Well, aren't you even going to see what I nearly broke my teeth on?" Kolinski complained.

"All right." He picked up the piece of bread and crumbled it a little. The gold coin shone out of the bread. "Holy Mother of God, would you look at that?" he exclaimed. "Is this real?"

"I have a feeling that those pieces of bread might be the same. Perhaps our two friends here would like to check them for strange ingredients?" Without waiting for an answer, he proffered the two pieces of bread to the two guards, who accepted them, puzzled. Their reaction was much the same as that of the nurse.

"What's this for?" asked one of them. "If you want to get out of here, it's going to cost you more than this."

"I don't have very much more," Kolinski lied. "Maybe I can manage the same again for each of you."

The guard scratched his head. "Maybe," he conceded. "Not sure that we can really help you for that amount of money, though."

"This is gold," Kolinski pointed out. "None of your paper shit."

"True," said the younger guard. "Sasha, I think this is worth thinking about, at least. My family could use the money, even if yours doesn't need it."

"Same here," agreed the nurse.

"We'll think about it," said the first guard. "Mind you, you're going to have to come up with some sort of plan. Don't ask us to help you there. That's nothing to do with us. We'll give you an answer tomorrow. We're off duty in an hour's time, and we won't see you until tomorrow morning."

"Agreed," said Kolinski, as he was left alone.

Now, sitting on the edge of his bed, he wasn't sure that he had done the right thing. He had let them know that he had more gold – to be sure, he hadn't let them know exactly how much was involved, but it wouldn't be hard for them to discover what remained of his store of gold now they knew it existed. He checked the spy-hole in the door once more, and lifted up his belt. He reckoned that after paying for his train and ferry tickets, the bribe to the village stationmaster in

Germany, and the money he had just given the guards and the nurse, he had more than enough money there for the additional bribes. He hadn't touched the money in his boots, so he knew exactly how much should be there.

He wasn't sure if he could remove the heels of his boots easily, since he had no implement to help him, but it seemed after careful examination that no-one had tampered with his boots since he had stuffed the heels with the gold pieces. Certainly the weight seemed to be about what he remembered it being. So that was all right.

He took the belt and fastened it round his waist. At least no-one was going to take that off him in a hurry. The boots were another matter. He had no wish to wear them in bed, but he decided to take them from their place on the floor, and keep them under the blanket, and be damned. At least they'd be in a place where he could stop them being stolen, even if they did dig into his side every time he turned over.

BRIAN WAS DRIVEN BACK TO THE DOCKS, where he returned to the submarine and informed Harry that his earlier suspicions regarding Petrov's identity had been correct, and that Petrov was definitely of a higher rank than he had previously claimed.

"So what is he? Some sort of prince or something like that?"

"Something like that," Brian confirmed. "Maybe a grand duke – he dropped hints that he's quite closely related to the Emperor."

Harry whistled in appreciation. "You mean, he's that high up? Royalty or something?"

"That's what it seems like. Can't be sure of it, but I'm pretty certain that he's a cousin or something like that." Brian then told Harry about his visit to the Catherinethal palace.

"What do I call him, then? I'm not used to talking to princes and dukes and that sort of person."

"That's just what I asked him, and he said that we could carry on calling him 'Colonel Petrov'. He said he'd got used to it and he liked it."

"I suppose you can get tired of being a prince," Harry remarked reflectively. "Not sure if I ever would, though."

"Not that you or I are ever likely to get the chance to find out," smiled Brian.

"What are our plans in Petrograd?" Harry wondered, changing the subject.

"You and I are meant to report to the Embassy and let them know that we've arrived safely. I expect there are going to be some more orders for us from London waiting for us there. Petrov also mentioned that we may have to attend some formal receptions with Russian high-ups and so on. Lord knows who we're meant to be meeting, or why, but that seems to be the way things are done round here."

Harry groaned.

"It's not as bad as all that. We'll probably run into some princes or dukes who aren't running around pretending to be colonels. You'll be able to write home and tell them that you're hobnobbing with royalty. Or at least, you'll be able to tell them when you get back, since we probably shouldn't be telling anyone where we are right now. Oh, and there's another nice little surprise for you, which I think you'll like. We're going to have a fellow-traveller with us at least to Petrograd. I think you'll be impressed with the Grand Duchess Maria, or whatever her formal title is."

"Oh no," groaned Harry. "First I find out I'm working with a prince, and then you tell me that I'm going to be sharing a train with a duchess. You know I don't bring it up that often, Brian, and I know that you never do, but you're one of the nobs and I'm not, though you don't like to talk about it. Anyway, I'm safe from her, because I can't speak Russian."

"She's one up on you then, Harry, because her English is as good as anyone's. She went to school in England. We had a bit of a chat after I'd finished my business with Petrov. She's not at all snobbish, it seems to me, and she thinks the world of England and the English. Maybe that's why Petrov is so keen on working with us. Anyway, you'll like her, and I'm sure she'll like you. And she's a real looker."

"Lucky you," said Harry.

"What's that meant to mean?"

"Well, maybe you'll end up marrying a Grand Duchess, but I don't think I'm going to, do you?"

"Me? Marry her?" Brian burst out laughing. "You're joking, old son."

"You've gone soft on her. I can tell it in your eyes," replied Harry. "How long were you with her?"

Brian considered. "About thirty minutes, I suppose. Maybe a little longer. Anyway, not long enough to 'go soft' on a girl, as you put it."

"That's plenty of time," replied Harry. "I saw it with my brother Sid. He hadn't met his Maggie for more than fifteen minutes, he told me, before he made up his mind that he was going to marry her."

"Rubbish. Complete rot," said Brian firmly, but when he thought about it, he realised there might be more to Harry's words than he wanted to admit. "Anyway, even if I did feel that way about her, there's no way on earth that I could marry a Grand Duchess. She's probably promised to some Russian prince or Austrian duke or something. Probably has been engaged since she was four years old or something. That's the sort of thing they do," he added morosely.

"See? You're already sounding jealous." Harry laughed.

"Me? Jealous? You're joking." But inside, Brian wondered a little. Something about Maria had struck him hard. It wasn't the first time it had happened to him, but it was the first time it had happened with someone of such a high social rank and so far out of his reach.

On the train to Petrograd, though their tickets had "First Class" printed on them, the usual class for all officers travelling by train, it seemed that their carriage was unoccupied except for their party: Petrov; Maria, who had the use of a compartment to herself at the other end of the carriage to those of the three men; and some servants, including two maids for Maria.

Much to Harry's embarrassment, Petrov had insisted that both Brian and Harry accept the services of two Russian servants each, at least until they reached Moscow.

"What am I meant to do?" asked Harry. "I'm not used to having servants waiting on me."

"Relax and enjoy the ride," Brian told him. "As far as I can tell, these blokes wouldn't be doing anything useful if they weren't looking after you and making sure that you had a clean shirt to wear every day."

"Well, I'm not going to let that one with the long black beard shave me," Harry had retorted. "I swear he drinks. Have you seen his hands shaking?" Harry came from a Nonconformist family, and claimed to have touched alcohol only once or twice in his life. Brian, who had no such scruples, appreciated that Harry never tried to convert others to this point of view, but simply claimed that it wasn't for him to judge others in these matters.

"Of course he drinks. Everyone in this country drinks. It's the only way to survive here. But you're right, I wouldn't let him shave me, either. It's something I've always done for myself, anyway."

❧

As it happened, the stay in Petrograd was less socially demanding than they had feared. Both Harry and Brian, whose formal wardrobes were nonexistent, were relieved. Harry, who had been instantly charmed by Maria's lack of pretension, which had almost helped him to forget her social rank, felt he could claim some credit for this avoidance of the social whirl. He had stammeringly explained to Maria that Brian and he were not important, and were not nobility in any shape or form, and therefore were unfit to join polite Petrograd society, especially in the clothes they had with them. Maria had taken the hint and passed the message on to her father.

They did, however, have to meet an aide to the British Military chargé d'affaires, a relation of a friend of Brian's, who seemed less than happy about their visit.

"Damn' funny business, if you ask me. Why didn't the blighters tell me straight off about whatever it is you're meant to be doing here, instead of sending this Colonel Petrov, whoever he may be, off to London to make a bloody nuisance of himself?"

Because they couldn't trust you to keep your mouth shut, said Brian to himself. Charles Featherington's inability to stay sober for more than a couple of hours at a time had been something of a cause for wonder throughout the whole Brigade of Guards when he'd been a serving officer. His secondment to the Foreign Office as a diplomat, following an incapacitating injury resulting from a riding accident, obviously hadn't changed things that much, thought Brian, noting the red nose and broken veins of the man sitting opposite him. He'd always liked him when they'd been growing up together, but despite having been at school with him, and his being a friend's cousin, Brian had little regard for Featherington's professional abilities, either as a soldier or as a diplomat.

"So can you tell me where you're off to? Just as a courtesy, in case we need to get hold of you?" demanded Featherington.

"Don't actually know the details yet, old boy," said Brian as airily as he could manage. "Somewhere outside Moscow, that's all we've been told."

"So you don't know what you're going to see?"

"We know as much as you do. Some sort of wonder weapon that the Russkies have cooked up. Probably a complete load of cobblers," replied Brian. "Waste of time sending us."

"What sort of wonder weapon are you talking about?"

"It's a—" Harry started to answer, but broke off as he received a sudden sharp blow to his ankle.

"It's a mystery," Brian continued hurriedly. "They're not talking a lot about it until we see it."

They had left the Embassy, and were sitting in the back of the staff car provided for them, when Harry turned to Brian.

"That bloody hurt," he complained, rubbing his ankle. "Did you have to kick me that hard?"

"Sorry about that. It wasn't meant to hurt that much. Just enough to shut you up," replied Brian. "But the less Featherington knows about this, the better."

"Why? He's on our side, isn't he? Why shouldn't he know?"

"That, Harry, is a question that has a very complicated answer."

"What are you talking about?"

"What I mean is that before we left, C called me in to see him alone. I have been saddled with another mission as well as the ones you know about, and I didn't want to tell you before now because, with all due respect, you're too damned honest. You're very bad at telling lies, so I didn't want you to know the truth."

"And the truth is?"

"That the Germans have been too lucky on the Eastern Front over the past few months. They seem to have known in advance exactly what they were going to be up against in terms of Russian forces, and the defences they were going to meet. Not every time, but a lot of the time."

"So what's that got to do with us?"

"C pointed out to me that the only operations where the Germans have known what was happening were those where the Russians had been discussing their plans with the military liaison of the British Embassy. I'm guessing that this all came through Colonel Petrov, and the whole business with this weird war machine is very secondary to his main purpose in visiting London, which was to get help from our side in finding the traitor in the British Embassy. It seems to be my job to find out who it is, and get him back to London."

"So what makes you think it might be Featherington? I thought he was your pal. And what a rotten thing, to ask you to do something like that. Couldn't you have refused?"

"And what would that make me if I refused? A party to treason?" replied Brian. "Believe me, this is not easy, and I am not at all happy about having to do it. Why does it have to be poor Featherington? Well, it doesn't have to be, but I'm afraid all the evidence seems to point that way. He's a weak man. He bets a lot on the gee-gees, and he has an infallible gift for picking losers. That and his drinking habits – and the drinking and the gambling are probably connected – mean that he's always short of money, and whatever moral fibre he has ever possessed has been weakened. He's a prime candidate for recruitment by the Germans."

"But you have no proof," objected Harry.

"And I'm sorry to tell you that it's our job – both yours and mine – to provide the proof," replied Brian. "It's a dirty job, and I am not happy about having to do it—"

"—so you're going to ask me to take over," interrupted Harry.

"Not at all," snapped Brian. "You know bloody well that I don't pass the dirty work over to you. That was a damned silly thing for you to say. " It was rare for Brian to speak that way to Harry, and there was an uncomfortable silence for about half a minute. "I was going to say that I will do it, with the greatest possible hope that C and Petrov are wrong, and that it is actually someone else who is passing all this information to the Germans. If they are right, though, and Featherington is guilty, then..."

"Then what?"

Brian encircled his throat with a finger and thumb and jerked upwards. Harry flinched.

"Really?"

"Unless they decide to shoot him." Brian rubbed his chin. "Harry, you're right. Featherington, damn it, despite all his faults, is a pal of mine. He's good fun to be around when he's sober, and he was one of the best wings in the house footer matches. I remember the time he broke into the school sanatorium one time with a box of white mice..." Brian grinned at the memory, but the grin swiftly disappeared as he spoke again. "He's the cousin of a good friend of mine, Henry Dowling. Don't like his mother much, but his father's a good man. This will break his heart, and the heart of the whole family." Brian stopped speaking, and his next words, which followed after a few minutes' silence, sounded as though they came from a different man. His voice was faint, as he turned to look away from Harry and spoke. "You know, Harry, I really don't want to do this. This really is too much for me. Just you be thankful you don't have to send one of your friends to the gallows." Brian put his head in his hands, and his shoulders began to shake.

"I think it's downright rotten of them, asking you to do the dirty on your friends like that," said Harry. "I think we should go straight back to England, and tell C that. And if you won't, I will."

Brian straightened up and looked Harry in the face with his reddened eyes. "I can't do that, and neither can you." His voice was so quiet that Harry had to strain to catch the words. "There's no way I can refuse to do this job. Believe me, Harry, I appreciate your thoughts and your sympathy. But we're both officers in His Majesty's Army, damn it. This is a foul thing for me to have to do, but it's orders.

If I have to do it, I will, but I'm going to hate myself for the rest of my life for doing it."

"It's C you should be hating, not yourself," replied Harry.

"It's C's job as well, and I'm sure it's no fun for him, either. His job is to keep the country safe and to beat the damned Boche. So he just moves us all round like pawns on a board. All of us, damn him." A long pause. "Harry, I'm going to need a drink when we get back. It's really too much for me to think about stone cold sober. A bloody great drink is what I need. I know you don't usually drink, but do you think you could break the habit of a lifetime, and keep me company? I drink a bottle of vodka, you drink one of those tiny little glasses? Will you do that for me, Harry? Keep me company? I don't want to drink alone. Make me feel like poor old Charlie."

Harry said nothing, but nodded silently. Neither man said anything more as the car continued its journey to their quarters.

FROM PETROGRAD, THEY CONTINUED TO MOSCOW. True to his word, Harry had drunk a thimbleful of lemon vodka at Brian's request, while Brian had finished the rest of the bottle.

"Did that really do you any good?" asked Harry, when Brian finally came to, moaning and clutching his head.

"I suppose not," Brian had replied. "Bloody stupid of me, really, I suppose. I feel like death warmed over. But at least I forgot about what I was meant to be doing for the time I was drinking."

"But it didn't make it go away for good, did it?" Harry couldn't resist a slight needling of his friend.

"True."

The luxury that they had enjoyed on their train journey to Petrograd was continued on the journey to Moscow. Their train was once again a sleeper, and their party, which continued to include Maria, again had a carriage to itself.

Brian, still groaning inwardly, was nevertheless appreciative of the comfort. "This is magnificent," he said to Petrov. "This is by far the most impressive train that I've ever travelled on," as the three officers and Maria sat together over a luxurious dinner.

"Ah, but we have more impressive trains than this," replied the Russian. "Before we go to see the *Netopyr*, I want you to take a look at one of them."

"Trains aren't really a passion of mine," replied Brian. "Lieutenant Braithwaite is the engineer, not me."

"Even so, I think you'll both find this one quite interesting," replied Petrov, with a smile. "It's not really very much like this train. However, I have something a little more serious and urgent to discuss. Lieutenant," he said, looking at Brian slightly quizzically, "are you in a fit state to talk about serious matters right now? Maria, you may stay or you may go, as you think fit."

"Is that a not-so-subtle hint that you don't want me listening?"

"If you stay, then I must have your word that nothing is to be said of this to anyone else. I know you have your friends in the Embassies in Petrograd. They must never hear of this."

"You have my word, Father."

"Very good. Now, Lieutenant," turning back to Brian. "Has our good Russian vodka robbed you of your ability to concentrate on serious matters? Are you ready to join us in the land of the living?"

Brian gave a rueful smile, and nodded.

"In that case, I'll come straight to the point. The drowning man whom we picked up in the submarine was, as I explained to Lieutenant Finch-Malloy, a Bolshevik agitator, or to be more precise, a terrorist. I placed him in custody in the Naval Hospital, with a view to his being questioned as to the whereabouts of his confederates as soon as he recovered."

"I explained this to Lieutenant Braithwaite," said Brian.

"Well, there are two new things that have only just been discovered and the report about them has only just been delivered to me. The first concerns that piece of paper typed in Russian that we found and which you couldn't make sense of, if you remember that."

"Yes?"

"Before I gave it back to you for you to return it to Kolinski's pocket, I copied the writing on it. It turned out to be a very simple code indeed. So simple that I'm not sure why they bothered to use it. I didn't bother trying to make sense of it while we were on the submarine, but turned it over to one of my officers when we arrived in Reval."

"And presumably this very simple code has been broken?"

"Indeed. It turns out that this terrorist is bound for the same destination as we are. Your old friend Lenin has all the details of the *Netopyr*, which have been passed over to the Bolsheviks."

Brian groaned. "Another traitor, sir?"

Petrov shook his head ruefully. "It would appear so. And a traitor working for the Bolsheviks is just as much of a hindrance to the Allied war effort as one working for the Germans. To continue... It seems that our friend Kolinski has orders to commandeer the *Netopyr* for the Bolsheviks, using a mixture of bribery and force directed towards the unfortunate inventor who directs the project."

"How likely is that to happen? His commandeering the machine, I mean."

"Not very likely, we think. As far as I am aware, Lebedenko is completely loyal to His Imperial Majesty, and we really don't consider that he would betray that trust. Indeed, I may tell you that the *Netopyr* is actually being funded out of His Imperial Majesty's personal purse. Lebedenko owes a debt of gratitude which is personal, rather than patriotic, in nature. I may be wrong, of course, but I don't think so."

"Well, let's assume that Lebedenko is loyal and refuses to bow to the pressure of bribery, and is brave enough to stand up against the threats of that Bolshevik monster. What then?"

"According to those coded orders, Kolinski is then to kill all the engineers working on the project, except for his informant, and then to destroy the prototype and all the plans."

"So," said Harry, "it would appear that we have one more job in front of us. We have to save the *Netopyr* and its inventors from these revolutionaries?"

"Absolutely, Lieutenant. And I also have my own personal reasons for wishing to see this project succeed. I have been promoting the idea of the *Netopyr* heavily to the General Staff, and much of whatever personal prestige and credibility I have rests on the success of this device. If the project were to fail, or God forbid, fall into the hands of the revolutionaries, my stock within those circles would be worthless."

"Well, it's not going to happen, anyway," Brian pointed out. "Kolinski is safely in a cell in the Naval Hospital in Reval, isn't he, sir?"

Petrov frowned. "I'm sorry to tell you that this is no longer the case. The report I received earlier was in two parts. What I have just told you was the first part. The second part described Kolinski's escape from where we left him."

"I thought you said he was in a guarded locked cell, sir?"

"He was, but we left the keys to the cell with him when we took him off the submarine." Brian frowned in puzzlement, and Petrov continued. "I am referring to the gold which we failed to remove from his belt and his boots. He bribed a nurse and his guards, as we have discovered from our interrogation of one of the latter. He gave each of them one of those gold pieces, and promised more in return for their promise to help him break out from the hospital."

"I take it he doesn't keep his promises?" suggested Brian.

"Correct. The nurse and the guards took the first instalment, and decided between themselves to accept his offer and let him escape. Their idea was simply to leave his cell door unlocked, as if by accident, and let the escape seem to be a matter of simple carelessness."

"From the way you're telling this, sir, things didn't go quite the way they planned," said Harry.

"They didn't. When the three entered the cell to inform Kolinski of their decision, he was ready for them. Apparently the stay in hospital had been good for his health and had allowed him to recover a large part of his considerable strength." Petrov smiled ruefully. "In any event, as soon as he was informed of the guards' and the nurse's decision, he told them he was going to present them with the rest of their bribe and showed them the coins. While their greed distracted them, he grabbed the nurse and one guard by the scruff of their necks, and smashed their heads against the foot of the bed with such force that he broke their skulls like eggshells. According to the report, blood and brains were scattered about the room. Death, of course, was instantaneous."

"The man sounds like a right monster, sir," shuddered Harry.

"And the third man?" asked Brian.

"He naturally moved away as fast as he could, but it seems that Kolinski had other ideas for him. As he tells it, Kolinski seized him by the throat and squeezed hard until he lost consciousness. Maybe Kolinski thought he was dead. We will never know, unless we can catch the man himself and ask him. Apparently the guard was almost as tall as Kolinski, though not nearly as massive, and he woke up stripped to his underwear, with his gun missing. Obviously Kolinski had disguised himself as the guard and simply walked out of the hospital, after he had locked the two dead men and the unconscious guard in the cell. Oh, and there was no trace of his boots or belt, which means he is still in possession of the gold, which is enough, as you saw, to be able to bribe his way past most obstacles when violence does not seem to be a suitable way."

"Well, that all certainly makes things more complicated," said Brian.

"But sir," pointed out Harry. "Don't I remember you saying that this Kolinski had an appointment in Petrograd to meet one of the revolutionaries? Do you think he will keep that appointment?"

"That's true. Thank you, Lieutenant, and well remembered. My theory is that his original intention was to cross over into Sweden from Germany, as we know from that ferry ticket, and then travel through Sweden and cross that border into Finland, and from there into Russia proper. That could have taken him quite a long time, particularly if he wanted to keep a low profile and travel by slow local trains."

"And now?" asked Brian.

"My guess is that he is ahead of his original schedule. To the best of our knowledge he has never operated in Petrograd, so it is quite possible that he has to depend on his contacts to take care of him, and he will keep the appointment as arranged. But in my personal opinion, he will try to make for Moscow and the *Netopyr* as soon as he can, in order not to stay in Russia for longer than he has to."

"Hardly cheerful news, is it?" said Brian.

Petrov smiled. "I think we will be able to hold off the threat of Kolinski for a few days. Please cheer up. I have a surprise for you tomorrow that I think you will both enjoy."

⊰⊱

PETROV'S MYSTERY WAS REVEALED when they arrived in Moscow the next morning. Brian woke up to find the train stopped in a siding. He rose, washed, and shaved, before getting dressed in the freshly valeted clothes that the ever-attentive servant had laid out for him.

Brian, whose digestive system had returned to something approaching normal, made his way in the general direction of the enticing aroma of coffee drifting along the carriage corridor.

"Feeling better?" asked Harry. Brian nodded in reply, and sat down at the table.

"Where's Petrov?" he asked. "He was here some time ago. He went off with Maria, saying something about a surprise."

"Oh God, not a surprise," groaned Brian. "I really don't need one of those." He looked at the food on the table. "What's this?" picking up a small dish.

"Something fishy and salty. Not too bad, actually."

Brian cautiously took a small amount and spread it on a slice of rye bread. "Oh, right. Never had caviar for breakfast before," he commented, looking at the plate.

"Oh, so that's what they make all the fuss about? Hardly seems worth it. Prefer bloaters, myself."

At that moment, Petrov returned. "Glad to see you up and about, Lieutenant. Can you be ready to go for a little walk in about fifteen minutes?"

"I suppose so. Why so mysterious, sir?"

Petrov merely smiled. "I'll wait for you outside the carriage. See you in fifteen minutes."

Brian and Harry finished their breakfast. "I'm just going to make sure I look smart," said Brian. "Lord knows what Petrov has planned for us, and who we're going to meet and where. From what we've seen of Petrov, it's probably a private audience with the Tsar of All the Russias. I'd advise you to do the same, Harry, and smarten up a bit."

At the appointed time, the two British officers made their way down the steps at the door of the carriage. Petrov was waiting for them, Maria by his side.

"Good. Come with me." He led them round the back of the train on which they had been travelling, where they entered a shed into which railway tracks stretched.

"What on earth is *that*?" asked Brian, stopping and looking in amazement at the massive piece of machinery in front of him. Harry likewise stopped in his tracks, and let out a whistle of wonder.

"That, my dear fellow, is the *Zaamurets*. It's the prototype of a completely new type of armoured train which has come all the way from Kiev. Some of the lessons from this will, we hope, find their way into the *Netopyr*."

"This is an impressive piece of machinery," Brian commented. "Now you tell me what it is, I can appreciate some of the strange beauty of this thing. It would strike fear into the heart of an enemy, for certain."

"Don't you need a special powerful armoured locomotive to pull it, sir?" asked Harry.

"Ah, this is the true beauty of this train," smiled Petrov. "It's self-propelled with its own petrol motors. It can even pull other armed and armoured wagons to add to its own firepower."

"And these here?" asked Brian, pointing to twin turrets on top of the train.

"We put 57-millimetre quick-firing guns in there. And it is equipped with searchlights and range-finders, so it can fix the enemy positions before attacking, even at night. And it has machine-guns and all kinds of other defences that we can add as needed."

"And the armour can withstand bullets?"

"Bullets and light artillery," explained Petrov. "It would be useless against heavy artillery, I admit. However, it does have the great advantage, as against ordinary field artillery, of being highly mobile."

"It's a remarkable machine," said Brian. "Maybe not a lot of use on the Western Front, where the distances aren't so great, but here on the Eastern Front, I can imagine that one or two of these could protect a troop movement or even be used for lightning raids into enemy territory."

"The only problem is that it can't move away from the tracks," pointed out Harry.

"And that is exactly why we have the *Netopyr*," pointed out Petrov. "The *Netopyr* can go anywhere. Not as powerful, of course, but the mobility will make up for that."

"Can we go inside, sir?" asked Harry. "I want to see how you've arranged things."

"We're going to do better than that. We're going to travel as passengers on the *Zaamurets* to see the *Netopyr* at Kubinka. I am pleased to invite you two gentlemen to join us as part of the exercise that we're going to be conducting using this train."

"Makes a change from the way we've been travelling up to now," remarked Brian.

"I suppose that's true. I hope you're not going to be expecting caviar for breakfast again," laughed Petrov. "Actually, it's not as far as all that, but as you can imagine, this train here doesn't go very fast compared to the express we've been travelling on. If we start off in about thirty minutes, we should arrive at the proving ground by early afternoon, and with luck, we'll have time to carry out a few exercises. So, if you gentlemen would like to pack some clean linen and some necessities for a couple of nights? I'd also suggest that you don't wear your best uniforms – the accommodation in the *Zaamurets* isn't up to the standards we've enjoyed over the past few days. We'll be returning here when we're finished at the proving ground, so there's no need to being all your baggage with you."

"Am I invited, too?" Maria asked her father.

Petrov seemed a little startled. "I wasn't expecting you to come.

You told me you had a lot of shopping to do here in Moscow." He smiled.

"I'd sooner come with you all," her smile encompassed all three men, but seemed to linger longest on Harry, "and see what's going on. It's so frustrating for me to only hear about these things and not to see them for myself."

"Very well, my dear," replied Petrov. "But you really must change out of those clothes. Do you have anything that isn't all frills and lace?"

"I could wear a soldier's tunic with my riding skirt," she replied.

"Very good," said Petrov. "It's highly irregular, but I suppose I can allow it this once. But don't take too long changing."

"Very good, father. Thank you." She turned and started back.

"Women," said Petrov to the other two, and shrugged.

THIRTY MINUTES LATER, Brian and Harry climbed aboard the *Zaamurets*. The interior was dark, and extremely noisy once one of the engines had been started.

"They need silencers on the exhausts!" shouted Harry to Brian.

"What?"

Harry shouted even louder, "They need silencers on the exhausts, and I can smell exhaust gas." He shouted the last words into sudden silence, as the engine sputtered and died. He turned to Colonel Petrov, and switched to German. "Sir, it really is essential that something is done about the pipes there leading from those engines. That noise is more than an inconvenience – we discovered in the trenches that constant noise like that can really get on a man's nerves, driving him a little crazy after a while. And it certainly makes people tired and less likely to respond."

"Noted, Lieutenant," said Petrov. "Is it possible to reduce the noise?"

"Believe me, sir, with the right materials, which I am sure I can find quite easily, I could solve this problem in less than an hour or so."

"Very good, Lieutenant. You can have as many artificers as you require."

"Thank you, sir. I usually work best on my own, though, sir. And there is one other very important thing. Quite frankly, I'm surprised that you haven't noticed it, sir."

"Go on."

"The exhausts are leaking, and the gas that these engines leak is poisonous. Hasn't anyone fallen sick while this train has been running?"

"Now you mention it, there have been some cases of sickness, but we'd put that down to the motion of the train on the rough tracks over which it was travelling."

"I'll look at this at the same time. I am surprised that no-one has died in this train, given the state of those exhausts."

"They may only just have worked loose," pointed out Brian.

"That's true," conceded Harry. He turned to Petrov again. "And I really have no idea why the engine stopped just now, and I doubt if your engineers do, either, sir. Now if your people can lend me a pair of overalls..."

Petrov appeared to be slightly shocked at the idea of an officer doing manual work, such as Harry was suggesting, but Brian drew him aside. "With respect, sir, I think it would be a good idea to let Lieutenant Braithwaite have his way. In civilian life he was chief chauffeur and mechanic to Lord Whitchurch, and in our infantry platoon, if there was anything mechanical that needed fixing, from a machine-gun to a lorry's gearbox, he was the man who could do it. He's a genius when it comes to working with machinery, sir, in a way that you and I can only aspire to. And I mean that with all sincerity, sir."

"Very good, then." Petrov shrugged, and shouted at one of the mechanics to find a spare set of overalls for the British officer.

Once clad for the task, Harry attacked the engine with gusto. "You're going to have to interpret for me," he said to Brian.

"Thank you very much," replied Brian sarcastically. "Once you get into these mechanical things, I hardly understand your English. How on earth am I meant to put this into Russian?"

"Just give it your best shot." Harry bent to his work, and through Brian, asked for some adhesive cloth tape. A roll was found and brought to him. "Shoddy stuff," he remarked to Brian, "but it will have to do." A few minutes later and, "That's fixed the leak. It looked like the joint had sprung loose. I tightened the bolts, and I've taped it up so it won't happen again. Now for the noise. Brian, ask them for a couple of silencers from lorry exhausts, would you?"

"You really make life difficult," complained Brian. He got the meaning over to the mechanics, but was met by shrugs and apologies. "They say that there are no spare ones."

"Then take them off the lorries in the transport pool," ordered Petrov. "They can be replaced later. This takes priority."

The two Russian mechanics saluted, and left the train. "And while they're doing that," said Harry, "I'll just check the engine that stopped." He bent over the carburettor, and fiddled around. "Oh dear, dear, dear." He sucked his teeth, and started unscrewing other parts of the engine. "There's meant to be a petrol filter here, and there isn't," he explained to Petrov. "Someone put this thing back together without the filter. Look at this." He thrust the carburettor under Petrov's nose. "Sorry, sir, but just look at the muck and filth here. It's disgusting."

"Damn fools – probably took it away to put in a samovar or something." When the two mechanics returned with two silencers that they had removed from the transport lorries, he greeted them with a blast of Russian, but both men shook their heads emphatically.

"Well, maybe it was never fitted, anyway," said Harry, "but either you strain the petrol when you fill this thing up, or you get proper filters fitted in the engine."

Brian translated this.

"And there are some valves here that really need adjusting properly," added Harry. He stooped to the engine again, examining it closely. A low whistle, and a sucking of teeth.

"That bad, Harry?" asked Brian.

"It's a disgrace," replied Harry. "This is meant to be a fine bit of machinery, and these idiots have let it go to rack and ruin."

"How long to fix it?"

"About a day."

Brian conveyed this to Petrov, who turned on the mechanics, and gave them a furious tongue-lashing in fast colloquial Russian, half of which Brian couldn't understand, but the general gist seemed to involve farmyard animals, excrement, and unusual sexual practices.

Petrov turned to Harry. "How long to get the engines running smoothly, if not perfectly, Lieutenant?" he asked in German.

"An hour or so, if those two will strip the other engine for me, sir. Is that going to be all right? I have to warn you that if we don't do something soon, this engine at least is going to become useless and require either major maintenance or replacement. And the other one is probably as bad."

"We can spend an hour or so," Petrov admitted grudgingly. He gave orders to the two Russian mechanics, who started asking Harry what to do, with Brian acting as interpreter.

"It's no good," said Brian, after a few sentences. "I don't even know what you're talking about in English, let alone know the Russian for these things." He was suddenly aware that Maria had entered the compartment without his noticing, and was watching Harry at work with a mixture of wonderment and what appeared to be admiration. He wondered if she had heard her father's tirade a few minutes earlier.

"Fine, then," said Harry. "Tell them to watch me carefully as I disassemble this engine, and then get them to do the same to the other engine. Do you think you can make them understand that?"

"I'm sure I can," said Brian.

Under the gaze of the two Russians, and watched with interest by Petrov and Brian, and with what appeared to be rapt fascination by Maria, Harry took the engine to pieces with the skill and delicacy of a surgeon performing a delicate operation.

"Understand?" he asked the Russians in English.

They nodded, and gave "*Das*" of assent before Brian could put it into Russian.

With the assistance of the two mechanics, who proved to be quite competent once they had been shown by Harry what they should be doing, the two engines were stripped, adjusted and reassembled well within the hour that Harry had promised.

"Now," said Harry. He adjusted the choke of one engine, and cranked the starting handle. The engine sprang to life with a soft purr. The two Russians stood aside as he moved to the other engine, and repeated the process.

"Truly remarkable," observed Petrov. "I suppose, Lieutenant, we can't offer you a higher rank and a commission in the Imperial Army as an engineer instructor?"

Harry smiled, and shook his head. Brian looked over at Maria, who seemed lost in amazement at Harry's skills. Ah well. You win some and you lose some, he thought to himself. It seemed that he'd lost this one even before he had started, though.

"Well, it appears we're just about ready to go, then," said Petrov. "We'll wait for the rest of the crew to come on board, and I'll make arrangements with the railway so that we have clear tracks to travel on, and then we'll set off."

"It's wonderful what you can do when you have that sort of rank," Brian whispered to Harry after Petrov had left the train. "Clearing a whole railway line for you to travel along."

"Almost makes me wish I was a member of the Russian Imperial family," replied Harry. "It obviously has quite a few advantages."

Such as being close to Maria, Brian thought, but didn't say. "What do you think of this contraption?" asked Brian, indicating the train.

"Well, it has its uses here, I suppose. But like you said, there's not really a lot of situations you could use it in on the Western Front. But from what I remember hearing when I was in Germany, there aren't a lot of roads between here in Moscow and the border, and the ground is pretty flat, so railways are the big thing, and it's got to be some sort of use here."

"I think you're right. If you could get something like this to go on ordinary ground without rails – a sort of land battle cruiser – it would be quite something. Put the fear of God into anyone meeting it for the first time."

"But it's a waste of time to build something like this, and let it go to ruin in this way." Harry's instincts as a first-class mechanic who loved machinery were coming to the fore. "It makes me wonder how much use this thing is as a fighting machine if they have let the guns get into the same state as the engines."

"We can check." Brian stepped over to one of the machine-gun ports. "Now that is really strange."

"What?"

"See this gun?"

"Yes?"

"It's not a real gun. It's wood, painted to look like a machine-gun."

"The Russians must be really desperate if they're building these fancy secret weapons without giving them proper guns to fight with."

"It seems like it. Quiet, they're coming back."

Petrov led a small procession of railway engineers and soldiers, who climbed through the hatches of the *Zaamurets*. The hatches were slammed and bolted shut, and Brian felt as he had in the submarine – shut in and sealed off from the world. The only light came from two electric bulbs, and a little daylight shining through the chinks in the armour.

"Is it possible to get a little more light and fresh air in here?" asked Brian.

"Certainly," said Petrov. "In fact, if you think you can manage to hang on tight, you can even travel on the roof. He shouted an order to one of the crewmen, who climbed a short ladder attached to the inside of the hull, and opened a hatch leading to the roof. "There you go."

"Thanks," said Brian. "Coming, Harry?"

The two Englishmen climbed the few steps to the ladder and found a convenient place to wedge themselves. Beneath them, they could hear the engines start, and a few shouted words in Russian.

"What's all that about?" asked Harry.

Brian smiled. "The railway engineers are saying that they've never heard the engines running so quietly, and they're thanking the army mechanics for their hard work."

"Well, I hope they're not taking the credit for what I did," said Harry.

"Don't worry, the army blokes are giving all the credit to the genius of an Englishman who's currently sitting up on the roof. And I don't think they're referring to me."

"We're off," remarked Harry, as the *Zaamurets* started to move off smoothly. As they passed a signal box, a loud blast sounded from the train's horn, startling both men. The exhaust fumes from the engines streamed behind them as they chugged their way slowly through the Moscow suburbs.

"What a way to travel, eh?" said Brian, smiling.

❧

KOLINSKI TOO WAS TRAVELLING ON THE ROOF OF A TRAIN out of Moscow, but in his case, no-one knew he was there. Or so he hoped.

His escape from the prison hospital in Reval had been ridiculously easy once he had disposed of the nurse and the marines and changed into the guard's uniform. Carrying the carbine, he had smartly saluted everything in sight that looked as though it should be saluted, and walked out of the door. The clothes he had arrived in were in the knapsack over his back, and as soon as he could find a place out of sight of the world, he changed out of the uniform into his own garments. He dumped the uniform into the river, weighted with the gun, which he abandoned with regret, but he had no illusions about being able to carry it around the city in civilian clothes without attracting attention. His knife had been removed from his belongings while he had been in hospital. Strangely, they had left his papers intact. He had to assume that they had been copied. Surely they wouldn't have been overlooked?

In any case, he had a lot of time to wait before the arranged meeting in Petrograd. For obvious reasons, Reval was not a suitable place for him to wait. He had to assume the authorities had read the note he was carrying, so it would be foolish to wait in Petrograd until the time of the meeting. Even if the paper didn't contain the actual date on which the meeting was actually to take place, the police might well assume that he was in Petrograd, waiting for the meeting, and would be on the lookout for him.

Best, he thought, for him to make straight for the *Netopyr* at the proving ground outside Moscow and skip the Petrograd meeting. Even if they had managed to break the code and read his instructions, they wouldn't be expecting him. And the Chief would be delighted if he managed to carry out his mission so quickly.

He had to assume that his description had been circulated, and that the railway stations and ferry terminals were being watched. Now he rather regretted having disposed of the uniform so quickly and having reverted to civilian attire. If he were to travel in uniform, no-one would ever question him. Especially if it were a police uniform...

He was lucky to be in a part of Russia where quite a few people were as tall as him, and, as he noticed, many of these tall men seemed to be in the police force. As he hung around outside the railway station, hunched over inside his thick overcoat, he noticed one strapping young policeman with a particularly vacant look on his face, who appeared to be bored with his job of standing outside the station. Time to arm himself. He went to a shop round the corner, returning with a bottle of vodka hidden inside his coat, and waited until his quarry was relieved at the end of his shift. Kolinski followed the off-duty policeman as he moved away from the station. As his quarry turned down a small side-street, Kolinski quickened his pace, and clapped the man on the shoulder.

"Ivan Gregorivich, how glad I am to see you!" he exclaimed heartily.

The policeman jumped, startled. "My name's not Ivan Gregorivich," he said. "Even if my name is Ivan, my father's name is Vladimir. I would trouble you to take your hands off me, you scum."

"My mistake," apologised Kolinski. "From the back, you looked exactly like my friend's nephew, Ivan Gregorivich. I am so sorry to have surprised you in that way. Nothing worse than being startled like that, is there, my dear fellow?"

"Well," said the other, accepting the olive branch. "I suppose it's my turn to apologize for my hasty words. As you say, I was startled."

"Of course, of course," cried Kolinski. "We should seal this with a drink. Are you on duty?" he enquired innocently.

"Just come off duty," explained the other. "I'm not altogether sure that I should be drinking, though. Not in uniform like this."

"Too bad," said Kolinski, pulling the vodka bottle from inside his coat. "In that case, I'll have to drink this by myself," winking.

"Hey! I meant I couldn't go to a bar or restaurant with you while I was in uniform. I didn't mean that I couldn't drink at all."

"That's good," said Kolinski. "I like a man who can be flexible." He opened the bottle and passed it to the other. "You first."

The policeman took a sniff of the bottle. "Good stuff," he remarked. "Your health, sir." He took a good swig, and wiped his mouth with the back of his hand before passing the bottle back to Kolinski, who took a drink in his turn before handing the bottle back.

"Are you sure?" asked the policeman. "I thought this bottle was for your friend's nephew. I shouldn't be drinking it."

"No, not at all," replied Kolinski airily. "I wasn't expecting to meet Ivan Gregorivich in any case – it just seemed to me that you looked like him. This was just for my personal enjoyment. But good drink is best enjoyed with friends, don't you think?"

A nod, and the level of vodka in the bottle dropped significantly. As Kolinski had guessed, the policeman's empty stomach and the long hours of standing guard had weakened his resistance to alcohol. He already seemed a little less steady on his feet, and when he spoke, there was a slight hesitation as he forced his mouth to frame the words.

"It really is most kind of you to let me share this. I wish there was something I could do for you in return."

"Actually, there is something," replied Kolinski. "I'm known round these parts as something of a joker, and I want to surprise my friend. He's going to be waiting for me just round the corner in a few minutes. If I was to turn up in a police uniform, and pretend to arrest him, it would be a bit of a shock for him, wouldn't it? Especially when we get close to the police station, and I let him see it's me?"

"That would be a good joke," agreed the policeman.

"And I notice that you and I are much of a size, so if you could lend me your uniform for an hour or so, that would give me time to play my joke. And then I could come back and give you your uniform back."

"I'm not sure about that. I mean, it is a police uniform, after all."

"That's what makes the joke better. But you didn't think I was going to ask you to do this for nothing, did you?" Kolinski produced one of his gold pieces.

"Well, as you say, it would be a good joke. Where do you want to change clothes?"

"As I say, my friend lives just round the corner, so why don't we change in this alley here behind the warehouse? I don't think anyone will be coming this way at this time of night." Kolinski led the way, and tried the warehouse door. "Better and better. Right out of the way. No-one will see us."

Kolinski started taking off his coat and shirt. "I'll keep my own boots, I think," he said. "Wearing another man's boots is never comfortable."

In a few minutes each man was dressed in the other's clothes. "You see, I was right," said Kolinski. "We are very much of a size, and this uniform could almost have been made for me, don't you think?"

"You certainly do look like a real policeman," smiled the other. "The only thing is that you kept your own belt, and you don't have my proper police belt. Here, let's change." He unthreaded his belt, and removed the pistol from its holster before holding out the belt to Kolinski.

"I think I'd better have the pistol as well, just to look the part," said Kolinski, unthreading his own belt and replacing it with the police belt.

"I'm not so sure about that," said the younger man.

"I'm leaving the bottle with you," said Kolinski. "And I'll bring another one with me when I return to change back into my own clothes."

"Oh, here you are," holding out the pistol, butt first, towards Kolinski.

"Thank you," said Kolinski, taking the pistol, flipping the safety catch, and shooting the other through the forehead in one swift fluid motion before thinking of any possible discovery. A passing tram rattled past on the other side of the wall; with luck, it would mask the noise of the shot, Kolinski hoped, but he stayed alert, revolver in hand, in case anyone had heard anything untoward and decided to investigate. He relaxed after a minute or so, "Thank you," he repeated to the corpse, stuffing his own gold-laden belt into the pocket of the police greatcoat and stooping to retrieve the gold coin from the pocket where the dead man had carefully stowed it a few minutes previously.

He took another swig from the vodka bottle, almost emptying it. "I told you I was leaving the bottle with you. See, I keep my promises," he told the dead body, tossing it onto the floor beside the corpse. It rolled, but didn't break.

Once again, Kolinski stooped down, this time to retrieve the coded papers that had been given to him in Zurich. He decided to leave the ruined Swiss and Russian passports in the pockets, though. They were useless to him now.

Next he looked at his new police identification, noting with pleasure that there was no photograph against which his face could be compared. Still, it might be a good idea if he were to trim his beard, or even shave it off. Maybe it wouldn't be such a good idea to entrust the operation to a barber. A pair of scissors should be an easy enough thing to come by, though, and he guessed he could always use a window of an empty shop in a side-street as a mirror.

⚜

AN HOUR OR SO LATER, he had put his plan into effect. His once luxuriant flowing beard was now neatly trimmed. He thought he looked quite dashing and handsome with this new look and the uniform. Maybe he'd keep his beard trimmed this way after all this was over.

He decided to try his luck and ask at the station for an official pass to travel to Moscow. A pity he'd killed the police officer, he thought to himself. It would have been amusing to handcuff the man with his own handcuffs and turn him into a prisoner being escorted under guard to Moscow, but he hoped that he would be able to travel at government expense to Moscow anyway. The idea was almost as amusing as taking along a policeman as a prisoner. And if they didn't give him an official ticket, what were they going to do? Call the police? He grinned to himself.

Forcing his way to the head of the line as he'd seen the police do so many times, he shoved an elderly woman who was buying a ticket out of his way, and demanded an official rail pass to Moscow.

"Where are your orders signed by your commanding officer?" asked the ticket clerk.

That was a nasty one. He'd never heard of this before, but decided to bluff it out. He felt in his pocket, and retrieved his police identification, laying it ostentatiously on the desk in front of him. A look of pretended horror came over his face as he continued to search fruitlessly in his pockets.

"I must have left it back at the station. I can't go back," he bluffed. "Superintendent Gretchkin will make sausage-meat out of me if I have to go back, and this is urgent. You know you don't really need the orders, do you?"

"Orders is orders," said the other firmly.

"Quite right," replied Kolinski. "And my orders are to be in Petrograd. And what's it going to look like when I tell them at the Ministry that I was late because of a stupid donkey of a railway clerk who couldn't recognise an official on urgent business when he saw one? Your name?" pulling out a notebook and pencil.

The clerk swallowed. "Very well," he said, writing out a travel pass in the name of the dead policeman. "When do you want to leave?"

"At last you see some sense," said Kolinski. "Maybe I won't have to report you after all. It's urgent, I tell you. The next fast train to Petrograd."

"In a little less than ten minutes," replied the other, with a slight edge of malice in his voice.

"Then you'd better write fast, hadn't you?"

The pass was written, and handed over. Kolinski pocketed it and strode away without a word of thanks, playing the arrogant police bully to the last.

On the train, he commandeered one of the best seats in the carriage, rudely forcing others out of the way. The combination of his size, the police uniform, and the scowl on his face meant that no-one was in any mood to argue with him.

It would be time to change identities once again in Petrograd. It was quite possible that the Reval authorities had discovered the body of the policeman and had telegraphed ahead to Petrograd to alert them of Kolinski's arrival. It might be a good idea to shave off his beard completely – he hadn't been clean-shaven since he was a teenager. At least it would be safer to have a barber shave him in Petrograd than in Reval.

The train eventually pulled into Petrograd, and Kolinski set out to look for a barber who could help with the transformation. He chose a small barber in a working-class district some way from the centre of the city, and explained that he had just been seconded from Reval, hence his uniform, but that his new commanding officer in Petrograd was not in favour of the policemen under his command wearing beards. He was surprised when the barber refused his offered payment after the operation was complete.

"It's brave lads like you who are keeping us safe from those so-cialist and communist scum," the barber had said, and went on at length about his love for the old regime and how it would protect his profits.

Bourgeois parasite, thought Kolinski, but kept his opinion to himself. Petrograd was not a place where he wanted to stir up more trouble than he had to. The ministries and national police headquarters were in the city, and he had no wish bring himself to the notice of the authorities. Still, he was grateful to the barber, who had not only shaved his beard neatly, but had also trimmed his rather long and shaggy hair, transforming him completely. In his own eyes, he looked even more like a police officer than he had done previously, but it was time to make yet another change of clothes and find a new identity. After leaving the barber, he made his way through the back streets, searching. He found what he was looking for in a few minutes.

Pushing open the door of the shabby pawnbroker's, with "A. Solomon" written over the front, he surprised the owner, a bearded Jew in a caftan.

"Your Honour, I've paid already this month. I can't afford any more right now." His eyes narrowed as he looked at Kolinski. "You're new here, aren't you?" He looked a little closer at the buttons on the police uniform. "You're not even from Petrograd, are you? You've got no business here."

"I might be a customer, you know. I'm not after your money. Are you prepared to help the government?"

"Of course, Your Honour. Why shouldn't I help? As long as it's not money. I pay my taxes like everyone else, and I pay the police to keep me safe. You want to know who brings me the things here? I can show you a list of names and addresses, all with dates and amounts. Here." He reached behind the counter and pulled out a large ledger.

"I'm not interested in that right now," said Kolinski. "I have special orders to track a very dangerous man, who has killed several people in Reval, and is believed to be making his way to Petrograd even now. My chief has ordered me here to find this man and arrest him, but I can't do it in uniform, can I now? I have to do it in plain clothes. Do you have any old clothes here to fit me?"

"Of course I do, Your Honour. A very good suit of clothes here, hardly worn, and it looks as though it was made for you."

Kolinski changed into the new garments. The shopkeeper was right. The suit was good quality, and it really almost did seem as though it had been made to measure.

"That will be five roubles," demanded the shopkeeper.

"Send a bill to the police department," replied Kolinski. "That is, if you still feel up to it after this," as his fist smashed into the jaw of the hapless pawnbroker. Kolinski stooped over the fallen figure, and encircled the man's neck with his massive hands. After a few minutes of squeezing, and a final twist that produced a snapping sound, Kolinski was satisfied that once again he'd proved the worth of the old adage that dead men tell no tales. He left the shop, carrying the police pistol in the civilian coat, and wearing his own belt and boots containing the gold.

Satisfied that no-one would recognise him now, he walked quickly to the station, where he bought a ticket for Moscow, first class again, as he had in Germany, again on the principle that no-one would look for him among the bourgeoisie.

O N ARRIVAL IN MOSCOW, Kolinski made straight for the railway depot from where military trains started for their destinations; the front, the armaments factories, and so on. He didn't think he would be allowed to travel on these trains in civilian clothes, and he was getting a little worried about the growing trail of corpses that he was leaving in his wake. Sooner or later someone might make connections, and he would be discovered. His best hope was to smuggle himself on board one of the trains making its way to the training area where the *Netopyr* was being developed. The alternative was to talk his way on board, and he had his doubts as to whether this last option would be possible. Kubinka was one of the Imperial Army's most closely-guarded and secretive installations, and it wasn't likely that he would be able to bluff his way through the security in that way. But first things first. He needed to get inside the depot. That would be a little easier than Kubinka.

He decided that he needed to improve his image a little. He left the area of the depot, and bought himself a smart-looking hat of the kind worn by civilian government officials. Next on his list was a stationer's, where he bought an official-looking notebook, together with a pen and ink..

He returned to the depot wearing the hat and ostentatiously brandishing the notebook. At the gate, the guard on duty demanded to see his pass.

"Here you are," replied Kolinski, putting his hand in his breast pocket. "Damn! It must be back in the office. Well, I've no time to go back and fetch it, unless you want to go and fetch it for me, that is? No? I thought not. Well, you'll just have to let me through, won't you?"

"I can't do that," replied the young sentry.

"Damn it all, you son of a donkey!" Kolinski exploded with simulated rage. "Do I have to call your officer and explain to him that you refused to let me do my job? After you've let me in here for the past week and you know my face by now?" Kolinski prayed that this guard actually had been on duty for the past week – his bluff would fall flat if the guard had only just been appointed to the post.

The sentry looked Kolinski up and down, seemingly checking his memory. At last he reached a decision. "Sorry, sir," he said, drawing himself up to attention and saluting. "Beg your pardon for having held you up, sir," letting Kolinski pass into the marshalling yard. Continuing his act, aware that the eyes of the gate sentry were still following him, Kolinski strode purposefully towards a pile of sacks, presumably containing grain, and started to count them ostentatiously, at times making notes in the book he was carrying and sneaking a look back towards the gate where he had just entered. Making a final entry in the notebook, and shaking his head regretfully for the benefit of the guard, who still appeared to be watching him, he moved to the next pile, a little further away from the gate. By the time he had reached the fourth pile, it appeared that the sentry's suspicions had been allayed, and he was able to start exploring without becoming an object of suspicion.

He made his way over the tracks, and through the piles of military supplies, stacked in seeming chaos around the area. For a moment, he pitied any genuine officials whose job it was to make order out of the muddle that surrounded him, but he realised that this inefficiency and disorder was the very sort of thing that would help the Revolution to succeed. He must remember this scene and tell the Chief all about it when he returned to Zurich.

As he made his way between crates of artillery shells, he came across a soldier smoking, leaning against the ammunition boxes. He decided to have a little fun. Striding up to the soldier, he smacked him hard across the face with the palm of his hand, sending the cigarette flying, and sending the unfortunate soldier sprawling on the ground.

"What the devil are you doing?" he asked the soldier. "Smoking near high explosives, you stupid swine. Pick that cigarette up. With your mouth! Hands behind your back, you ox!" he ordered, giving the man a sharp kick.

The soldier obeyed, cringing.

"Now eat it," ordered Kolinski. "Maybe that will teach you to put the lives of all around you in danger. You swine, you imbecile don-key, you piece of rotten offal, you!"

Unhappily, the soldier chewed and swallowed the muddy ciga-rette. His face turned pale as the last shreds of coarse tobacco went down his throat.

"Right. Now run as fast as you can, ten times around the perime-ter. I want you never to forget this for as long as you live. Drop your gun. Now! At the double!" As the luckless soldier, now green in the face, jogged off unhappily, Kolinski picked up the rifle. He consid-ered keeping it, and decided against it, but detached the bayonet, which he tucked into his coat. He still had the police revolver, and before he'd changed out of the police uniform, he'd discovered a car-ton of ammunition in one of the pockets. The bayonet, though, was a silent weapon, and one that often had more effect when used to threaten victims than a pistol, as he had found in the past.

He looked over at the soldier, painfully making his way around the wire fence surrounding the rail yards. Time to move on.

He passed a closed shed that obviously held locomotives, and as he did so, the great double doors at one end opened, and a strange vehicle emerged, making its almost silent way past him. Painted a dark Army brown, it looked like some sort of giant tortoise, with a rounded front and back, and two turrets mounted on the top. What appeared to be machine-guns stuck out of ports on the sides of the strange train, which seemed to consist only of a single car. The train made a soft purring sound, like that of an expensive motor-car. Kolinski watched, entranced, and imagined himself commanding one of these armoured monsters driving into Petrograd and terrifying the Tsarist soldiers as the shells from the guns did their awful work. That and the *Netopyr* between them would win the Revolution for the Chief and the Party. He took out his notebook and, not without a certain skill, sketched the shape of the strange train that had just passed him. The Chief would be pleased with what he had just found out, he thought. If he could somehow get control of that train, or at least discover how it could be controlled, as well as the *Netopyr*, he would almost certainly be promoted within the Party organisation.

A sudden thought struck him. It was just possible, he felt, even likely, that the tortoise was on its way to the testing fields where the *Netopyr* was being developed. All he had to do was follow the train. Fifty kilometres was really no problem – a matter of two or three days' forced march – but the major problem was that he didn't know which way he should go. If the tracks divided at some point on the way to Kubinka, he would have no idea which path to take.

The tortoise seemed to have come from the shed. Perhaps there was another train in there that would also be going to Kubinka. He looked back, and saw that although the main train doors had now been closed and were guarded by sentries, there was a small un-guarded door at the side. He decided to try his luck. With a jaunty confident stride, he walked to the door and pushed it open. To his amazement, the shed was full of armoured trains, some of them single-vehicle affairs, little more than locomotives with steel plates bolted to their sides, and some with many carriages and trucks be-hind a locomotive, which looked as though a whole troop of artillery had been attached to an ordinary train. There was no other train that looked like the tortoise that he had seen, though. Obviously what had passed him was the newest and the most formidable of these monsters. But all these massive machines could strike power-ful blows against the Revolution, if the Party ever fought the Tsarists in an extended military campaign.

Kolinski's worry was that none of these trains appeared ready to move out. The shed seemed almost deserted, except for a few me-chanics who seemed merely to be going through the motions of ser-vicing the iron monsters.

As he stood pondering his options, one of the mechanics came up to him.

"Can we do anything for Your Honour?" he asked. Obviously the clothes and the hat that Kolinski was wearing had had the desired effect on him.

Kolinski was inwardly amused by the title he had so easily acquired. "Yes, as it happens. I have orders to go to Kubinka, and I was told to catch the special armoured train, but I seem to have missed it. I think I saw it go past me as I came here."

"Ah, you mean the *Zaamurets*?" said the mechanic. "Yes, the rail cruiser left here only a few minutes ago."

He seemed to be waiting for something, and Kolinski, who had himself been in the man's position many times before, fished in his pocket, and brought out a coin which he displayed, but not too ostentatiously. This, as expected, loosened the mechanic's tongue.

"If Your Honour can wait another hour, there is another train due to set off for Kubinka from here, and I am sure the Colonel could easily find room for Your Honour to travel on it." He stood there stolidly, and Kolinski inwardly cursed the greed of the Russian proletariat which forced another coin out of his pocket.

"Ah, thank you, Your Excellency," replied the mechanic, pocketing the money. "If you'll just follow me." He led the way through the maze of massive iron machines. They reached one of the larger trains, painted a dull grey, with a steam locomotive clad in flat metal plates, and several wagons, bristling with guns, coupled to the back of it. The mechanic gestured towards the train.

"This one, Your Honour. You may want to wait in the command car at the back. When the Colonel arrives with the crew, I will let him know you are here. What name should I give him?"

"Simply tell him that Kharitonov is here, from the Ministry. I'm sure he'll understand." Kolinski had picked the name of one of the Okhrana's most brutal interrogators, whose name was a feared byword for cruelty among revolutionaries. "Now show me to the command car," he ordered.

Obediently, the mechanic led Kolinski to one of the central wagons, and opened a heavy steel door. "This way, Your Honour," he invited. His hand was half held out, but no more money materialised. Slightly sulkily, he climbed up the steps. "This way," he repeated. Looking quickly around him to ensure no-one was watching, Kolinski bounded up the steps. For such a large man, he could move very quickly and quietly, and as a result, the mechanic had no forewarning of the arm that gripped him from behind like a vice, nor the bayonet that sliced his throat open. Kolinski dragged the body to a locker, which he guessed was usually used to hold ammunition, and stuffed the corpse in there, kicking the door shut. He moved forward to one of the fighting compartments in the front carriage of the train, and hid himself in a cramped position in one of the main gun turrets, where he guessed there was a good chance he would not be seen when the crew eventually turned up.

Chapter 9: Kubinka, Imperial Russia

*Brian had leapt to his assigned machine-gun, and was squinting
along the sights, as soon as the Zaamurets started sliding to a halt.*

THE JOURNEY TO KUBINKA took most of the morning. The
weather was mild, and Brian and Harry enjoyed sitting on the
roof, once they had found a place out of the wind. Petrov puffed his
way up the ladder once or twice, but declined the invitation to join
the two British officers. Maria stayed below for the whole journey.

Eventually, after a long stretch through birch forests, the train
stopped.

"Hello?" said Brian, standing up to see what was happening.
"We've come to a damn' big fence with a gate, running across the
track, and there are some fellows pointing their guns at us." He put
his hands above his head and shouted something in Russian.

"What's that?" said Harry, who had likewise raised his hands.

"I'm telling them that we're friends, and they should be talking to
Colonel Petrov about us if they are worried about who we are and
what we're doing here."

At that moment, Petrov himself, attracted by the noise, put his
head through the hatch.

"Ah, Colonel," said Brian. "Would you mind explaining to those gentlemen below us that we are not spies or Bolshevik agitators, and we would welcome the chance to put our hands down soon?"

Petrov came up onto the roof. The sight of his colonel's uniform seemed to make the rifle muzzles waver a little, and the stream of Russian abuse directed at them had even more effect. The guns were lowered, and Brian and Harry put down their hands with a sigh of relief.

"Thank you, Colonel," said Brian. "I'm glad to see your chaps are on the ball and all that but it would have been dashed annoying if we'd been shot as spies or something."

"Not to mention embarrassing," said Petrov. "Still, as you say, it is a relief to know that at least this part of the Imperial Army is carrying out its duties efficiently. There are certainly days when I have my doubts."

The *Zaamurets* started off again and crept forward into the test area – a huge clearing surrounded by dense forest. Petrov stayed on the roof with the two British officers, obviously proud of what he was showing them.

"This is impressive," said Brian. "You're re-creating different kinds of terrain here, it seems?"

"Yes, we have a trench system over there," pointing to one corner, "based on the trenches where we have been fighting against the Austrians. We also have forest terrain, as you can see all around you; and we have steppe here. In winter, this is all covered in snow, so we can test winter warfare plans and tactics. And there's a river and small lake just over that ridge to test amphibious assaults and river-crossing tactics."

"Am I right in assuming that all this is your doing, Colonel?" asked Harry, waving a hand at the area surrounding them.

"Yes, Lieutenant, I suppose this is my contribution to the Imperial Army. I am not happy about throwing thousands of under-equipped peasants into the meat-grinder of the battles we have fought, and I want to make sure that our Russian soldiers have an advantage in quality as well as quantity when they face the Germans. I can tell you I have had to fight hard against some of our more conservative generals, but I am pleased to say that his Imperial Majesty has been pleased with some of the results we have obtained here. Even more important, to my mind, is the fact that through our program of practical testing here, we have stopped many thousands, if not millions, of roubles, being spent on crackpot ideas that would never have come to a practical conclusion. But now, lunch. We can't do our work on an empty stomach, and I think you'll agree that the cook we have in the officers' mess here is the equal of any working in the restaurants in Petrograd."

"When will we be meeting the inventor of the *Netopyr* and his assistants?" asked Harry. "I'm really excited to meet him and to see what he's come up with."

"Well, that depends on how ready the *Netopyr* itself is to receive visitors," said Petrov. "I'm afraid Lebedenko is a little touchy about his invention, and if it's not working to his satisfaction, then he's very reluctant to show it to any visitors at all, including me. Unless the visitor happens to be His Imperial Majesty, of course, but that's a rather different matter."

"You let him take that attitude?" asked Brian, curiously.

"My dear fellow, we don't have a lot of choice in the matter. Nikolai Nikolaivich is one of those temperamental geniuses. One day he's full of life, singing like a bird, and working nineteen to the dozen. But one word of criticism, and he's down in the dumps, and it's all we can do to get him to even grunt out answers to questions, let alone do serious work. But mark my words, he really is a genius. Wait till you see the *Netopyr* for yourselves. When you see it, you'll agree that only a genius could have dreamed it up and brought it to a working state." His eyes almost glowed with excitement.

The meal, as Petrov had promised, was of a high standard. At the end of it, a servant came up to Petrov and whispered in his ear.

"Show him in, then," said Petrov. "Damn it man, can't you think for yourself?" He shrugged as the servant departed and switched back to German to address Brian and Harry. "You see, this is one of the problems we face. A lack of initiative. If only some of our people could learn to make their own decisions instead of waiting to receive orders for everything." He sighed.

A young man in oily mechanic's overalls came into the room. "Sir," he said to Petrov, while standing in a pose that suggested, without actually quite being, military attention. "Engineer Lebedenko sends his regrets, but the project is encountering some problems, and the demonstration will have to be postponed. He is, however, confident that tomorrow morning, he will be able to demonstrate the *Netopyr* to its full capacity." His tone did not in any way suggest regret.

"Thank you, Alexander Alexandrovich." The engineer took the hint and left the room.

"One of Lebedenko's nephews. Apparently a good engineer, but not always the easiest person to work with. It must run in the family." Petrov sighed.

"Since the *Netopyr* seems to be off today's menu, maybe you would be good enough to show us around the proving ground this afternoon, sir?" suggested Brian.

"I can certainly do that, but I have another suggestion. There's another armoured train joining us here. I want to test the *Zaamurets* against this more conventional type of train. I believe that the greater mobility of the *Zaamurets* will compensate for its relative lack of firepower."

Brian coughed. "Excuse me, but sir, I couldn't help noticing that the guns in the *Zaamurets* appeared to be made of wood."

Petrov nodded sadly. "That is true. They were indeed wooden

replicas. However, they have now been replaced with the real thing. The armourers have been working since we arrived."

Harry raised his eyebrows.

"Why? you are asking, I believe," Petrov continued. "The reason is painfully simple, I'm afraid. We don't have enough machine-guns to go round, and we Russians are not a very honest race sometimes, even in the army. If we left the *Zaamurets* unattended with the guns in place, we would find nothing in the gun ports when we returned. We keep the guns here at the proving ground, under lock and key."

"What sort of tests will you be conducting today?" asked Brian.

"A very simple one," replied Petrov. "Timed target practice for the machine-guns and the artillery pieces. Each train will start along the straight test track at a set speed, and as soon as the targets pop up, the train must do whatever it needs to do – slow down, stop, whatever, to fire at them. The targets will be between 200 and 500 metres away, and will appear for exactly two minutes. We will count the number of shots fired, and the proportion that actually hit the target."

"There is obviously some reason for this?"

"Of course – I believe that the lighter, faster *Zaamurets* has more of a future in the Imperial Army than the slower, more expensive and somewhat cumbersome conventional armoured trains. It presents a smaller target to the enemy, creates less wear on the track bed, it's more flexible and cheaper, of course, and is more easily controlled by a central commander. Of course, there are others who believe that the thickness of the armour and the weight of the firepower are more important considerations. The only way to settle the argument is by a practical application of the devices, don't you feel?"

"There might be a use for both types of train, though, sir? Different circumstances may demand different weapons," suggested Harry. "After all, you don't build a navy simply out of dreadnoughts. There is room for battle cruisers, and light cruisers, and destroyers and torpedo boats in a fleet, as well as the battleships."

"Of course you are right, Lieutenant. This is why we describe the *Zaamurets* as a 'rail cruiser'. The more conventional type of train is a battleship. But there are those who argue that there is no room even for a cruiser in this war. I want to prove that they are wrong."

"He's got a bee in his bonnet about this sort of thing," Brian said to Harry after Petrov had left them to make some further arrangements for the afternoon.

"I wish some of the senior officers in our army were the same way," said Harry. "The things he's worrying about are all things we should be thinking about in the British Army. It's a crying shame the way our lads are stuck in the mud, with no way of moving. I'm not saying that this rail cruiser thing is the answer, or that this *Netopyr*, whatever it turns out to be like, is the way to win a war, but Petrov seems to be thinking about new ideas, at least. It's what our generals should be doing, instead of all ordering these mad charges against machine-guns and barbed wire."

"You're right there, Harry. But while you have officers like Wobbler Wilkins in charge, I don't see any changes happening soon. And the cavalry are worse. They're not going to give up their smart uniforms and all the horsey business to become mechanics. You'd have to start a special section of the Army to make all these new machines work properly."

Petrov returned. "Let's be off and see the *Zaamurets* in action, if you're both ready to go."

"I'd like to see it from the inside, sir, if you don't mind," said Harry.

"And why not?" smiled Petrov. "That sounds like an excellent idea. I'm only a little worried that you don't speak Russian."

"In which case, may I also request that I see the exercise from the inside of the *Zaamurets*?" requested Brian.

"Excellent. I'll be happy to have a report from you on what it's like inside when the cruiser is in action. Maria and I will be observing from the outside."

THE HIDING PLACE that Kolinski had found for himself in the armoured train was none too comfortable, as he discovered while waiting for the crew to arrive. However, he could find nowhere more suitable, and he was forced to remain, cramped and uncomfortable, in the main gun turret of the front car.

After about thirty minutes, he could hear noises from the locomotive as coal was shovelled into the firebox, and pipes hissing as the steam pressure built up. There was a slight vibration from the pent-up power of the locomotive, which he would normally never have noticed, but in the otherwise silent metal tomb of the armoured car it was disturbing, and his head rattled gently against the steel of the turret. A blast from the locomotive's whistle startled him and made him jump, banging his head painfully. He swore to himself, but not too loudly, and settled down again. Noises from the rear of the train told him that the train crew were boarding. He hoped that it would be only a skeleton crew, and that the front carriage would remain unoccupied, as it seemed to him that he would never be able to straighten his limbs again if he had to remain in the turret for very much longer. On top of everything else, he felt a need to urinate, and there was no way that he could do that if the carriage was occupied.

Whatever luck he been enjoying up to this point now deserted him, as the carriage filled up with a noisy crowd of soldiers. He could see nothing from his perch high in the turret, and he doubted whether they could see anything of him, but he still drew his legs up higher to keep them out of sight, though the cramp became worse, and the position put extra pressure on his bladder.

The sound of the soldiers' chatter continued, and the smell of smoke from coarse tobacco filled his nostrils, which he had to pinch to avoid sneezing. He heard a rattle and a clatter from in front of the carriage, and a lurch as the train started, nearly throwing him off his perch. There were a few cries from the soldiers below, who had obviously likewise been caught off balance, and then another sudden jerk as the train stopped again.

"It's Major Strepkin, I bet," came a voice from below him. "Probably forgotten his scent bottle or his lace hankies."

There was laughter, and another high-pitched effeminate voice. "Now, my good men, I want you all to behave yourselves properly and listen to me," it said, presumably parodying the unfortunate Major Strepkin. More laughter.

"Time for a drink," called out another voice.

"What have you got, Volodya?"

"The usual. Want some?"

Kolinski now heard the sounds of a cork being drawn and a bottle being passed round with healthy sighs of appreciation. The sound of gurgling liquid put an extra psychological pressure to his bladder, and he started to become desperate. He looked around frantically, and noticed a steel helmet on a shelf just below his feet. It would do, if he could manage to retrieve it without being seen by the men below. Would it be possible? he asked himself.

Just then, the train jerked into movement again, this time without stopping. It was noisy up in the turret, and also uncomfortable, with smoke and ashes from the locomotive's boiler blowing in through the gun mounting, irritating his eyes, and making his nose itch. A change in the noises from below. Leaning forward, he could just make out what was going on. A pot of soup and some bread had appeared, and the soldiers were crowding round, dipping their mess tins into the pot and arguing with each other about the bread. Quickly he reached down, straining a muscle in his back, and picked up the helmet. It was then the work of a moment to unbutton himself, and a sense of relief filled him as the helmet filled in its turn.

Now he was faced with another problem, but not for long. There was an observation hatch at the rear of the turret, and he undogged it, emptying the contents of the helmet out of the hatch to be carried away by the slipstream of the train. He decided not to refasten the hatch, allowing the coal smoke from the engine to escape from the cramped turret, and rested the helmet on his lap, not daring to put it back where he had found it.

After a little while, the noises of eating ceased, and the smell of cigarette smoke again assaulted his nostrils, but this time, with the ventilation from the open hatch, the urge to sneeze was nowhere near as strong as it had been earlier.

The journey went slowly, and the pain in his cramped limbs turned imperceptibly to a dull ache, which he ceased to notice after a while. He knew, from similar experiences in the past, that his arms and legs would be in agony for some time after he emerged from his hiding place, and that he would be unable to move quickly, or indeed, do anything which required any physical exertion for at least ten minutes. There was no chance of a sudden spring down from his perch to overpower the soldiers below, even if that had ever been a possibility.

His chance came after what seemed like half a day after the train had started, but was in reality probably closer to a couple of hours. The soldiers below were dozing or resting; at any event, there was no sound of conversation coming from below, and he fancied he could hear snoring from time to time, but he had no way of knowing if they were all asleep, so he dared not move.

The noise of the train seemed quieter than it had done when they had first started off, so he could hear the metal door to the car opening and a new voice shouting.

"All right, you load of peasant swine! On your feet! I'll teach you to sleep on duty, you pigs." There was the sound of a blow, and a cry. "We'll be taking part in a live fire exercise against the *Zaamurets*, and the Colonel is expecting you all to do better than last time. All of you, on the double. To the command car where the Colonel will give you all your orders. On your way, scum." More blows, more cries, and then blessed silence. Kolinski uncurled his cramped legs, and almost screamed with the agony as the circulation crept back into them while he dangled his feet below him. His arms were not in quite as bad a state, but they still pained him as he used them to massage his thighs and calves. Since the NCO had talked about a live fire exercise, it was pretty clear that his turret would not be a suitable place for him to continue hiding. He had to find somewhere else. Come to that, the corpse of the railwayman that he had stuffed into the ammunition locker would probably also be discovered soon, but he wasn't so worried about that. No-one would be looking for the killer on the train itself, he was pretty sure.

He noticed a roof hatch that he could reach if he climbed a short ladder. The catch was stiff, but he managed to open it after some effort, and climbed onto the roof of the moving train, closing the hatch behind him. Although the roof was smooth metal with little to hold onto, he managed to get some sort of a grip on the hatchway from which he had just emerged.

Worse, though, was the fact that he would be in plain view of the main turret's still open rear observation hatch, not to mention the clear view from the two machine-gun cupolas behind him. And if he looked back, he saw that he was exposed to the field of fire of most of the train's gun turrets.

God damn it all to hell, he was going to have to find some way to hide or get off the train before the turrets were manned.

Thinking about it a bit more, he relaxed a little, realising he was actually quite safe. The big guns couldn't fire at him at this short range, and they wouldn't dare use explosive shells. The turreted machine-guns wouldn't dare fire at him, either, for fear of hitting the locomotive or the main gun turret, and if he kept his weight on the hatch, there was no way that anyone could come from there. The only possible danger was if any soldier could be persuaded to go out onto the roof of another car and make his way to meet Kolinski face to face. He decided to close the turret observation hatch, all the same. No point in courting fate unnecessarily, he told himself.

He had just returned to his position on top of the hatch, with some difficulty, as the train was going over a series of points, making the car rattle and jerk, when he noticed with horror that the main gun turret was now turning to left and right. Although he could not now be seen from that turret unless it turned round to face the rear, it showed the turret was now manned. Someone would discover the damp and probably smelly helmet that he had left there. Even worse, he realised, was the fact that the machine-gun turrets behind him would probably be manned by now.

He stole a look behind him, and saw faces peering out of the observation slits in both cupolas. As he watched, there was a puff of smoke and a bang which he could hear clearly over the noise of the train, and a bullet whanged off the roof of the train, only about thirty centimetres from his nose. Too close for comfort, he told himself. Although he was probably right in assuming that they wouldn't use the machine-guns against him, there was still the risk that there was an officer with a pistol in the turret, or worse, a Siberian sharp-shooter with a rifle, waiting for the opportunity to finish him off with a single well-aimed bullet.

He carefully slithered over to the side of the car, clinging as best he could to the rivets forming the only protrusions on the roof. Several times he nearly lost his grip and slipped off as more bullets sped past him, one actually passing through the sleeve of his coat. He flattened himself still further against the roof, but a few more bullets cracked past him, another parting his hair as he gripped the rivets as tightly as possible, and reached the edge. He swung his legs over the side, using his finger ends to hang on to the shallow lip formed by the armour plates bolted to the side of the car. He was now dangling from the edge of the car, his legs swinging against the side as the train rolled and rattled its way along the track. He swayed his way, hand over hand, towards the locomotive, until he could drop onto the platform between the tender and the front car. With a sigh of relief, he massaged his aching arms, and prayed that he was now safe, at least for the moment.

Almost for the first time, he looked around at the scenery, noticing that the train was passing through a birch forest. There was no sign of human habitation other than the railway, and he wondered how far the train was from its destination. He didn't have long to wait. Within a few minutes, he could hear the squeal of the brakes as the train started to slow down. Kolinski craned his head and saw a high wire fence running through the forest, and gates blocking the train's path. Obviously the train was required to stop, and if there were guards and soldiers at the checkpoint as well as the train's crew, this spelt trouble. Once again this journey, he was going to have to jump from a moving train. Luckily, the ground on either side of the track appeared to be soft, and the train, which had been running along a slight embankment, was now on the level of the surrounding ground, so there appeared to be no danger, as long as he jumped well clear of the track.

He landed on soft ground, narrowly avoiding hitting his head on a birch tree, and rolled into a shallow ditch as the train rattled past him, slowing to a stop as the locomotive reached the gates. As the train stopped, several men jumped out of the command cars, and rushed forward to the car from which he had just jumped, brandishing guns. One of them ran forward to the gates, and started talking to the sentries. A blast from a whistle, and about twenty armed men spilled out of a guardhouse beside the gates. He had to move fast to avoid being spotted, but there seemed to be no way to move without exposing himself to the view of the guards and the train crew. Now he could see figures on the roof of the train, scanning the surrounding forest with binoculars, adding to his problems. If he didn't move fast, all would be lost, and there was little hope of his ever reaching the *Netopyr* and either acquiring it for the Revolution or disabling it.

His only hope, strange as it seemed, was to get closer to the gates and the fence. The soldiers had been concentrating on searching the train and the immediately surrounding area, but were now spreading out, away from the gates, leaving only a couple of sentries there. So all he had to do…

He crept as low and as quietly as possible towards the gate, picking up a handful of large stones on the way, and stuffing them into his pocket. When he was only about five meters from the gate, behind a screen of vegetation, he was still unobserved by the sentries. He pulled the stones out of his pocket and lined them up in front of him as silently as he could. He aimed the first stone at a post about ten meters away from him on the other side of the gate, and it hit the post with a satisfying thunk, dropping to the ground, and rolling away noisily. Both sentries immediately turned towards the sound, presenting their backs to Kolinski. He threw the next stone, a little further this time, and the sentries moved away from the gate to investigate. A third well-aimed stone, and they called to the other soldiers that they had the fugitive cornered. Kolinski grinned to himself, and continued throwing the rest of the stones in a pattern that led the sentries away from the gate and drew the rest of the soldiers in that direction. A quick look round, and Kolinski slipped out of his hiding-place towards the gate. He could see no-one outside the guardhouse or in the sentry boxes, and made his way through the gate, crouching almost double as he passed the windows.

He had just reached the edge of the woods on the far side of the fence when a volley of shots rang out, and bullets cracked past him. He was grateful for the low standard of marksmanship in the Imperial Army, but soon realised after the second volley that he couldn't escape for long. One bullet actually hit his boot. The shock threw him to the ground, and he picked himself up, noticing as he stood that the heel had been removed by this fluke shot. No time to stop and pick up either the heel or the gold in it, though, he thought. He ran clumsily, on account of the unevenness of his boots, into the cover of the woods, and moved behind the cover of a large tree trunk to protect him from the bullets of his pursuers. He noticed the tree's branches were arranged almost like a ladder, and it occurred to him that if he were to climb the tree and lie full-length along one of the thicker branches, it was unlikely that anyone would spot him.

Thought was action, and in a few seconds he was stretched out face-down along the branch, looking back at his pursuers, screened from them by leaves and by the branch on which he was lying. As he watched them run towards the wood, the leaders of the pack stopped abruptly and stooped down. The soldiers following them all did the same when they came to the same spot, and then, to his surprise, started fighting among themselves. He realised that this spot was where the heel of his boot had been shot off, and the gold coins had presumably spilled out. He smiled as he watched one of his pursuers lead with a right to the jaw of one of his companions, only to be felled by a roundhouse punch from another of the soldiers.

Eventually a portly officer came waddling up to see what was happening, and though it was too far away for him to hear what was being said, Kolinski had little doubt as to the content. The soldiers straggled into line and stood at attention. Much to his relief, the officer started to march half of them – presumably the train crew – back to board the train. The locomotive got up steam, and started off along the tracks into the compound, with the guards closing the gates behind it. Although the odds against him had just got markedly better, Kolinski was under no illusion that he was safe. The sentries and guards at the gate were still hanging around the area, and were still presumably under orders to continue searching for him. There was nothing for it but to continue hiding up in his tree. He considered ruefully that he seemed to have spent most of the day hiding away in cramped positions, but he had had little choice.

The other soldiers had spread out now, and were moving in an extended line towards the forest. As they reached the undergrowth at the edge of the woodland, they slowed down and started prodding in the bushes with their bayonets. They kept their eyes on the ground, moving forward slowly and grimly in silence, obviously listening for the crack of twigs, or the rustle of leaves. Kolinski thought he might just escape the search if his luck continued. Sure enough, the line went past his tree, and continued searching deep into the forest. Kolinski continued to lie still, guessing that they would return the same way that they had come.

His guess was right. In about an hour's time, the line of soldiers returned past his tree, heading back for the gates. They were still searching, but not nearly as thoroughly as when they had set off. They had nearly reached the gatehouse, and Kolinski was just about to climb down from his perch when a straggler appeared from within the wood. He was limping slightly, supporting his weight with the butt of his rifle, which he propped against Kolinski's tree, as he sank down and lit a cigarette. Kolinski considered his options. The man looked a little smaller than Kolinski, but then it seemed that none of the soldiers he had seen had well-fitting uniforms. Kolinski felt there was a very good chance of turning himself into one of the guards with this soldier's uniform. His victim was now sitting and smoking peacefully, massaging his ankle, which he had presumably twisted.

Silently as a panther, Kolinski slid from the branch, timing his movements to coincide with the noise of the wind in the branches, so that even the faint sounds that he made would be perceived as part of the forest.

Once again the bayonet did its deadly work, and the red blood dripped onto the forest floor. Kolinski had taken care to prevent the dying soldier's blood from staining the uniform, but he had not been careful enough, and a large bloodstain adorned the front of the tunic. He guessed it would look less obvious when dry, but the bright red splash would make a highly visible target. He'd have to keep hidden until the blood dried or he could clean it off.

Still, the uniform fitted tolerably well, and he felt it would now be impossible to recognise him, given that his appearance had changed so dramatically and so many times recently. He believed that he would actually achieve his goal and accomplish his mission. All he had to do now was follow the train tracks to the depot he was sure was at the other end. Time enough for that after dark. For now, it was enough to move away from the stripped body, over which he kicked some dirt and dead leaves, and wait for nightfall.

Brian and Harry were enjoying themselves. Though the interior of the *Zaamurets* was quite noisy and cramped, and Brian kept bumping into projections and parts of the machinery, as he had done on the submarine, the general feeling within the rail cruiser was one of high excitement.

Despite Harry's initial impressions of the mechanics who had been servicing the *Zaamurets* in Moscow, he soon realised through a mixture of pantomime and Brian's Russian that they were skilled workers, who had been too frightened to ask for the materials, or even the tools needed to do their work properly. The gulf between officers and the other ranks in the Imperial Army seemed great enough to place a serious strain on the capabilities of the army as a fighting unit. The mechanics were astonished to see the British officer literally roll up his sleeves and get his hands dirty alongside them, but once they had got used to the shocking idea, they seemed happy to work with him, and the *Zaamurets* purred happily along the test track at its set speed. Brian was working alongside Harry, acting as interpreter, but warned him that when the targets appeared, Harry would lose his interpreter, as Brian would have to move to his post at one of the machine-guns, as had previously been arranged by Petrov.

The lookouts in the top cupolas were scanning the target range for the appearance of the targets, and when they spotted the red flag break out from the signal mast and the white wooden squares flip up, they shouted down to the engineers to stop the train. There was a loud metallic squeal as the brakes were applied, and the sound of the engine revolutions grew less as the motors were throttled back.

Brian had leapt to his assigned machine-gun, and was squinting along the sights, as soon as the *Zaamurets* started sliding to a halt. Even before the train had reached a full stop, he was firing in short accurate bursts at one of the wooden targets, and by the time the train had actually stopped, the target was so damaged by the bullets that even as they watched, a light gust of wind snapped it off its supports, where it lay on the ground.

Immediately after this, the other machine-guns started their mechanical clatter, bucking and kicking in their mounts.

"No, no!" shouted Brian, knocking the gunners' hands away from the triggers. "Short bursts. Like this. A light touch," and demonstrated once again what he had achieved with the first gun. The other gunners tried to follow his lead, with less success than Brian had achieved, but hitting their targets more often than they had been doing earlier.

The two 57-millimetre Nordenfelt cannon in the turrets fired in quick succession, deafening the crew, and throwing the machine-gunners off their aim as the recoil caused the car to rock. The gunners reloaded and fired again. One of the cannon targets went down, and there was a cheer from one of the turrets, but before they could fire again, the red flag was lowered, indicating that the targets were no longer available. The engineers released the brakes and let

in the clutches, and the *Zaamurets* continued its journey to the end
of the line.

⁂

"IMPRESSIVE," SAID BRIAN. He and Harry were sitting round a
table in the officers' mess, together with Colonel Petrov and the
commander of the *Zaamurets*. Maria had made her way to bed after
dinner when the vodka bottles had come out.

"But if I may make a suggestion, Major?" he said to the *Zaamurets*
commander. Receiving a nod in answer, he continued. "Your machine-gunners are waiting for the train to stop before they open fire.
It seems to me that because the *Zaamurets* almost glides to a halt
compared to a normal train, they can start firing effectively well before the train actually stops moving. I managed to destroy a target
while the train was still braking. When the cannon fire, there is a
lot of recoil, and the noise is disorientating, so it's good if the machine-guns can get their shots in before the cannon start up."

"It's a good idea in theory," replied the Major, "but we don't all
have your skill. It's going to take some time before we can come up
to your level."

"Well, that was my other point," said Brian. "Your men seem to
find it very difficult to fire in short bursts. Instead, they seem to just
point the gun in the general direction of the enemy and hope for the
best. Quite frankly, that isn't going to get very good results, especially
with those Maxims. They need to practice static firing, but they
need only a little practice, I think. They got much better as soon as
they started firing in short bursts, rather than trying to run through
the whole belt in one go."

"It sounds good," said the Major. "We'll start practising that sort of tactic tomorrow. Now, if you gentlemen will excuse me, I must retire."

He made his farewells and left.

"Lieutenant," said Colonel Petrov after the vodka bottle had passed between him and Brian once more. "I've been worried for some time about the traitor in the British Embassy in Moscow. It seems to me that we have to bait a trap for this man, and the *Zaamurets* is one way to do it."

"You do realise, Colonel, that the man in our sights as the main suspect is a relation of one of my good friends?"

Petrov gave a start. "No, I was not aware of that. I wish you had told me this earlier. I am genuinely sorry if this is causing you personal difficulties. Would it be better if this were assigned to somebody else?"

Brian shook his head. "I can't honestly say that I find this a pleasant task, Colonel, but it is my duty, and I will perform it to the best of my ability. And in any case, I am here in Russia now, and valuable time would be wasted before a replacement could be sent out here."

"I am sorry," repeated Petrov. "May I, however, present my idea about the *Zaamurets*, for you to pass judgement on?" Brian nodded in assent. "First, may I ask your candid opinion of the rail cruiser?"

"I was impressed, despite myself," admitted Brian. "I have to confess that when I first saw the machine, and heard about the concept, I had severe doubts as to its feasibility. But having seen how fast the train can travel, even over sustained periods, and how quickly it is able to become a dangerous fighting machine, I can see that two or three of these could create havoc in the right places. Given a little more training of the crew, of course."

Petrov turned to Harry, questioningly.

"If I may add my opinions?" said Harry. "Your mechanics are actually much better than I first gave them credit for, but there seems to be some sort of gap between them and your officers that prevents them from doing their job as well as they might."

Petrov sighed. "You're perfectly correct, and it is a fault of our Army that the officers tend to regard all those without a commission as illiterate peasants who can only be kept in order with blows and kicks. Major Tchukalski is definitely one of the better officers as far as this sort of thing is concerned, but you are right – the rail cruiser crews must act as one unit, not a collection of officers, soldiers, and mechanics travelling together." He made a note in his notebook.

"Your ideas regarding the traitor, Colonel?" invited Brian.

"My suggestion is that you make a report on the *Zaamurets* to your people in the British Embassy in Petrograd that deliberately underplays the capabilities of the cruiser. Make the armour a little thinner than it is in reality, the speed slower, the machine-guns fewer, and the cannon of a smaller calibre than the real thing. And then add that a troop of them will be dispatched to a certain area of the front. We will soon discover, from the sort of reception committee that the Germans prepare, whether the leak has come through the British Embassy or not."

"Yes, that may well be true," agreed Brian, "but it really won't help us find out who the traitor is."

"Oh yes it will," said Harry, grinning. "If we send copies of the same message to all those people at the Embassy who might possibly be passing on the information to the Germans, we can find out who it is." Brian frowned, and Harry continued. "All we have to do is to change the information about where the *Zaamurets* will be dispatched to in each message. And when we see the Germans getting ready to meet the train, we work out which message they had read by seeing where they are assembling."

Petrov smiled. "Exactly the idea I had in mind, Lieutenant. Well done." Harry smiled back.

"I suppose I should have thought of that myself," grumbled Brian. "Good thinking, Harry." He still seemed troubled.

"I'll give you the names and locations of half a dozen likely locations where the *Zaamurets* might be dispatched," said Petrov. "Each is roughly equally strategically important, and all are distinctly feasible locations. None of them, by the way, is the place we have picked for the first actual *Zaamurets* raid."

"I wish I could feel a little happier about all this business," said Brian.

"I can sympathise with your feelings, believe me," said Petrov. "If you want to feel a little better, I can point out that this will make it almost certain that only the guilty party is punished, with very little risk of the innocent suffering."

"That's true," sighed Brian. "What's the word on the *Netopyr?*"

"Ah, there I am able to give you some good news. Lebedenko has sent word that the problem holding things up now appears to be fixed, so we will be able to see the *Netopyr* in action tomorrow. However, I have something to counterbalance that good news. We Russians would never be completely happy without a little gloom and misery to enliven our days." He smiled without humour. "I don't know if you were listening to any of the conversations this afternoon, but there was a strange sort of incident earlier today."

"I heard a little," confessed Brian. "But I felt it wasn't my business to be listening."

"Actually, it was very much your business, but I really didn't want to bring you into it until I had more details. It concerns the train the *Zaamurets* was competing against. Just before it reached the perimeter gates here, it seems a man was spotted on the roof of the train – not a member of the crew, as he was in civilian clothes. The officer in charge fired at him with his pistol, and thought he had hit the man, who then fell off the train."

"They thought it was a spy of some kind?" asked Harry.

"That was their assumption. Anyway, when they stopped the train, there was no sign of the man on the train, and no sign of him anywhere near the tracks. It seems that the officer was mistaken about his shooting. The mystery man seems to have slipped off the train as it stopped, and hidden in the bushes at the side of the track. He then distracted the gate guards from their duty and slipped through the gates. He was spotted going into the woods and a few shots were fired at him."

"Hitting him?" asked Brian.

"I'll come to that in a moment. That's one of the rather interesting things about all this. Anyway, he made for the woods, and there was a sweep made through the woods by the sentry company. They found nothing. My guess is that he'd climbed a tree or something, but the fools were only looking on the ground. When they returned to their barracks, they discovered that one of their number was missing. The search party sent out to find the missing man found their comrade with his throat cut, and the body stripped of his uniform."

"Very nasty indeed," said Brian. "And what was so interesting about the shooting?"

"It appears that one bullet missed the man himself, but knocked off the heel of his boot, which they discovered as they were chasing him. They also discovered that the heel was hollow, and contained gold coins, which had spilled out."

"Our friend on the submarine," said Harry.

"Whose orders, if you will remember, were to come here to this establishment and spy on the *Netopyr*. From the sketchy descriptions that the train crew provided, it would appear that our friend Kolinski has indeed managed to follow us all the way from Reval."

"That's not cheerful news, to be sure."

"There's actually a little more. Just before the train was due to begin its practice shooting against the *Zaamurets*, they had to take on ammunition, having none on board during the journey from

Moscow. When they opened one of the ammunition lockers, they discovered a corpse in there, again with a cut throat."

"One of the train crew?"

"No. They made enquiries, and it seems this was one of the railway workers in the yard in Moscow. As yet no definite identification has been made, but this seems to be the most likely explanation at this time."

"Well, it would be hard to mistake friend Kolinski for anyone else, with that dirty great beard of his, and that mass of shaggy hair. It's going to be easy to spot him. Surely he can't hope to pass himself off as one of the guards here?" asked Harry.

"That, I am afraid, is where you are wrong. According to the officer who spotted the man on the roof of the train, he was clean-shaven, and his hair was short. However, judging from the general size and physique, it does indeed look as though the man was Kolinski. Maybe you haven't noticed, but most of the guards in this area have been selected for their height and general strength. Kolinski won't stand out as much here as he would in a normal group of soldiers. We're just going to have to be extremely careful, and challenge anyone suspicious. We're all going to have to keep our eyes open until we catch him, and I'm counting on you gentlemen to do your part here. Please don't trust any of the ordinary soldiers that look to you anything like your memories of Kolinski until you have had an officer verify them for you. I don't think that he'll be able to pass himself off easily as an officer, so that's not something that worries me very much. I have arranged for the officers commanding the guard units to make surprise inspections of the sentries as often as possible – at least once an hour, but not at fixed intervals, to identify personally all the men on duty."

"Not much more you can do, is there?"

"I can't think of much at the moment. I'm tired. It's been quite a day." Petrov yawned. "And on that note, gentlemen, I will bid you both a very good night. Many thanks to you both for your invaluable assistance today."

⚜

When Harry came down to breakfast the next morning, Brian seemed to have disappeared.

He was halfway through his black bread and jam when Brian came in, looking a little muddy.

"It's not really my place to tell you how to behave," said Harry. "But I think you should make yourself a little more presentable before Petrov joins us."

Brian laughed. "Give me a moment, will you?" he replied. "It's chilly out there and I need some of that tea. Petrov's been out there with me. He may be a Grand Duke or whatever, but he knows what he's doing here, and he loves doing it. It's a pleasure to work with him."

"What were you up to?"

"Looking for traces of our friend Kolinski." He gulped his tea. "Ah, that's better. That Kolinski's a vicious bastard. I saw the two bodies he left behind him yesterday. They're not a pretty sight. He seems to have no conscience at all about killing. Petrov feels that these two are not the only bodies Kolinski has left behind him. There are probably some in Petrograd and Moscow that we haven't heard about. Then we went to the woods to look at the place where the guard's body was found. Petrov's good. He sometimes notices things even before I do, and I've always been regarded as being a bit of a Sherlock Holmes. He spotted some marks on the tree bark where Kolinski had climbed up it, and the place where he must have jumped down on the poor sod whose throat he cut. We saw which way he'd taken off, but then we came to a stream, and the dogs lost the scent."

"Dogs?"

"Yes, a couple of bloody great monsters. Look more like wolves than dogs. Vicious-looking brutes, but Petrov says they're nice as pie once they get to know you. And they're as good as bloodhounds at following a scent, it seems. Anyway, we know which way the beggar went, even if we don't know where he is now. And now I will go and wash and brush up. I caught a sight of the *Netopyr* as we were coming back, by the way. Bloody amazing thing. You're going to love it."

About an hour later, a freshly cleaned up Brian made his way with Harry and Petrov across the proving ground. As they reached the corner of one of the huts and turned towards the open space, Harry's jaw dropped, and he stopped dead in his tracks.

"Bloody hell! Sorry, sir," speaking to Petrov, "but that's it?"

"That, Lieutenant, is the *Netopyr*," said Petrov proudly. "The only one so far, but we hope it will be the first of many."

Harry looked at the two massive spoked wheels with the sponson between them. "How big are those wheels?"

"Nearly nine metres," replied Petrov.

"That's nearly thirty feet! Bloody hell," he repeated. "This is amazing. How is the engine power transmitted to the wheels?"

"Well, I'm not really the expert on this," said Petrov. "Engineer Lebedenko is the man you should talk to. He speaks a little English, so you should be able to communicate with him without too much difficulty, I think."

As if on cue, a tall gangling man approached the group. "Ah, Engineer Lebedenko," Petrov greeted him. "Here is Lieutenant Braithwaite of the British Army, who is an engineer himself, and would like to know all about the *Netopyr*."

"You English? Good. I like English very much," in thickly accented English. "Come with me. I explain all about *Netopyr*."

"I was wondering how you transfer the energy from the engines to the wheels," asked Harry.

"Come." Lebedenko led the way up a gangway leading along the "tail" from the rear trail wheels to the central compartment between the two main wheels. Harry followed cautiously, but Lebedenko was obviously used to doing this, and almost skipped ahead. "Now, look," he said, opening a hatch.

Harry looked and tried to make sense of what he saw. "You're using that spring to press that wheel against the rim of the main wheel, and transfer the energy that way?" Lebedenko looked blank, so Harry pantomimed the need for a pencil and paper. Lebedenko pulled out a notebook and a pen, and Harry sketched a quick diagram. "Engine here. Gearbox here. Main drive shaft and wheel here. Spring here. Presses against wheel here, and turns it."

"Yes, yes. You have it," said Lebedenko.

"I like it," said Harry. "It's pretty simple, but it should work. How do you steer?"

"Look," said Lebedenko, leading Harry to another part of the massive machine. "Here." There was a small compartment for a driver that looked a little like the helmsman's position on a ship. "Throttle here. Both engines," pointing to a lever beside the steering wheel. Harry examined the lever and the cables that led to the left and right engines. "Now turn wheel," Lebedenko commanded Harry, who obeyed. "See this?" he asked. There was a complex system of wires and pulleys which seemed to be attached to the throttles of the two engines.

"So if I turn the wheel to the left, I increase power on the right engine, and decrease power on the left?"

"Yes, yes."

"And that works well?"

"Yes. We have much success with this."

"What about brakes?"

"*Netopyr* is so heavy that he stop when no engine. So we have clutch only and no brake. Here we need two people because of strength of spring. Look."

"No dials or instruments to tell you about the engines?" asked Harry. The only instrument he could see was a rather primitive compass that looked as though it had come from a ship.

"Two engineers in crew, one for each engine," explained Lebedenko. "They watch temperature and revolution and when there is problem they tell steersman or captain."

Harry said nothing, but thought to himself that this did not sound like an ideal way to keep things running, especially in an emergency.

"Can we have a look at the engines now?" asked Harry.

"Certainly. My two nephews are now with us, I think," replied Lebedenko. He led the way along a cramped gangway, with armour plate on both sides and overhead.

"This is Boris Sergeyevich Stechkin, my sister's son," introducing a grinning young man, as blond as Lebedenko himself was dark. "This port engine here is his duty."

Harry examined the massive Maybach, and nodded approvingly. From what he could see, the engine was in excellent condition, and had been well maintained. "Do you speak English?" he asked the young man, who shook his head in reply.

"My other nephew at the starboard engine speaks English and German. Come," said Lebedenko, and he and Harry bent almost double to traverse the low corridor joining the two wheels.

"Alexander Alexandrovich Mikulin," he introduced the other mechanic. "My brother's son." He added something in Russian – Harry could make out his name, and the word "mechanic", which seemed to be the same in Russian and English.

"Another engineer who loves motors? Wonderful. Please call me Sasha, or even Alex if you prefer," said the young man in English that was much better than his uncle's. Harry recognised him as the bearer of the news of the delay the previous day. His surly mood of the day before seemed to have vanished, and his smile appeared genuine and unforced. He was about the same age and height as Harry, and even looked somewhat similar to the English officer. "I spent a little time in London and in Yorkshire after I had graduated from the Technical Institute. It is good for me to speak English again." He held out his hand for Harry to shake, and then withdrew it before Harry could grasp it. "My apologies." He wiped his hand with a rag. "I had oil on them from changing the plugs."

"Don't worry," said Harry. "I bet I've had as much oil on my hands in my time. May I look?" He bent over the engine and examined the valve tappets. "I've never seen this model of engine before, and I understand there's a new development here."

"Indeed there is," said Alex. "Look," pointing to a complex spring arrangement. "This really improves the efficiency of the exhaust system." The two men went into a complex discussion about the mechanical virtues of different engines, and Lebedenko turned away, smiling.

On the ground below, Brian and Petrov were standing below the monster, looking up at the giant mass of steel towering above them.

"I can see how this could work," said Brian. "It would certainly scare the living daylights out of any enemy that it approached. Is that a gun turret that I see in the centre, above the cross-beam?"

"Yes, that's right. Much the idea same as the main gun turrets on the *Zaamurets*, but we have no gun mounted as yet, as we're still testing the basic concepts. It will probably hold a smaller gun or maybe a cluster of machine-guns."

"And those would be machine-gun mounts on either side of the main sponsons?"

Petrov nodded. "They are there to provide cover for the flanks of the *Netopyr*. And if you look, you'll see another belly gun underneath to stop anyone from attacking that way."

"You will have to put in some sort of mechanism to prevent the main gun turret from firing through the wheels. It would be a disaster if the crew were to shoot off their own wheels. Some of the aeroplanes on the Western Front have an arrangement to stop them shooting off their own tails or propellers."

"That's something where we may have to ask for assistance from you British. The Russian aeroplanes aren't very sophisticated, though we have some wonderful designs from Igor Sikorsky and his team, but we lack some of the practical details that I am sure you have developed on the Western Front, and I doubt if our mechanics have the necessary experience to develop such a system quickly without a little assistance."

There was a shout from above. "We're ready to set off," Lebedenko called down to the two men below. "Will you ride in the turret, while the British lieutenant and I control the *Netopyr*?"

"Well, this is a first for me," said Brian. "I've never been in anything like this before."

"It's the first time Lebedenko has ever allowed me to be inside the *Netopyr* while it's moving," confessed Petrov. "Usually he's been too worried about something to allow me inside. It must mean that he is fairly close to completing his work."

The two men climbed up the ramp at the rear of the machine, and squeezed through the hatch that Lebedenko was holding open for them.

"If you two will go into the top turret," he said, hardly bothering to look at the two visitors.

"That sounded like an order," said Brian, when he and Petrov were alone in the turret.

"Lebedenko's a little like that. Rank really doesn't seem to mean anything to him. He was one of the best designers in the artillery division in the company where he worked, and I think it went to his head a little. He knows that I am something more than a Colonel, of course, and that I have a title, but I guess he's never given it more than a moment's thought. His nephews, though, are a completely different matter. Young Stechkin in particular is a very well-behaved and pleasant lad. Always respectful and willing to help. I'm not so sure about young Alexander Alexandrovich at times, but generally he's co-operative and observes the social niceties."

There was a loud bang, as one of the engines kicked into life, quickly replaced by a low roar. The sounds were repeated from the other side, and the whole structure started to vibrate.

"I feel like a pea in a tin," Brian shouted to Petrov.

"I know what you mean," replied Petrov. "This is not at all comfortable."

"And it's not going to help with aiming the guns, either."

Petrov nodded. There was a mighty lurch, and both men staggered, Petrov almost falling, but Brian moved to catch him before he actually hit the floor. Petrov nodded his thanks, and both men stood at the port where the gun would be mounted, looking at the ground more than five metres below them.

"It's a splendid observation platform," Brian shouted over the roar of the engines, which had increased in volume since the *Netopyr* had started to move. "This would be invaluable to see over ridges and to see what was happening in trenches."

"I'm impressed that this is moving at all," replied Petrov. "Quite frankly, after all the disappointments over the past few months, I didn't really expect us to be on our way today. But yes, I agree that this is a wonderful mobile observation platform, if somewhat large and heavy for the purpose. But it's been designed as a fighting vehicle."

There was another great lurch, and Brian and Petrov, who were now gripping supports inside the turret, kept their balance better this time. "What was that?" asked Petrov, who had been thrown back away from the gun port.

"We moved off the paved road. We're now travelling cross-country."

"But there's a great ditch between the road and the field," said Petrov. He moved to the rear observation point. "Good Lord, we seem to have crossed it." Brian moved to join him.

"That's quite some ditch," said Brian. "More like a trench on the Western Front, and we crossed it without too much difficulty. I don't think barbed wire would be much of a barrier to us, either."

At that moment, the hatch to the turret opened and Lebedenko's grinning face appeared.

"Nikolai Nikolaivich," exclaimed Petrov. "What are you doing here? Who is controlling this infernal machine of yours while you are talking to us?"

"The Englishman," replied Lebedenko. "He wanted to try for himself, and I let him. I made the *Netopyr* so simple to operate that even an Englishman can use it after a few minutes."

"That's very impressive," said Brian. "Well done. I would prefer it if you were to take the helm, all the same. I hate to think of the international consequences for Anglo-Russian relations if Harry damaged this amazing machine."

"I understand," replied Lebedenko, with a flash of surprisingly white teeth. "Colonel Petrov, we have enough fuel for about an hour's travel. Is there anywhere you would like us to go?"

"The trench system is less than two kilometres away," replied Petrov. "We will have enough fuel to get there and back?"

"Easily. I estimate that we can travel at about sixteen or maybe even twenty kilometres an hour along a good road, and perhaps half of that over fields and so on."

"Very good. You know the way?"

"Straight over there, I think, past that undergrowth." Lebedenko had entered the turret, and pointed to the west, towards a swath of low bushes.

"That's right. Those bushes will be a good test for the capabilities of the *Netopyr*."

Lebedenko laughed. "I promise you, you won't even notice as we go over them." He left the turret.

"That's probably true," said Petrov. "We're shaking around so much that we probably won't notice anything, even if we collide with an elephant."

"Mind you, an elephant probably wouldn't survive the impact of a collision with us," laughed Brian.

Petrov peered out of the turret. "We're moving at quite a speed, and this is pretty rough ground," he commented. "I wouldn't like to ride a horse this fast over this terrain, would you?"

"I don't know," replied Brian. "I'm not a horseman, but I certainly appreciate that this thing is moving much faster than infantry can advance, and I'd feel a lot safer going up against the enemy in this, rather than on foot."

There was a sudden loud bang from the left side of the *Netopyr*, and almost immediately both engines stopped. Brian and Petrov heard a rapid exchange of Russian between Lebedenko and his nephews.

"We have a problem with a fan belt," said Lebedenko, popping his head into the turret a few minutes later. "It broke on one engine, and we daren't risk overheating the engine by running without it. We can repair the belt, but it will take about ten minutes or a little more." His head disappeared, and Brian and Petrov could hear his voice shouting to his nephew.

"What do you think so far?" asked Petrov.

"I feel shaken to pieces," said Brian. "I think there's going to have to be some sort of suspension in the final model. Maybe the crew compartment can swing from wires or something. I don't know, I'm not an engineer. Maybe Lieutenant Braithwaite can come up with something."

They waited, and after a few minutes, Lebedenko sang out, "We'll be on our way, gentlemen." The engines re-started, and the *Netopyr* staggered off again.

"That didn't take very long," said Brian. "I'm guessing we're nearly there now."

"We're nearly at the brushwood," said Petrov. "Getting closer. We're in it now."

"Didn't feel a thing," said Brian. "Other than this continual infernal shaking."

"That undergrowth would stop an infantry advance dead in its tracks," said Petrov. "And cavalry would certainly slow down or even grind to a halt when it came to it. And we never even noticed. I don't think we've even slowed down at all."

"It's an interesting way to travel," agreed Brian.

"The trenches are just the other side of the ridge," said Petrov. "We're slowing down a bit as we climb, but I suppose that's only to be expected, really. Ah, here we are," pointing.

"Complete with wire fortifications and everything," remarked Brian. "As I said, this makes a wonderful observation platform."

There was a shout from Lebedenko from his place at the helmsman's station. "Look out! Hang on tight and brace yourselves. We're about to go over the first trench!"

Brian wedged himself against the side, and braced himself with his arms. Petrov did the same on the other side of the turret, and there was a sickening jolt as the floor seemed to drop away. Brian hit his head painfully and swore, repeating his words as the floor seemed to rise and hit him with considerable force. Petrov avoided hitting his head, but lost his footing as the *Netopyr* climbed out of the trench, and slipped to the floor.

"Everyone all right?" called out Lebedenko, cheerfully.

"Just about," replied Petrov. He sounded winded.

"Can you stop this thing for a moment?" shouted Brian.

"Yes. In a few seconds," and sure enough in a very short time the *Netopyr* had shuddered to a halt. Brian reached for the exit hatch on the turret.

"What are you doing?" asked Petrov.

"I want to see how this thing looks from the ground as it goes across the trenches."

"I'll come with you. But I want to make sure that we get picked up again." He shouted an explanation and instructions to Lebedenko. Brian led the way out of the hatch and down the walkway to the trailing wheels.

"We make a mess of the ground," commented Brian, pointing to the deep ruts left in the mud. "How much does this thing weigh?"

"It's too heavy to travel very far under its own power, I fear," Petrov answered. "Lebedenko has been instructed to design it to be disassembled and transported in sections, and reassembled close to where it will be used."

"The wheels are going to be a problem, though. They're nearly nine metres tall, and that's going to cause a lot of problems when you try to move them. They're not going to fit into any railway tunnel that I can think of, or even go under most bridges."

"He says he has a way to take even those giant wheels to pieces and put them back together again, but I am not sure if he's put those ideas into practice on this prototype. Let's get him moving, anyway." He looked up at the observation port where the steersman was located, and waved. An answering hand waved out of the port, the engines roared, and the giant machine shuddered into motion, trailing black smoke from the engine pods at each side.

"Well," said Brian, laughing, "there's no way that you're going to be able to mount any kind of surprise attack with a squadron of these things."

"That's true," said Petrov. "What with the noise and the smoke—"

"Not to mention the size of the bloody thing. It seems even bigger than when we saw it on the road."

"On the other hand, just think of the speed," Petrov pointed out.

The *Netopyr's* engines changed note, and the massive vehicle moved forward, turning in a wide semicircle.

"Is that the tightest turn it can make?" asked Brian.

"I think so. The trailing rear wheels don't make it very easy to turn in a tight circle, I think. But don't forget that the turret can turn fast to engage any enemy."

"I was thinking of escaping enemy artillery fire. It seems to me that those wheels might be quite vulnerable to high explosive."

"Hmm." Petrov considered this. "You may be right, but let's watch it cross a trench."

The gigantic wheels crunched across the barbed wire entanglements in front of the trench as though they did not exist.

"If the wheels were wider, they'd clear more wire for any supporting infantry and the weight would be better distributed," remarked Brian. "But then again, the whole thing would be heavier. I suppose there have be some compromises."

The massive wheels dipped into the trench, but because of their great diameter, hardly sank into the trench at all, and, engines straining, the *Netopyr* hauled itself out over the parapet on the other side. The rear trail wheels then entered the trench, and were left rotating uselessly in mid-air as the engines screamed and the giant drive wheels strained to pull the whole machine forward.

"This never happened when we crossed the trench just a little while ago," said Petrov. "I'm sure we would have heard the engines making that sort of noise."

"Maybe the rear wheels rolled onto a firestep or something last time," said Brian. "Right now, they're resting on nothing, and the engines are just dragging the trail along the ground until the rear wheels can touch solid earth again."

With a final bellow, the *Netopyr* pulled itself out of the trench and continued lumbering on its way.

"Wait for us!" Brian shouted, but Petrov had already pulled out a Very pistol and fired a red flare ahead of the *Netopyr*, which lurched to a stop. "Good thinking, sir," said Brian, as they walked to the rear and started climbing up to the turret.

Just before they entered the small hatchway, Brian caught at Petrov's sleeve. "Sorry, sir, but do you see something?"

"Where?"

"I don't see anything now, but I could have sworn that I saw a man there, at the edge of that undergrowth. I can't see anything now."

"What was he wearing?"

"Infantryman's uniform, as far as I could tell. Do you think it's our friend Kolinski?"

"Who else could it be? This area's fenced off, and the guards are all accounted for. I think we'd better get back as quickly as possible. Let's see how fast Lebedenko can make this thing go."

KOLINSKI WATCHED THE MASSIVE MACHINE sputter away in a cloud of exhaust fumes, moving at a pace he had no hope of matching. He had seriously considered rushing the two men whom he had seen outside the *Netopyr*, but he realised that there would be other men inside, and he had no idea of the interior, or how many men would be crewing the monster, or how they would be armed. He would have to get more information from his contact.

At least he'd found the beast in this massive testing area, thanks to an immense stroke of luck. The soldier whose uniform he was wearing had been carrying a map of the testing ground in his pocket. Once Kolinski had identified his location from a unique configuration of railway points and the confluence of two streams, it had been easy to find his way to the main machine shop, where he had stood out of sight as he watched the enormous machine. The size had awed him, and he realised that regardless of how well or badly it actually worked, just the sheer bulk and power of a *Netopyr* would intimidate the other side in a battle. He watched as four men, two in unfamiliar uniforms, and one in civilian clothes, approached the machine and stood around talking before walking up the tail of the *Netopyr* and entering the main cabin. After a short while, the engines started, emitting clouds of black smoke as they roared into life, and then, with a lurch, the *Netopyr* moved in the direction of the proving grounds.

When it had lumbered off and was almost out of sight, he had tried to follow it, but it had quickly outpaced him. Truly an impressive machine, he told himself, panting along the trail, trying to keep up. The noise and the dark smoke pouring from the *Netopyr*'s exhausts made it easy to keep track, even when the vast machine disappeared from sight behind a ridge. Without warning, the noise of the engines stopped, and the smoke slowly dissipated in the breeze. Cautiously, Kolinski made his way forward towards where he had last seen the *Netopyr*. Peering over the hillock, he saw the stationary monster. A mechanical failure of some kind, perhaps. As he watched, with load bangs and puffs of smoke, first one, then the other, engine fired up once more, and the *Netopyr* lurched off.

By following its tracks and taking advantage of the path created by its enormous wheels crushing the bushes, he was able to follow the machine through the undergrowth lying immediately in front of the trench system. He ducked into the forest beside the clearing and watched as the *Netopyr* successfully crossed a trench, and then stopped.

Two men got out and descended to the ground, watching the machine go across the trench, this time with a little more difficulty. It was very hard to tell, but one of the men looked somewhat familiar, though Kolinski was unable to put a name to the figure. He racked his brains trying to remember where he had seen him before, but failed. After re-crossing the trench, the *Netopyr* stopped again, and the two men went up the gangway into the cabin. Again that nagging feeling that he knew one of them, but he was still unable to place the man.

As the great machine started back along the way it had come, Kolinski knew that he would have to talk to the engineer who was his contact within the project, to find out more about the machine, and explore the possibility of taking control of the *Netopyr* for the Party, or else destroying it so that the Tsarists were unable to use it against the Revolution. He had noticed that there were no guns mounted in the turrets, so there was no hope of his walking off with a working war machine, however impressive the monster might appear.

The way back seemed easier, and the *Netopyr's* tracks were easy to follow, but they led him towards the area where the machines were stored and repaired, and the soldiers' barracks – an area he wished to avoid for the time being. The fact that dogs had been set to follow his trail the other day was a sure sign that his presence in the compound was known, and that there would be more attempts to find him and flush him out in the near future. As if his mind was being read, he could hear the sound of what sounded like a search party in the distance, similar to the sounds he had heard previously. The dogs sounded closer than was comfortable.

Yesterday he had gone into a stream and waded along it, in an attempt to shake the dogs off his trail, but today there was no stream nearby that he could see. Nor, he felt, would climbing a tree work again for him – he could only pull that sort of trick once or twice. The only thing to do was to bluff it out and hide where they would least expect to find him. He ran, panting heavily, towards the machine shops, where there was a chance to blend in with the other men who were working there. At least there he wouldn't be a lone soldier in the middle of a field. The searchers appeared to be coming from the opposite direction, and he gave thanks for that small mercy.

At last he could see the sheds where the experimental vehicles and motors were housed. The sound of the approaching soldiers sounded closer than before, and he hurried, now gasping, towards the largest and tallest of the sheds, guessing it was the one containing the *Netopyr*. A group of men was leaving the shed through a small door, the main doors through which the *Netopyr* had presumably entered having been closed. As the last man left, closing the door behind him, Kolinski waited as long as he dared before seizing the door handle, darting through the door and closing it behind him. He desperately looked around him for crates and oil drums to block the door and shut out his pursuers.

The exertion of creating the barricade, following his frantic run, left him exhausted. Obviously he was not fully recovered from the time he had spent in the sea, and the activities of the last few days hadn't helped, either. It occurred to him as well that not having eaten for over 24 hours was doing nothing for his stamina. He sank to his knees and almost collapsed onto the hard-packed earth floor of the shed. To his horror, he realised that the shed, which he had assumed was empty, actually contained another occupant, who was coming towards him. He felt for his bayonet, having left the rifle concealed in the forest before he had started out to track the *Netopyr*, and re-alised that it must have fallen out from his clothing while he was running. He was defenceless, and he had little strength left in him to fight.

THE OTHER CAME CLOSER, and bent over him. Kolinski could see he was not in uniform, but that meant nothing. Anyone here was a government agent, and was there to enforce the Tsarist will over the people. Suddenly the other stood up straight.

"Greetings, Comrade," he heard, to his amazement. "Welcome. You seem more than a little tired."

Kolinski realised that the other must have recognised him as a member of the Oupinski gang from the star tattoo on his neck, but although many of the gang had allied themselves to Ulyanov and his party, membership of the gang by no means implied automatic membership of the Party. In fact, he fully expected to be turned in for the sake of the reward that he expected had been offered for his capture.

He looked up to see if the welcome had been meant ironically – it was hard to tell from the tone of voice – and saw nothing but concern on the other's face.

"Who are you, to call me 'Comrade'?" he growled.

"I know who you are, Kolinski," replied the other. "Even if I hadn't received a message from Zurich letting me know you were coming, you were the subject of conversation earlier today. You're a popular man."

"I know," said Kolinski, his brain racing. "There's a search party after me right now."

"So my suggestion is that you hide behind these here," indicating a pile of boxes, "and I'll talk to the soldiers when they arrive. Go on, hurry."

Kolinski was in no state to protest, and moved quickly to the spot indicated. The other was halfway through dismantling the barricade that Kolinski had set up by the door when a furious knocking on the door started up.

"Wait a moment," he called out. "Some idiot left some boxes piled up here, and I'm just trying to get them out of the way. There," he grunted, as he opened the door. "Now, what can I do for you, Corporal?"

"We're chasing after that man they were talking about this morning, sir," replied the NCO. "He's somewhere in this area. You haven't seen anyone, have you?"

"Well, apart from the big doors there," he pointed, "which are shut and bolted, this door's the only way in here. And I haven't seen anyone come in through here. I'd know if there was someone in here, don't you think?"

"I suppose so, sir," replied the corporal. Well, sorry to have bothered you about this, sir. Please call out and raise the alarm if you do see anything or anyone suspicious, won't you?"

"I'll be sure to do that. Goodbye." He closed the door, smiling. "You can come out now," he called.

"Thank you," said Kolinski. He was feeling quite a lot better now, but still felt hopelessly confused. "Why on earth are you helping me like this?"

"Haven't you guessed? I'm the man who brought you here. Officially, I'm supposed to be helping my uncle develop the *Netopyr* for the Tsar, but I'm working for the Party. Comrade Zinoviev wrote me a message to tell me you were coming, and that you were here to do something about the *Netopyr*."

"That's right," said Kolinski. "Good to meet you, Comrade." The two embraced.

"But you're quite a lot earlier than I expected," said the other. "I wasn't expecting to see you here for at least another week or maybe even two."

"It's a long story," said Kolinski, "and it involves a ferry in the North Sea and a British submarine." He proceeded to give an abbreviated account of his adventures since leaving Zurich.

"It sounds as though you've really left a trail of blood and destruction behind you," said the engineer. "If they catch you, they're not going to show you any mercy at all."

"I wasn't expecting any before I set off," replied Kolinski. "I've done enough in my time to get me hanged many times over. I came here to do a job, though. Can we take control of the *Netopyr* for the Party?"

"It's not really finished yet. A lot of work to be done before it's ready."

"You say you're an engineer, right?" The other nodded. "So if we were to take the plans back to Zurich, you could work from the plans and make the thing perfect?"

The other laughed. "Comrade, you don't understand the way these things work. First, I don't have the plans; my uncle keeps them under lock and key, and I only see them when there's work to be done. And then how are you going to get this monster," pointing to the *Netopyr*, "back to Zurich for me to work on?"

"Well, then, would your uncle consider selling the plans to me to take back to Zurich? Maybe you could improve them and build a new *Netopyr*."

The engineer shook his head. "Uncle Kolya may not be in love with the Tsar, but he wouldn't want to help the Party, I am sure of that."

"Even for money?"

"Even for money. He doesn't work for money."

"He doesn't work for money, and he doesn't work for the Tsar. What does he work for, then?" asked Kolinski, puzzled.

"He's an engineer. He exists to build perfect machines. As do I," said the other, "but I design my machines only for the good of the people, and not for the machines' own sake."

Kolinski shook his head. This was a species of human being with which he'd never previously come into contact. "I see," he said, though he didn't.

"And the other thing that you seem to be overlooking, Comrade, is that building a *Netopyr* takes a lot of money."

"How much?"

"So far, I heard the figure of two hundred and fifty thousand roubles. And it's not finished."

Kolinski whistled. "That *is* a lot of money, to be sure."

"And the other thing is that you need skilled workers and a place to build it, as well as some sophisticated assembly processes and plants. Where does the Party have access to armour plating, for instance? And even if you did manage to build the thing in Zurich, what use would it be there to help with the Revolution here?"

"I suppose you're right, Comrade." Kolinski heaved a huge sigh. "Why didn't you tell Zinoviev all this before he sent me here?"

"I did. Several times. Maybe he just thought he knew better, or he didn't believe me."

"What would happen if we were to destroy the *Netopyr*? Would your uncle build another one?"

"I don't think he would be able to get the money for another one. The Tsar has given most of the money so far out of his own pocket. He was really impressed by a model of the *Netopyr* that my uncle showed him once, and has been providing the funds to develop it ever since. It's not really a government project, you know."

Kolinski craned his neck and looked up at the monster looming over them. "It really is a big thing, isn't it? I saw it out there today, and it looked big then. Close up like this, it's enormous. I don't want our people to be fighting it when we start the Revolution. If we can't buy it or make it for ourselves, we have to destroy it and stop all the work on it so that it can never be built again."

"Easier said than done, Comrade. My uncle has designed it to be pretty tough. That's armour plate protecting it up there, you know. Not just any old metal."

"The wheels look pretty fragile, though."

"You'd need something the size of an artillery shell to destroy them, but yes, if you knocked out the wheels, the whole thing would come crashing to the ground."

"So where are the explosives we could use to destroy it?"

"All the ammunition and so on is locked away, and it's only released on Petrov's orders."

"Who's Petrov?"

"Colonel Petrov. He's the one in charge of this whole place. You said that you saw us taking the *Netopyr* out today?" Kolinski nodded. "Well, he was the little fat one who came down and watched us while we went over the trenches."

A thought came to Kolinski. "Who was the other one, the tall one who was with Petrov?"

"Some Englishman who's come over with another English officer to look at the *Netopyr* and make suggestions to Petrov or something like that."

"Aha!" The parts of the puzzle fell into place. Now he knew why the face was familiar. It was the same English officer who had escorted him in the ambulance from the submarine to the hospital in Reval. What an extraordinary coincidence that he should be travelling in the very same submarine that picked him up out of the Baltic. Or was it coincidence? Kolinski couldn't be sure, but he would take money on a bet that the submarine knew of his existence and had been following him across the ocean. But how could they know he was there on the ferry, or in the lifeboat, or in the water? "You're going crazy!" he said to himself, but out loud.

"What?" said the other.

"Nothing, just talking to myself," he replied. "You said there was another Englishman?"

"Yes. He seems to be an engineer. My uncle let him control the *Netopyr* for a while, and he certainly knows his way around engines and motors. He came in on the *Zaamurets* yesterday." Kolinski frowned in puzzlement. "The *Zaamurets* is another of Petrov's toys. He calls it a rail cruiser. You say you came in on that armoured train yesterday?"

"Yes, that's right."

"Your train had a locomotive and carriages, right? Well, the

Zaamurets is only one car with guns and armour, and it's its own locomotive."

"Looks a bit like a tortoise?" asked Kolinski.

"I suppose you could say that. It can go quite a lot faster than the usual type of armoured train, and it can fight better. Yesterday Petrov held a target shooting competition between an ordinary armoured train and the *Zaamurets*. The *Zaamurets* won hands-down, I heard."

"What sort of guns?" asked Kolinski.

"Nordenfelts. Two of them. I know, because that's the sort of thing we're thinking of putting in the *Netopyr*. And a lot of machine-guns."

"Can you drive a train?" asked Kolinski. "Could you drive the *Zaamurets*?"

"I've never driven a steam train, but the *Zaamurets* uses very similar engines to the *Netopyr*. Why?"

"If we could get the *Zaamurets* close to this shed, I could probably manage to get the guns working, and we could blow up this shed and the *Netopyr*."

The engineer shook his head. "The railway doesn't come close enough to this shed," he said. "Uncle Kolya was pretty angry about it, because it means that all the parts for the *Netopyr* have to be carried about five hundred metres by the soldiers on handcarts, and they are always dropping things or damaging them. He's asked for some other way of doing things, like a small railway, but because the *Netopyr* isn't really an official project, there's no money, they say."

"Then we have to make sure that the *Netopyr* comes close to the railway," replied Kolinski. A smile spread over his face. "Maybe we can do the world a favour, and introduce the *Netopyr* and this *Zaamurets* thing to each other?"

Petrov, Brian and Harry were sitting round the table, drafting their almost identical reports on the *Zaamurets* to trap the suspected traitor in the British Embassy. Maria had been persuaded that it was not in her interests to be privy to this part of the operation, and though she protested, she had gone off reluctantly, leaving the three men hunched over a pile of papers.

"We have to make the whole thing specific enough to be believed, and also to make sure that the Germans are responding to a threat of the *Zaamurets*, and not to anything else," said Brian. "Otherwise there's no point in doing this."

"I don't think you need to worry about that too much," answered Petrov. "Basically, the Germans are facing infantry most of the time, and they seem to have moved most of their artillery to the Western Front. Since the *Zaamurets* is tied to the rail lines, which the Germans typically avoid, any new concentration of German troops around the rail network, especially supported by machine-guns and artillery, is going to give the game away."

"All right," Brian agreed. "How much time do we give the Germans to move their troops into position? I mean, when are these supposed *Zaamurets* attacks going to take place?"

"I'd say about four weeks from now should do it," said Petrov.

"But you only have the one *Zaamurets*," pointed out Harry.

"I know that, and you know that. The Germans don't know it, though, and I am sure that your people in the embassy have no idea either. Let's say three *Zaamurets* cruisers in four weeks. It's perfectly feasible, I think. Here is a list of the locations," passing over a piece of paper. "And this is where they are on a map," opening another folded sheet. "As you can see, all of these are places where it would seem reasonable to make a breakthrough spearheaded by a *Zaamurets* attack."

"Can't argue with that reasoning," said Brian. "Very good, we'd better get writing."

"If you don't mind," said Petrov, a few minutes later. "Can I leave you gentlemen?" He yawned. "I'm tired, and I will bid you good night." They all rose to their feet as Petrov walked to the door.

"Is this really going to work, do you think?" Brian asked Harry.

"You're asking me?" replied Harry. "It seems a bit unlikely, really. If the worst comes to the worst, I suppose it will narrow the field a bit."

"I don't want it to work," said Brian. "I don't mean that I want the traitor to continue with what he's doing – don't get me wrong about that – but this seems to me to be the wrong way to go about things."

"Any better ideas?"

"I'm damned sure that it's Charles Featherington. If there's a train back to Moscow from here tomorrow, I want to be on it, and then back to Petrograd to confront the man face to face."

"And if you're wrong?"

"Then I've wasted a few days and a railway ticket. But if I'm right, then at least he's been caught fair and square and not by some trap. Do you understand what I'm trying to say?"

"I suppose so. What do you think Petrov's going to say about you just walking out on us here?"

Brian put down the pen he had been writing with, and looked Harry in the eye. "Harry, you're a lot more use than I am here. You know as much about trench fighting as me, and you know much more about the mechanical side of all of this than I do. I want you to take care of the *Netopyr* business here. And there's another thing…" His voice tailed off, and Harry looked at him questioningly. "Damn it, Harry, what are you going to do about Maria?"

"What do you mean?"

"Harry, she can't take her eyes off you."

Harry laughed embarrassedly. "Brian, you've gone bloody daft."

"I'm serious, Harry. Have you really not noticed how she always arranges things so that it's your arm she leans on as we go up steps and so on? You're the one she always talks to at dinner."

"That's ridiculous. She's a well-brought up girl, being polite to her father's visitors, that's all," protested Harry. Brian snorted. "And in any case," Harry went on, "even if what you are saying is true, there's no way a Grand Duchess or whatever she may be is going to have anything to do with someone like me. Look what she did to that poor nephew of Lebedenko's when he tried to take her arm and guide her round the place."

Brian laughed. "Poor lad. I've never seen anyone look so embarrassed as when she turned her back on him and started talking to her father. I tell you, Harry, I have some bloody snobs in my family – the sort of person you wouldn't wish on your worst enemy – but she could give lessons in showing the cold shoulder to any of them. But she's definitely showing a different kind of shoulder to you. I can tell."

"I think you're making this up as you go along. I haven't heard you come up with such a load of cobblers since I don't know when."

"Just saying, Harry, that's all. Just saying."

Harry started to laugh. "I still don't believe you. You're pulling my leg."

"Then open your bloody eyes."

Harry hadn't stopped laughing. "I do believe you're jealous."

"I am not—!" Brian caught himself and continued in a quieter tone. "All right, I admit it, perhaps I am, just a little. But believe me, the gap between her and you isn't that much bigger than between her and me. Face it, lad, she's out of your class and she's out of mine as well. As I said to you some time back, she's probably been promised to some prince or duke or something since she was four years old." He sighed. "Anyway, changing the subject… How are those letters getting on? I've done one, and I have two left on my list here."

"Same here. Finish them off, and then we'll call it a night."

"No, don't bother doing them. If I'm going to Petrograd, there's no point in sending these letters, is there?"

"*If* you're going," Harry reminded him.

"I'm going," said Brian, with a set jaw, and a determined look on his face. "Don't worry about that."

⁂

O NCE HE'D REACHED PETROGRAD, Brian soon made his way from the station to the British Embassy, where he caused some consternation by loudly demanding to see Charles Featherington.

"I regret to inform you that he hasn't arrived here yet," the porter at the front gate informed him, after Brian had given his name and Army rank.

Brian made a show of pulling out his watch and looking at it. "I suppose quarter past ten is a bit early for old Charlie," he admitted. "Maybe I can wait for him in his office?"

"I'd have to check whether that would be possible," replied the porter. "Sir," he added, as Brian glared down at him from his full height. "I'll be with you in a moment, sir," as he scurried off.

Brian wondered for a moment whether he should make his own way to Featherington's office, but decided that this was not the ideal time for him to start making waves. He tapped his foot impatiently on the stone floor as he waited. After a few minutes, the porter returned, in the train of one of the Embassy diplomats.

"Now then, Lieutenant Finch-Malloy, I don't know who the devil you are to come in here and start demanding a private audience with one of our most respected diplomats—"

Brian held his temper in check, but cut the man off in mid-flow. "Sir, if we could step aside a little?" He jerked his head towards the porter, to emphasise the need for privacy.

The other took the hint. "You're being most mysterious, Finch-Malloy. I hope you have a good reason for all of this."

Brian had come prepared. "Indeed, I do, sir." He reached into an inner pocket, and withdrew a stiff official envelope, clearly marked with the Royal coat of arms. "If you would, sir." Brian had his doubts as to whether the man actually rated so many "sirs", but it seemed like a wise move.

The bureaucrat took the envelope gingerly, and extracted the paper from within it. His eyebrows raised as he perused the letter from C. "'To whom it may concern," he quoted. "Well, I suppose it concerns me. You hush-hush fellows seem to get everywhere. Name's Crofts-Lavery, if it's of any interest to you. I suppose there's no point in my asking you why you want to see young Featherington?" Brian shook his head. "I supposed as much. In which case, I suppose there's nothing for it but to ask you to wait in his room." He turned to the porter. "Thank you, Smithers. I will show Lieutenant Finch-Malloy to Mr Featherington's room myself. Follow me," to Brian. Brian followed the heels clacking down the hallway. "In here," he was told. "Need anything, Lieutenant?" Brian shook his head again. "Fine," replied the frustrated Crofts-Lavery. "I'll leave you here, then."

The door closed, and Brian sat in the chair behind the desk. He resisted the temptation to look through the drawers, or shuffle through the papers on the desk, but rested his chin on his hands, rehearsing the forthcoming conversation in his mind.

After about ten minutes, the door burst open, and Charles Featherington entered the room, looking somewhat the worse for wear.

"They told you'd pushed your way in here," he said, more quietly than his words and the expression on his face suggested. "What the hell are you back here for?"

"Shut the door and sit down there," Brian ordered in reply, pointing to a chair on the far side of the desk.

"Why on earth are you sitting in *my* chair at *my* desk?" asked Featherington in reply, seemingly only just having taken in the fact.

"Never mind. Please do as I say."

Featherington closed the door, and sat as directed, wincing a little. "Rough night last night." He grinned feebly. Brian didn't return the grin. "So what's all this in aid of?" he asked, returning to seriousness.

Brian avoided the other's eyes. "I really don't know how to tell you this," he began, forgetting all the speeches he had been rehearsing in his head. "The long and short of it is, that someone's passing on our information to Jerry, and the finger seems to point in your direction. Give me your word of honour that it's not you, and I will go back to London and tell them, with the greatest pleasure in the world, that they were mistaken." He watched the other's face carefully as he made his speech, noting the shock that appeared in Featherington's bloodshot eyes.

"Just my word?" asked Featherington, biting his bottom lip. "You wouldn't want any proof?"

"How could you prove that you're not a traitor?" shot back Brian. The word "traitor" had a further effect on Featherington, who squirmed in the chair, and looked down at his shoes.

"Silly of me to imagine I could do that, I suppose." He looked up, almost defiantly. There were now tears in his eyes, Brian noticed. "No, I can't give you my word." Brian remained silent, continuing to stare at him. "It's a blasted relief to admit it, I have to say. Who are you, anyway? You're not police. Are you? Are you going to be giving evidence against me or something?" He was almost crying by now, and the words came out disjointedly.

"I'm not the police. I have no power to make an official arrest or anything like that. I was sent here to trap you by a rather underhand trick that I didn't want anything to do with. I thought it was better if you admitted it all yourself – if there was anything to admit. And

I'm sorry to see that there does seem to be something to be confessed. Want to talk about it?" he added, after a pause.

"Not really. Well, maybe. You know I have damnable bad luck at picking winners? If they gave money for picking losers, I'd be a rich man, I tell you. And Pater's been pretty generous with my allowance, I have to say, but even so..."

"And so you found someone who would help you over the bad patch?" Featherington nodded silently in reply. "And they started charging a little more interest than you were expecting?" Another nod. "And then?"

"It all came through the moneylender. He knew that I wouldn't be able to pay off what I owed him without some help, and put me in touch with someone he said would be able to pay off my debts for me."

"German?"

"No. One of those Confederates, but with a German sort of name."

"And you thought that it didn't really matter too much, because we're not at war with the Confederate States of America? And anyway, it was only Russian information, not British? Correct?" Featherington nodded silently. "Didn't it ever occur to you that he might be passing your information along to the Huns?"

"Maybe," muttered Featherington.

"You damned fool. And did he pay off your debts?"

"Not all of them. There was always enough owing that I had to keep giving him what he asked for."

"I won't ask you who he was or what he was asking for. You can tell them all that in London."

"You might at least leave me here alone with a pistol or something. Let me do the honourable thing?"

"Sorry, Charlie," replied Brian, using the other's Christian name for the first time. "They need to know in London just how much of the shop you've given away. And who knows, maybe it's not enough to justify your killing yourself, after all? I don't know, and I don't want to know. Besides, if you kill yourself here in Petrograd, it's going to look pretty messy for the Embassy here."

"And what's it going to be like for my family if I go back and they shoot me or hang me or whatever?" He paused. "Look here, Finch-Malloy, I know it's early and all that, but I think I need a drink. Do you mind?" Brian shook his head, and Featherington pulled a hip-flask out of his pocket and swigged from it. "Believe me, I need the stuff now. Another thing for me to be ashamed of, I suppose." He repeated his question.

"They'll do it very quietly, I am sure. It will be better for you and for everyone if you cooperate this way."

"And how do I get back to London?"

"The same way that I came here. Max Horton and his magic submarine. He's still here in Russia, in Reval. It's not a comfortable journey, but you'll get back safe and sound. We can arrange things here so that no-one need know why you've left. And no-one at home need know what's happened to you, either. Maybe you were just re-turning home on leave from here and you slipped overboard from the submarine. It could be arranged that way if you— if you don't appear in public again, and you don't want your family to know what's been going on."

"How many other people know about all of this?"

"The chap I'm working with, one of the Russians – I think it's only him on the Russian side who knows anything – and my chief in London and some of his people. I'm afraid your cousin Henry Dowling knows – he works for the same people as me. It's not going to go any further than it needs to. For one thing, you're a bloody em-barrassment to us all. We really don't need to tell the world about it."

Featherington had broken down completely by this point, and was sitting sniffing in his chair, his shoulders heaving. "Sorry about this," he said. "I mean, not about the – the treason." He seemed to choke on the word. "I mean about me sitting here like a shivering jelly. What do you think is going to happen to me?" He stared at Brian with bloodshot eyes.

"That's not my business," replied Brian. "My job was to make sure that you returned to Blighty to face the music, but I don't know what tune they'll be playing for you. It's not going to be 'See the Conqu'ring Hero Comes' though, I can tell you that right now. So, I am going to tell the pompous little rat who brought me here – Crofts-Lavery, I think his name was – that I am going to escort you to HMS *E9*, Lieutenant-Commander Horton's submarine, currently in dock at Reval, and see you safely on board to go back home, as the result of a sudden death in your family. And I want your word of honour that you are not going to do anything silly like run away or try to hurt yourself while I'm gone, or indeed, at any time before you get to talk to the people you've got to talk to in London."

Featherington smiled ruefully. "You trust my sense of honour after this?" he asked.

"Of course. You had your chance to break your word when I asked you earlier, and you didn't take it. Of course I trust you."

"You have my word."

Brian left the room, and returned after about thirty minutes. "That's it. All fixed. We're on our way."

"What? Now? Don't I even have time to pack a toothbrush or something?"

"Time, tide and Max Horton wait for no man. We'll take the train to Reval, and you'll be on your way back to Blighty an hour or so after we arrive."

The two men left the room together, Featherington a few steps in front of Brian.

F ROM HIS FELLOW PARTY MEMBER and protector, Kolinski discovered that the *Netopyr* was always crewed by at least three people: two engine-men (and sometimes four) and at least one helmsman and clutch-man.

"It's pretty cramped in there," he was told. "Quite frankly," his informant continued, looking him up and down, "I don't think you would be able to move around in there at all fast. Not fast enough to overpower them all. My uncle always carries a gun with him, and so does my cousin."

"You don't?" Kolinski asked.

"No," shaking his head. "I wouldn't know how to use one if I did. Something I've always managed to stay away from."

"So what you're telling me is that there's no easy way I could take over the *Netopyr* by force?"

"That's right."

"Supposing I took your place in the crew?"

The other shook his head, smiling. "I don't think you're a trained mechanic. Have you any experience with engines of this type?" Kolinski shook his head back in reply. "It really wouldn't work. Those engines are so temperamental that they need a nursemaid all the time, and if you're not experienced in these things, it just wouldn't work at all."

"So there's no way of capturing the *Netopyr*?" Kolinski asked again.

"Basically, that's correct. Unless we can find several Party members who are also mechanics, and train them in the operation of the machine."

"And are there any other Party members here?"

"The only three I know here are soldiers without the education or training that we need for something like this."

Kolinski paused in thought. "Then I have to destroy it, don't I?" His grin, displaying the wreckage of his teeth, was a terrible thing to see. "You'll have to arrange to be sick or something so that I don't destroy you along with it, won't you?"

"I guess so," the other had replied. "How will you destroy it?"

"I'll find a way, don't worry. This is an Army base, after all. Full of things which are meant to explode and blow up other things. You talked about the armoury before. Don't suppose you could find your way in there, could you?"

"I could get hold of the key, I suppose. I know where it's kept, and it should be easy enough for me to get in and out without anyone noticing if I time things right."

"That's good news."

"What do you need?"

Kolinski scratched his chin thoughtfully. "Grenades. About ten of them." The other nodded. "And a rifle for long range work, and some ammunition for it, of course. Twenty or thirty rounds should be enough. I've got enough ammunition for my pistol."

"That's it?"

"Make sure that I have a bayonet as well. Useful things, bayonets." Kolinski smiled without humour.

"Fine. I'll try to get these things to you really early in the morning, before sunrise. You stay here – I have keys to this place and I'll lock you in here. No-one's going to come here before I come back anyway, but just in case, it's best if no-one can get in. Then you've got to leave here while it's still dark."

"What's going to happen tomorrow with this thing?" Kolinski gestured towards the *Netopyr*.

"I don't know yet. There's a meeting to discuss plans in," pulling out his watch, "about an hour's time. I'll know then, and I can tell you in the morning where you should make your ambush."

"Good. Once the monster's out in the open, I can start the fireworks."

"You could destroy it here," the other pointed out.

"Too easy for me, and too easy for them." Kolinski's hideous grin re-appeared. "I want this to happen a long way away from tools and repair workshops. Otherwise it might be too easy to put it back together again."

"I see your point. In any case, I want that fat little bugger Petrov to go up with it. He's too dangerous to be allowed to continue with what he's doing, but I would really like you to leave my uncle alive, if you can. He's not dangerous to the Party. He doesn't believe in what you and I believe in, it's true, but he's not really a bad man – just in love with his machines."

"And your cousin? And the Englishmen?"

"My cousin can go to hell for all I care. Drunken Tsarist fool. One of the Englishmen left the other day without telling anyone. The engineer Englishman told us he'll be coming back, but we don't know when. It would be a shame to kill the engineer, though. He seems quite intelligent and could almost be useful."

"He's an English officer," Kolinski objected.

"But he's not one of their aristocracy, he told me. In fact, he's one of the proletariat."

Kolinski was confused. "You mean the English army makes officers of proletarians?"

"Not always, but this is because of the other one – the one who's gone away – they made the proletarian engineer an officer. I don't pretend to understand everything about it, but it seemed to be that way when it was explained to me."

"So you want me to spare the two most valuable engineers on the project?" Kolinski growled. "I suppose you're going to want me to save the life of the young lady as well?"

"I have no love for her, but if you kill her, you're going to have to kill everyone. They're not going to show any mercy to you if you dispose of her and leave the rest alive."

⚜

KOLINSKI WAS STARTING TO FEEL the same sort of excitement that he had experienced as a teenager, hunting wolves in the taiga. There was the same element of danger, from something larger and more powerful than Kolinski himself, but without the intelligence that Kolinski knew he possessed. Although he was not in any shape or form an intellectual, and would have argued violently with anyone who suggested that he was, Kolinski believed himself to be the equal or superior of anyone he had ever faced when it came to matters of practical tactical cunning. Although he hardly seemed to have slept for the past few days, and his stomach was now almost empty, as it seemed to have been for at least two weeks, his mind was alert and his senses were on edge, attuned to any movement or noise out of the ordinary.

He was now waiting at the edge of the forest by the trench system. He had been told early in the morning that the *Netopyr* was due to make another trench-crossing trial some time in the afternoon. His informant had given him this information along with the requested grenades, a rifle and several magazines of ammunition for it, along with a bayonet, all of which had been secretly removed from the armoury, and then once again repeated his request for Kolinski to spare the lives of his uncle and the English engineer officer.

Kolinski grinned to himself. He wasn't going to spare anyone if he could help it. He had his pistol as well as a rifle. His primary weapon, though, on which he was relying to complete the job of disabling the *Netopyr*, was the knapsack of hand grenades. He had constructed a sturdy and powerful catapult to act as a grenade launcher, using a forked branch and a rubber fan belt he had discovered in the workshop. Testing it with stones of the same size and weight as the grenades, it propelled its projectiles with an almost flat trajectory up to about 50 meters. It wasn't as accurate as Kolinski would have liked, but he guessed that the explosive force of the grenades would compensate for this, by bursting and damaging anything nearby. And, as an ace in the hole, he also had the bayonet hidden under his jacket.

The air was still. A few birds called from inside the forest, but otherwise there was silence, broken as he listened by the faint sound of what sounded like the *Netopyr*'s engines. Kolinski raised a pair of stolen binoculars to his eyes, and scanned the horizon in the direction from which he expected the *Netopyr* to arrive. Sure enough, two columns of dark smoke indicated the imminent arrival of his prey. He turned to his knapsack and withdrew the grenades, arranging them in a neat row in front of him, and placed his grenade launcher carefully at the end of the line. He turned his attention to the rifle, making sure that there was a round in the breech. Lastly, he rechecked the pistol, thrusting it into his belt, after ensuring that the safety catch was on. Now he felt ready for anything.

Waiting was always the hardest part for Kolinski at these times. He wanted to smoke, but he'd run out of cigarettes, and the last of his bottle of vodka had disappeared down his throat that morning. Still, there'd be enough when he finished this job, he guessed. He watched the horizon, and soon he could see the massive shape of the *Netopyr* lurching towards him. The details were too far away to be clearly distinguishable without the binoculars, but the general shape and appearance were unmistakable. Even though he'd been assured that there were no guns mounted in the machine, he was still struck with a sense of awe as the green metal monster approached.

He had worked out that he would attack the main axles first, which he considered to be the Achilles heel of the beast. The rest of the machine was too well armoured and the observation and ventilation slits too small for him to be sure of doing any damage with a grenade. If he could stop even one wheel from turning, the *Netopyr* would be unable to proceed, and he would be able to finish it off at leisure with the rest of the grenades, or simply wait for the occupants to emerge, when he could pick them off one at a time with the rifle. Maybe he could just wing them with the rifle and finish them off at close range with the pistol. Yes, that would be the most satisfying, especially if they could watch his face while he was doing it.

He picked up the first grenade and fitted it into the catapult. He crouched behind one of the bushes, where he was fairly certain he could not be seen. The monster lumbered closer, and the roar of the engines became louder, drowning out the birdsong behind him in the forest.

He drew back the grenade, stretching the heavy rubber fan belt, and when he judged the time was right, let go. The grenade soared through the air straight towards the *Netopyr*… and bounced harmlessly off the metal flanks of the beast, coming to rest in the grass below the wheels as the behemoth rumbled on, seemingly without noticing this pinprick.

Kolinski swore foully to himself as he realised he had forgotten to pull the pin out of the grenade before sending it on its way. He'd forgotten this basic action when he'd practised with stones. Never mind. He picked up the next grenade in the line, and fitted it into the rubber belt. With a little effort, he was able to remove the pin with his teeth, before pulling back the rubber, and letting fly with the grenade. This time the grenade let out a small pop while it was still on its way to the target, and Kolinski instinctively ducked to avoid the expected shrapnel from the casing, which never arrived. Another foul oath emerged. Obviously only the detonator had exploded. The grenade crashed against the *Netopyr*'s armour with a loud clang. Surely the crew must have noticed something by now, Kolinski told himself.

They had noticed, obviously. After about ten seconds, the sound from both engines dropped in volume and pitch, and the machine slowed down. The belly turret under the main body of the *Netopyr* now started to turn, like a wolf scenting its prey, Kolinski thought to himself, and for the first time he noticed what appeared to be the muzzle of a Pulemyot Maxima machine-gun protruding from the gun port. He had been specifically told that the *Netopyr* was unarmed, and was likely to remain so for some time. Why was this happening to him now? The oaths were coming fast and furious as he fitted another grenade into the catapult and pulled the pin, working a little faster now to ensure the grenade exploded against the axle of the *Netopyr*. This time, both his aim and his timing were accurate. The grenade sped straight to the gap between the main body and the axle and lodged there for a second before exploding, but once again with no more than a puny pop.

Kolinski had exposed himself to the view of the *Netopyr* as he stood up to launch the grenade, and the belly turret was now definitely pointing in his direction. A loud voice came from within the body of the halted *Netopyr*, obviously amplified by a megaphone.

"Kolinski, we can see you, and in case you had failed to notice it, there is a machine-gun pointing straight at you. We give you ten seconds to throw down all your weapons and walk slowly towards us with your hands in the air. Ten … nine …"

Without pausing to think how they came to know of his presence, Kolinski flung himself flat on the ground, dropping the catapult and snatching up the rifle. He wormed away from the place where he had been hiding, using the long grass and the undergrowth as cover.

"… five … four … "

He peeked through the grass at the *Netopyr*. The machine-gun still appeared to be pointing at the spot he had just left, now five meters away. He had to move faster.

" … two … one … Belly turret. Fire at will."

With a loud chatter, the machine-gun started spitting slugs into the vegetation where Kolinski had been hiding, spraying the bullets over an area a few meters in diameter. He was certain that if he had remained in his original position he would have been killed. As it was, some of the ricochets seemed to come uncomfortably close at times. After about five seconds of firing, the gun stopped. Kolinski reached for his rifle and flicked the safety off, nestling the butt into his shoulder. As far as he knew, there was only one hatch on the *Netopyr*, at the back, leading onto the rear trail wheels, and he sighted the rifle in that direction. To his surprise, however, a hatch at the top of the vehicle opened, and a man's head and shoulders emerged. The man's hands followed, grasping a pair of binoculars, which he used to scan the ground where Kolinski had been hiding. Kolinski debated with himself whether to shoot, and betray the fact that he was still alive, possibly betraying his position into the bargain, or to keep low and hope to slip away unseen and unnoticed. His hunter's instincts got the better of his caution.

He let out his breath, sighted the rifle on the observer's head, and squeezed the trigger. Another pop, rather than the sharp crack he had been expecting. A misfire? He threw the bolt, ejecting the unfired round, but no new round took its place in the rifle's breech. A jam? Kolinski quickly removed the magazine. Why was it empty? He checked the other magazines in his pocket. All seemed to contain only one round. What in the name of all the saints was going on? He mumbled several obscene oaths to himself, and realized that by now, he had probably given away his position, anyway. As if to confirm this fear, the belly turret swung round in his general direction. He couldn't expect ten seconds' grace this time, he was sure, and he rolled to one side, bracing himself for the rain of bullets that he was sure would come his way. To his astonishment, however, there was no such rain. Instead, the voice came booming out of the *Netopyr*'s belly once again.

"Our patience is wearing a little thin, Kolinski. Throw down your weapons and advance towards us."

It took Kolinski little time to make up his mind and move towards the *Netopyr*. Not that he had any intention of surrendering.

His plan was to get inside the machine, and, armed only with the bayonet, to kill all inside before wrecking the vehicle with the remaining grenades which were still on the ground where he had been lying in ambush.

He stood up slowly, and ostentatiously dropped the useless rifle. He moved his right hand towards his waist.

"No tricks," warned the voice of the *Netopyr*. Kolinski smiled inwardly. The sort of trick he was planning was a little more subtle than simply pulling a pistol from his belt and firing it. He pulled the Nagant by the butt from his waistband and dropped it beside the rifle.

"Stay where you are," came the voice. There was a clanging sound, and two figures appeared on the rear trail and started to walk down towards the back wheels. One seemed to be carrying a rifle and one a pistol, but neither appeared to be wearing a Russian uniform.

"Don't move," one of them called. It was a woman's voice. Surely, Kolinski thought to himself, the *Netopyr* was not being crewed by women? The two guns never wavered as the two walked towards him. The one carrying the pistol was definitely a woman – a girl, in fact – and rather a beautiful one, Kolinski thought to himself. In a way, it was a pity that she was going to have to die. The rifle carrier was wearing a military uniform, but not a Russian one. He seemed young, and appeared to be strongly built. He might be a problem, Kolinski reckoned, working out his chances as they neared him. He hadn't forgotten the belly gun in the *Netopyr*, which was still pointing straight at him, but he'd already worked out there were several blind spots where the gun was unable to fire without damaging the machine itself. He reckoned that if he played his cards right, he could reach one of those spots before the crew of the *Netopyr* had time to react.

The man appeared to be wearing an English army uniform, as far as Kolinski could tell, but he wasn't the same man who'd escorted

Kolinski in the ambulance to the hospital in Reval. Presumably this was the proletarian engineer officer he's been told about. The girl was a different matter. She was wearing a riding skirt and a Russian infantry tunic, but of much better cut and material than the usual private's uniform.

"Turn around, put your hands in the air, and put your feet apart," she ordered. The pistol was pointing directly at Kolinski's head. Slowly, he did as he had been ordered, and he felt what seemed to the be muzzle of the pistol pressed against the back of his neck.

"One false move and your head comes off, Bolshevik scum," she hissed at him. How had he ever thought her beautiful? he asked himself. "The Lieutenant is going to search you. Stay absolutely still."

He felt hands patting his tunic pockets, and feeling under his arms. They were the hands of someone who had done this kind of work before, it seemed, and they were carrying out the task quite rapidly. They would reach the bayonet soon. It was now or never.

With a sudden ducking twist, he turned to face the girl, and knocked his hand upwards against her wrist. The pistol went flying out of her hand as Kolinski ducked down, and grabbed the ankle of the British officer, who went flat on his back as Kolinski heaved at his leg. The confusion gave Kolinski the few vital seconds he needed to reach inside the waistband of his tunic and pull out the bayonet, which he flourished in the face of the girl.

"Come with me, darling," he leered. "Stand right here," indicating a point immediately in front of him, between him and the *Netopyr's* gun. She obeyed, seemingly hypnotised by the bright shining steel of the bayonet. Kolinski grinned his horrible grin at her. "Now, you're not going to make trouble, are you?" She shook her head. "And what about you?" he asked the Englishman, who just stared at him as he struggled back to his feet.

"He doesn't speak Russian," explained the girl. "I'll tell him."

The Englishman said something to Kolinski, who understood not a word.

"What was that?" he asked the girl.

She shook her head and said nothing.

"Come on, damn you. Or one of those pretty little ears of yours comes off." The bayonet flashed to emphasise his words.

"It wasn't exactly a compliment. And he added that he promises that if you hurt me, you will die. Very slowly."

Kolinski laughed. "I spit in the face of threats like that, little one. Tell him that."

She spoke to him, and to Kolinski's surprise, the Englishman laughed back in his face, but without saying anything in reply.

"What do you want, anyway?" the girl asked Kolinski.

"Justice for the workers," he replied, repeating a phrase he had heard at Party meetings. "Or to be more exact, I want to see the death of that monster, and all those connected with it," jerking his head towards the *Netopyr*.

"And is this what you call justice?" she flashed back at him. "You know, there are people like my father who might even listen to what you people have to say, if you would just behave like civilised human beings instead of like animals."

"And who is your father, then? Even if he listened, would he take any notice? Would he agree with what we told him? Even if he did agree with us, could he persuade anyone else to listen and agree with him? No, my pretty little one, we don't believe that talking to your father will do any good. Action is the only way forward for us." Kolinski was now a little confused. Intellectual debate was far from being his strong point, and he had almost run out of words. Now he was even less sure about whether he was going to be able to kill this girl in cold blood. It wouldn't be the first time he had killed a woman, but his previous victims had been of a somewhat different class, and the circumstances had been more heated.

He must have relaxed his grip while he was considering all this, because suddenly she twisted in his arms to face him, and brought her knee up sharply between his legs. Kolinski reacted to this in the same way as most men do when hit hard in the testicles. He doubled up sharply in agony, but still managed to keep his grip on the bayonet, though losing his hold on the girl, who managed to wriggle completely out of his grasp. As Kolinski desperately sucked in air, he noticed through the black spots dancing in front of his eyes that the Englishman was making a dive for the girl's pistol lying on the ground where it had fallen. Still bent almost double and gasping for breath, he debated his best course of action. The girl was still within reach, and he made a grab for her arm, seizing it, and dragging her in front of him once again as a shield between his own body and the Englishman. Now, with the pain between his legs sending waves of nausea surging through his body, he had no qualms about slicing the bitch's throat open, and he lifted the bayonet to her face, pressing the edge against the skin of her neck. He bared his teeth in a snarl of pain and ferocity.

Before he could tense himself for the final stroke to cut her throat he saw the Englishman raising the pistol, seemingly about to fire. He swiftly switched his attack to counter the immediate danger from the pistol, and hurled the bayonet at the Englishman's face. As if in a dream, he watched the blade spinning end over end, and realised it would go low, and miss its target. The Englishman automatically dodged, but did so clumsily; too slowly to avoid the bayonet's point, which lodged itself firmly into the side of his neck, just above his shoulder. He slumped down to the ground, dropping the pistol. Kolinski was still drawing his breath in massive heaves and trying to make sense of what was going on round him, when the sudden noise of a firearm behind him made him start. A bullet cracked past him from behind and his hand felt the wind of its passing, too close for comfort. Before he could react to this new development, the sound of another shot rang out, and a sudden sharp pain in his right hand distracted him from the ache between his legs. Dazed and shocked, he looked down at his hand, and was horrified to see that it was covered with blood. He tried to move it, and quickly gave up the attempt. Even a slight movement of the fingers sent waves of agony shooting through his body to mingle with the pain spreading from his groin.

⁂

"THERE, THAT TOOK YOUR MIND OFF BEING KICKED in the balls, didn't it?" came a new voice. Kolinski couldn't see the speaker, but the voice didn't seem to be coming from inside the *Netopyr*. Rather, it seemed to be coming from behind him. Looking around him cautiously, he noticed that the girl was now bent down over the injured Englishman. "Don't worry, we'll meet soon enough," said the voice behind him. "Just keep perfectly still and don't move a muscle."

With the pain in his groin and in his shattered hand, moving was one of the last things on Kolinski's mind. He stood and waited, hearing footsteps coming from the woods behind him.

The footsteps passed him and halted in front of him. Raising his eyes, Kolinski saw another English uniform, worn by a man as tall as Kolinski himself, but considerably slighter, carrying a sniper's rifle fitted with telescopic sights.

"By God, if you've killed Harry..." said the stranger, fixing Kolinski with a pair of cold green eyes. Now Kolinski recognised the Englishman who had ridden with him in the ambulance to the hospital in Reval. "Maria, how is he?" without taking his gaze from Kolinski's face.

"Breathing," came the girl's voice. "But he needs a doctor."

"Damn it, there's no wireless or telephone here, is there? Can he be taken back to the base in the *Netopyr*?"

"I'm not a doctor, but my feeling is that he shouldn't be moved any more than necessary, and the *Netopyr* isn't really suitable as an ambulance."

"I'll run back and fetch help," came a voice from behind them. "I used to be the champion long-distance runner at school, and I've kept in training since then. I can take short cuts that the *Netopyr* can't manage and I promise you I'll be faster than any machine."

At the sight of the speaker, a strange look came over Kolinski's face. "You here, Comrade?" he asked curiously. "You told me that you wouldn't be on the *Netopyr* today."

"I'm not your Comrade, you piece of Communist garbage," spat back the other.

"Do you mean to say that you know this maniac, Alexander Alexandrovich?" asked Brian.

"Indeed he does," came another voice. Kolinski looked up to see what appeared to be the whole crew of the *Netopyr* emerging from the hull of the monster, led by a short portly man in Russian officer's uniform, presumably Colonel Petrov. It was he who had spoken. "I'll explain later. Are you all right, my dear?" to the girl. She nodded dumbly. "Lieutenant, keep your rifle to that man's head. Alexander Alexandrovich, start running now. Get a doctor and an ambulance. Bring the doctor here first on a horse or a motorcycle if you can, and let the ambulance follow. You two," pointing to two other men, "bring the handcuffs and irons that we brought with us – you'll find them in the top turret – and make sure this bastard can't get away."

"Not much danger of that for some time," said Kolinski, attempting a feeble grin. "This bitch here has wrecked my manhood, and this bastard here has wrecked my right hand."

The Englishman strode forward and slapped him twice across the face, so hard and fast that Kolinski's ears rang. "That's for calling me a bastard," he said. "And this," driving his fist into Kolinski's face, "is for calling her a bitch." Kolinski heard something crack – either his nose or his cheekbone, or maybe both. He wasn't going to lift his hands up to his face to find out – it was just too much effort.

"Leave him to us, Lieutenant," were the last words Kolinski heard from the fat officer before the black spots in front of his eyes joined up to make a solid impenetrable black veil, and he slumped to the ground in agony as he passed out.

❧

"GOOD SHOOTING THERE, Lieutenant, and good timing," said Petrov to Brian, who was ruefully rubbing the hand he had used to hit Kolinski.

"Not good enough on either count, sir," replied Brian. "Harry looks as though he's in a bad way, and I was far too late."

"At least you were here." Brian had returned from his mission to Petrograd, having delivered Featherington to the submarine, just in time to see the *Netopyr* being fuelled and armed with a machine-gun. Since Harry had briefed him already about the trip, Petrov had not asked too many questions, but had simply handed him a sniper's rifle, and explained that he was to hitch a ride on the rear trail of the *Netopyr*, and jump off at a point which Petrov indicated on a map, before circling round to the rear of where Kolinski was expected to be lying in wait.

Brian was too surprised by Petrov's apparent knowledge of Kolinski's movements to argue, and did exactly as he was told. However, until he had seen Maria coming out of the *Netopyr* with Harry, he had had no idea that she was on board. What, he asked himself, was Petrov doing allowing her to come out and meet Kolinski like this? Brian had met men like Kolinski before, though none had been quite as vicious or remorseless as the Russian, and he had no intention of under-estimating Kolinski's ruthlessness or his cunning.

The way that Kolinski had been standing had made it impossible for him to take a clean shot for fear of hitting either Harry or Maria, until Kolinski, obviously still incapacitated from Maria's knee to his groin (Brian had been unable to stop himself wincing in unconscious sympathy), had drawn his arm back to throw the bayonet at Harry. Brian, for all his skill, had been unable to draw a bead on his target before the throw, and had had to content himself with firing two quick shots at Kolinski's hand after the event. He felt sick at the way that he had let Harry down. If only he'd been a bit quicker, he told himself. He forced himself to look at Harry, who was breathing regularly, but shallowly. The wound in his throat looked as though it had missed the vein, but there was an obscene sucking noise as Harry breathed. Brian had heard that sound before, from men who had been shot in the throat. They usually died quickly, and sometimes very painfully. I should have managed better, he told himself again. I should have been quicker.

"You couldn't have been any quicker than you were," said Petrov, reaching up to put a sympathetic hand on his shoulder. Brian realised that he must have been speaking aloud. "Don't worry," Petrov told him. "You did more than I would have believed possible, under very difficult circumstances."

"I've seen this sort of wound in the past," Brian said. "It's never good news."

Maria was still tending to Harry. She'd taken off her tunic and rolled it up to put under Harry's head. Better her than me, thought Brian. He was amazed that tears were blurring his eyes. After all those months in the trenches. All that mud and blood. All those deaths. This one was different.

"Where's Kolinski?" he asked. Anything to take his mind off Harry.

"He's there, under the *Netopyr*. Don't damage him any more. We are going to want to find out more about him and his organisation and we want him to be able to speak. After we've finished with him, we'll shoot whatever's left of him."

"Shooting's too kind for that bastard," said Brian.

"Come now," replied Petrov. "Where's that sense of British sportsmanship and fair play we hear so much about? If we break the rules of decent behaviour, that makes us no better than them."

"Sod decent behaviour. I just hope that the doctor arrives soon."

"He will be here in a few minutes. Worrying about it won't do a thing to help Harry. Maria's trained to look after wounds – she's been doing some volunteer nursing in the hospitals, and she knows what she's doing. You and I would only be in the way."

"And I think she has a strong personal interest in making sure the patient recovers," added Brian.

Petrov shot him a sharp look. "Yes, I'd noticed that, too. If it wasn't for damned social conventions, I would say that they'd make a good match. You look surprised, eh? I have to tell you, I am regarded as a dangerous radical by many of my extended family. That's one reason I'm not wearing a uniform covered in gold braid and prancing up and down on a white horse in front of regiments of cannon fodder. I think they fear I might infect the troops with revolutionary ideas or something."

"But you don't go along with lunatics like Ulyanov and his gang of Bolsheviks?" Brian was curious. This was a side of Petrov that he had only just discovered.

"No, of course not. They're crazy dreamers. You know, they say they're for the working man, but most of them have never done a day's work in their lives. Ulyanov, for example. A few months at most working as a lawyer, and he talks about the 'dictatorship of the proletariat.' What does he know about the Russian proletariat, living in Zurich? I would wager that I come into closer contact with the Russian proletariat every week than he does in five years. But even so, I would like to see more democracy in our country, and less reliance on one person and his personal whims and fancies. And an end to the corruption and the lies and thievery that make this country weak. I can tell you all this because I can trust your discretion." It was not quite a threat.

Brian nodded. "Thank you for the confidence."

Petrov cocked an ear. "I think I hear the sound of an engine."

"You're right. A motorcycle?"

"I think so," Petrov agreed.

A few minutes later, and Alexander roared the machine to a stop. The army doctor, looking somewhat the worse for his bumpy cross-country ride, dismounted shakily, tightly clutching his bag of instruments.

"This one first, doctor," said Petrov, pointing to Harry.

The doctor bent over the patient and went into consultation with Maria.

"Excuse me," said Brian to Petrov, and walked away from the scene, ostentatiously turning his back on everyone, and staring blindly into the forest.

After about ten minutes, Brian felt a gentle tap on his arm. "Lieutenant Finch-Malloy?" He turned to look into Maria's face. Her eyes were swimming in tears.

"It's not good news, then?" Brian asked. He felt helpless.

"Not bad news, either." She forced a smile of sorts. "At least, the doctor seems to think so. It looks as though he is in a very serious condition, but with proper treatment and care, he should make a perfect recovery. At least that's what the doctor told me." There was an element of doubt in her voice.

"And you're not so sure?"

"I don't know what to believe. I've seen many men with similar wounds in the hospital. Not many of them survived."

Brian said nothing. The tears were starting to his own eyes. He sniffed. "Maria, we have to pull ourselves together. This is not going to help Harry. We have to get him back to the sick bay."

"An ambulance is coming. But they'll have to carry him on a stretcher to the road. The doctor does seem confident he's going to live, though."

⁂

HARRY DIED AN HOUR AFTER he was put to bed in the sick bay, without regaining full consciousness.

"Loss of blood," said the doctor. "And shock. I did all I could."

"I know you did. Thank you, doctor," said Brian, but there was no gratitude, or indeed, any emotion at all discernible in his voice.

Petrov said nothing, but sat impassively. Maria burst into tears and fled from the room. Brian half-rose, but Petrov waved a hand, and Brian sat down again.

"Believe me, Lieutenant. She's better without us at a time like this. Leave her alone for now. Her maid will look after her better than you or I could manage."

"I think we need a few explanations here, Colonel," said Brian, after the two men had sat in silence for a few minutes, each ostentatiously avoiding the other's eyes. "You were expecting that maniac, obviously. You told me that he was waiting to ambush the *Netopyr*. You knew he was armed. Why the hell, begging your pardon, sir, did you send out only Harry and Maria to meet him and deal with him?"

"I also had you as a backup," pointed out Petrov. "To answer your question, because they were the two I trusted most. I trusted your friend's honesty and competence more than I could trust anyone else on the *Netopyr*, and of course I trust my own daughter, and I know she is neither a fool nor a coward."

"And how did you know he was there?"

"We have Alexander Alexandrovich Mikulin to thank for this. When he was studying in England, he made friends with a group of Communists there. Through them he became acquainted with Ulyanov's group, which he joined, and for a while, he was an active member. However, he saw what they were after – and believe me, it's not the class struggle that they would have you believe. Ulyanov is a ruthless seeker after power, and has little interest in the proletarians that he claims to represent."

Brian nodded. "So he agreed to become a police informer?"

"Correct. Not only on account of his personal revulsion against Ulyanov, but also because of the violence that his gang uses. I told you that Kolinski, along with other thugs, has carried out bank robberies, which they call 'expropriations', in a number of towns in Russia and in Georgia. There's one revolutionary, a Iosif Dzhugashvili, whom the police would dearly love to keep in prison. He keeps escaping and returning from exile. He's one of the worst. But he's more the brains of the operation. It's murderers without consciences like our friend Kolinski who are the killers."

"And Mikulin has been in contact with Ulyanov in Zurich?"

"I've been telling him what to write. The Bolsheviks are probably now convinced that we have many more kinds of terrible weapon to crush any attempt at a revolution than actually exist. And Zurich's idea of the *Netopyr* is almost certainly of a more fearsome war machine than the reality."

"Did you know Kolinski was going to come here?"

Petrov shook his head. "No, and when we picked him up on the submarine coming here, I still didn't put two and two together until you noticed his tattoo. Then I was pretty certain that Ulyanov had taken the bait we'd prepared for him. And Mikulin informed me when we arrived that he'd had a message from Zurich informing him that Kolinski was on his way here."

"And you let Harry walk into that?" Brian was still quietly fuming with rage and grief, mixed with more than a little guilt.

Petrov shrugged. "I let my own daughter go there as well," he reminded Brian. His tone was still quiet. "I believed that with a machine-gun pointing at him from the *Netopyr* and a pistol pointing at him from Maria, and an experienced combat soldier to handle him, there would be little danger from Kolinski. He had asked Alexander Alexandrovich to raid the armoury for him, and of course I was informed of all of this. Before Kolinski was presented with all his weapons, I arranged for the main charges to be removed from the grenades, as well as leaving only one round in each of the rifle magazines, again with the propellant removed. In retrospect, we were lucky that Kolinski didn't check everything before he set off to meet the *Netopyr*. And then," he added, rising from the bench where they had been sitting, "there was you to watch over everything. It is fortunate that you came back from Petrograd when you did."

"Hardly fortunate. I let them down," said Brian. "I let Harry down, I let Maria down. I let Harry down," he repeated. He rose to join Petrov, and the two men walked together out of the wooden hut which served as hospital, and now as a mortuary. The sun was low, half hidden by the birch trees surrounding the building.

"You did nothing of the sort," said Petrov. "If your shot hadn't gone through his hand, Kolinski would almost certainly have killed Maria and probably finished off Lieutenant Braithwaite immediately. And I am not convinced that we could have used the machine-gun against him. He'd chosen his position too well for that. There's no way you could have worked miracles on your own, you know. If there's any blame, it's on my side. I underestimated Kolinski, I failed to provide adequate backup, whatever. But I don't want you to go around blaming yourself for something that isn't your fault.

Understood, Lieutenant?" The last words were spoken in a tone that was only half joking.

"Yes, sir."

"So now, we hide our grief. We stiffen our spines, and we work to make this whole sorry business work in our favour. Believe me, Lieutenant, I am not unfeeling, but I have found for myself, as I am sure you have also done in situations like this, that one of the best cures for grief is hard work. And I would suggest to you that when you go back to London, you make it a priority to defeat these Bolsheviks."

"That's not a matter for me to decide, sir." Brian spoke formally. "The British government will make its own decisions on Russian internal political affairs without my help or advice."

"I quite understand, Lieutenant. But I can help provide you with some material that will help convince your superiors. The death of Lieutenant Braithwaite will surely help to persuade them, or so I would imagine. But there are important strategic elements as well. As you know, the current rulers of Russia, as incompetent and venal as they may appear at times, are still managing to tie up large numbers of German and Austro-Hungarian troops on this front. I do not think that the Bolsheviks, should they ever be in a position where they can influence the course of Russian politics, would prosecute the war with the same vigour. Indeed, they might even be in a position where they could force the Russian government into an armistice. And you can guess for yourself what a disaster that would be for the Allies fighting on the Western Front. How many German divisions would that free up to fight in France and Belgium?"

Brian nodded in reluctant agreement.

"And, I remember you telling me in London, what seems like a long time ago, that you knew Ulyanov when you were younger. Let's use that. Let's make the bastard sweat a little. I think we're going to get to know quite a lot about the Bolsheviks by the time we've finished with Kolinski."

"You're not going to use torture, are you?" asked Brian. "Not that I have any liking for the man, but as you told me earlier, that would just be going down to their level."

Petrov shook his head. "I am almost certain that this won't be necessary. Of course, there are those in the Okhrana who would beat all the information out of him, but as long as I am in command here, nothing like that is going to happen. Kolinski is feeling very sorry for himself. He is in considerable pain, thanks to you—"

"—and Maria," Brian added.

"Indeed." Petrov smiled to himself. "He is hungry, exhausted, and in pain. He is extremely vulnerable to any kind of pressure, and I foresee his telling us many interesting things about the Bolsheviks and their activities in the near future. I am sure he saw himself as almost invulnerable and invincible before today. Now he is weak and helpless."

"We thought that in Reval," Brian pointed out.

"But the main difference is that we weren't there to take care of him. We know this man. We know how dangerous he is. And I think we can find his weak spots, don't you?"

Brian nodded.

"And so we are going to carry the fight forward. Weep in a little while if you must, my friend." Brian was astonished by the form of address, as well as by the fact that Petrov had used the familiar form of "you" rather than the formal form of address. He looked up, and Petrov continued. "Yes, I want us to be friends. I would like you to think of me and Maria as your family whenever you come to Russia. So weep later. But now we have work to do. And I am sure that is what our friend Harry Braithwaite would want us to do now."

Chapter 10: Whitehall, London

"I'm afraid we're stuck with each other, whether you like it or not."

"It goes without saying, Finch-Malloy," said C, as Brian sat in the armchair on the other side of the desk, "that we are extremely sorry about Braithwaite. It does seem to me, though, that both you and he acted in the highest traditions of the service, and I am sure that I can persuade the War Office to provide a posthumous medal and a generous pension for his family, at the very least. A medal of some sort for you, as well. And you are now Captain Finch-Malloy, by the way, with all the privileges that appertain to that exalted rank."

"Thank you, sir." Brian was tired. He still felt Harry's loss keenly, but the wound was healing fast.

"And for you, young Finch-Malloy, I want you to keep up with our friend Petrov. I received a glowing letter from him about you – and Braithwaite. We are going to need to keep up our links with Russia, and a personal link like the one you seem to have established is exactly what we need. You may well be meeting Alexei again, and the beautiful Maria."

Brian raised his eyebrows questioningly.

"Yes, I know Alexei of old. My daughter was at school with Maria, and sometimes went to Petersburg, as it was then, for the summer holidays, and Maria sometimes stayed with us. Alexei and I discovered we had a lot in common, and our daughters helped to carry useful information between us without any of our Whitehall friends being any the wiser. You look surprised, young Finch-Malloy. Believe me, after a few years with us, it will be your turn to surprise raw young subalterns with your guile. So any relationship you care to develop with my old friend Alexei and his family will be greatly appreciated at a very high level indeed. Your old chess-playing partner and his gang of revolutionaries are beginning to worry my lords and masters. We need you to help keep an eye on them and to frustrate their knavish tricks. You appear to have made a good start there. Petrov told me about that as well."

"So you want me to join the Embassy staff in Petrograd, sir?"

C laughed, and then stopped abruptly. "No, Finch-Malloy, I don't think that would be in your interests or those of the Embassy. After what happened to young Featherington, I can imagine that you would be less than popular, and receive very little in the way of co-operation from the others there."

"About Featherington, sir. I haven't heard anything. Is he. .?"

"The trial was two weeks ago. He was found guilty. Execution two days later. He could have appealed, but chose not to."

Brian swallowed.

"I know. If it's any consolation to you, I have to congratulate you, if that's the right word to use here, on the way you handled that business with Featherington. A horribly dirty and disgusting job, I know, and you handled it admirably with both initiative and tact. The two don't always go together. Your introduction to the Service has been an unusually bloody and unpleasant one, I'm afraid. But," rising, and leaning forward to look into Brian's eyes, "we need people like you. I'm afraid we're stuck with each other, whether you like it or not.

You've done well, Finch-Malloy. Damned well. Let's carry on the good work together." He held out his hand and Brian took it. "Glad to have you on board."

Chapter 11: Zurich, Switzerland

"After all that we have done for the scum, he betrays me!"

ULYANOV PUT DOWN his pen, and stared at Zinoviev.

"A package from whom?" he asked.

"Comrade Michelov brought it from Petrograd."

"And where's Michelov now?"

"Outside. Waiting to give you the package."

"Let him in." As Zinoviev went to the door, and called for Michelov, Lenin's fingers drummed a tattoo on the desk.

Michelov entered, followed by Zinoviev, who closed the door behind him.

"Sit down, sit down," invited Lenin. His testy mood seemed to have vanished, replaced by an affable friendliness. Zinoviev was not deceived by this. He knew that this affability of Lenin's often masked a towering rage. "You have something for me, I believe, Comrade?" Lenin was still smiling.

"Yes, Comrade," replied Michelov. He was a small man, and Lenin's unblinking gaze seemed to shrink him even smaller inside his ill-fitting jacket. He held out a small square package, wrapped in brown paper. The single word "Lenin" was written in large Cyrillic letters on the top.

"Later, later." Lenin waved away the proffered parcel. "First, I want to know how you came to have this."

"I explained to Comrade Zinoviev here that it all started when I was arrested."

"Arrested? Where? How?"

"As I was returning from a Party meeting. Just outside my front door. They were waiting for me. I was carrying all the papers and notices from the meeting, so there was no way I could pretend to them that I had nothing to do with the Party."

Lenin shook his head in sympathy, but whether real or pretended, there was no way of telling. "So they took you to the Okhrana headquarters?"

It was Michelov's turn to shake his head. "No, Comrade. That really surprised me. I was taken to the Imperial Nicholas Military Academy."

"The devil!" burst out Lenin. "Who arrested you, then, if it wasn't the Okhrana?"

"Comrade, I have to tell you that I have no idea. They were not in uniform, and they didn't salute the sentries as we entered the Academy. And the sentries didn't salute them, either. I notice these things." Lenin said nothing, but made a note on the paper in front of him, and nodded for Michelov to continue. "They took me to an office."

"Which floor?"

"Second. Near the front of the building. Room 282."

Lenin wrote this down, as well, and smiled at Michelov "Well done, Comrade. You certainly do have your wits about you."

Michelov seemed to grow a little taller at the praise. "A man in colonel's uniform was waiting for me. My guards saluted him, all right. One of them called him 'Your Highness,' but he didn't seem too pleased by that."

"Do you know who he was?"

"No, Comrade. But I'm pretty sure that he is connected to the Imperial family somehow, and he's a higher rank than a Colonel from the way that they were behaving round him. They never addressed him by name, so I can't tell you that." Michelov waited for a comment, but there was none. He ploughed on. "He spoke to me politely, and used my full name and patronymic. Offered me tea."

"Which you refused, of course?" asked Zinoviev sarcastically.

"Of course I refused." Michelov was indignant. "I wasn't going to drink their tea. He asked me to sit down. I refused. I didn't want to accept any favours from those people. 'Very well,' he said to me, and stood up himself. Not a tall man when he stood – maybe a little taller than me, but not much."

"And the guards?"

"Right behind me. I couldn't have done anything, even if I had been armed. They'd taken all my papers and my revolver when they first picked me up."

"And then?"

"He told me that he knew you, Comrade, and proceeded to describe this very room to me. This room here in Zurich. He described it perfectly." Lenin frowned. "That inkwell on your desk there," pointing. "That picture of Karl Marx there. The way that your coat – forgive me, Comrade – is thrown so carelessly over the pegs there."

Lenin's face twisted into a bitter scowl. "We have a traitor among us. A spy or an agent provocateur, it would seem." He glared at Zinoviev. "I charge you with discovering the swine and dealing with him appropriately."

"Comrade, that was also my thought," said Michelov. "And I asked this colonel who was the traitor. 'When you next see Vladimir Ilyich,' he told me, 'tell him that I needed no spy to tell me these things.' He was smiling. So of course, I asked him how he knew all this." Michelov paused for dramatic effect, or perhaps out of fear of the consequences of being the bearer of bad news. "They captured Kolinski, Vladimir Ilyich."

Lenin's face contorted in a scowl and his fist smashed down on the table, causing the inkwell to jump, and pencils to fall to the floor. "The devil they did! But Kolinski's tough – he never would have told them a thing about us, even under torture."

"I hate to tell you differently, Comrade, but Kolinski told them all. Apparently even without torture."

The fist smashed down on the table again. "The swine! The treacherous piece of shit! After all that we have done for the scum, he betrays me! The counter-revolutionary weakling!"

Michelov held out a hand, seemingly in supplication for the torrent to cease. Lenin seemed to relax a little, though it appeared to cost him some effort, and Michelov continued. "Kolinski was very badly injured, I was told. His right hand was completely shattered by a bullet, and he received several other very painful injuries. He was given medical treatment, this colonel assured me, and while he was under the anaesthetic that they gave him to lessen his agony, he talked a little." Lenin slumped back in his chair. "When he awoke, they repeated what he had told him, and gave him the impression that they knew much more, and so tricked him into telling them everything that they wanted to know."

"Did they know who he was before he talked? That he was with the Party?"

Michelov nodded. "They did. There was indeed a traitor, Comrade, but it was no-one from here. This officer told me that one of the engineers on the military project that Kolinski was to gather information about had told him that Kolinski was coming."

Zinoviev drew in his breath sharply. Lenin gave him a cold stare. "This, I take it, Comrade Zinoviev, was your trusted source who told us all about your ridiculous machine?" Zinoviev nodded silently. "You really do have a turd for a brain, don't you?" Zinoviev remained silent. "Did no-one out of you herd of incompetent useless swine ever think to check this 'trusted' comrade's loyalty? Am I the only one round here who can think?" There was no answer that could be given to this scream of rage. Lenin let out a massive sigh of exasperation and turned back to Michelov. "Does it get worse?"

"I don't know if this counts as 'worse', Comrade." Michelov was wary, even though Lenin's anger seemed to have been deflected slightly away from him. "This colonel or whatever he was gave an order for 'the Englishman' to join them, and one of the guards who'd brought me went out to fetch him. He arrived in a minute or so. Big tall officer with these green eyes that looked at you like a wolf. He came in and stared at me with those eyes of his for two or three minutes without saying anything to me. Scared me really badly just by looking at me like that."

Lenin, who himself often produced this effect on others, nodded. "No name for this one either?"

"No, he told me he was called Brian Finch-Malloy. He claims that he knew you when you lived in London. You taught him how to play chess, he told me."

The Bolshevik leader's fingers rasped through his beard. "I remember the lad. Good player for his age when I knew him. What the devil is he doing in Petrograd?"

"He's in the English Army. An officer. Working with the Russian Army." Michelov hesitated. "He told me Kolinski had killed his best friend and he had sworn to avenge him."

"So he killed Kolinski after they'd squeezed him dry?"

Michelov shook his head. "Not at all. Kolinski is dead, though, I was told, but he died of shock and weakness. Apparently he'd been through a lot on his way to Kubinka and he was weak from hunger and exhaustion when he was captured. This Englishman gave me this package. It contains a photograph of Kolinski's body in its coffin, he told me. There's also a letter for you explaining what they had learned from Kolinski, including the details of his journey from here. But even if he hadn't died the way that he did, they would have hanged him. He'd killed enough people on his journey to have him executed several times over, even if he hadn't been a Party member."

"And then?"

"He gave me this package. And the colonel gave me a safe-conduct pass and tickets to reach here through France. They told me that they could pick up my family at any time and send them off to Siberia, so I wasn't to think of running away anywhere else. Not that I ever would," he added hurriedly. "So here I am. I told Comrade Zinoviev about the details of my own journey here."

Lenin held out his hand in silence, and beckoned for the package with the other. He accepted it without a word, and gazed at his name written on the brown paper.

"Get out," he said to Michelov after a minute or so. There was no expression in his voice. Michelov looked at Zinoviev, who jerked his head towards the door. Michelov backed away from Lenin, who remained looking at the package, and opened the door, fumbling behind him, before slipping out and closing the door silently.

Zinoviev coughed.

"Yes?" snapped Lenin, who hadn't lifted his eyes from the package.

"What shall we give Michelov for his trouble? He's been through a lot."

"A bullet in the back of the neck," growled Lenin. "He's been turned. You heard him say it himself. They have his family as hostages. He's an Okhrana agent."

"You have no proof, Comrade," protested Zinoviev.

"And you have no proof otherwise," countered Lenin. "Dispose of him as soon as possible." Zinoviev turned to leave. "Not this minute, idiot. Open this package for me." He thrust the package into Zinoviev's hands, and Zinoviev started to unwrap it carefully.

"A black chess piece – a knight," said Zinoviev, laying it on the side of the desk. "A photograph – yes, it's almost certainly Kolinski, but he looks exhausted and hungry. Look – the bastards put a crucifix in the coffin with him. Can you believe it?" He snorted. "Another photograph. This is unbelievable, Comrade. This is the machine that we asked Kolinski to find for us. Look at it."

Lenin took the photograph and examined the picture of the massive machine, with three men posed proudly on it, standing in a clearing against the backdrop of a birch forest. "It's a machine," he sneered. "Only a machine. Revolutions are won with the will of the people, not machines. What else is in there?"

"A letter, Comrade. Presumably the one from the Englishman. Written in Russian, but not by a Russian, if I am not mistaken."

"Give me that letter!" Lenin snatched it out of Zinoviev's hands. He read in silence, punctuated by outbursts of "a load of shit", "the devil take them all" and other choice phrases. Finally he came to a stop.

"It passes all belief, Grigory Yevseevich. Listen to this. This is how he ends his message to me." He read out, " '...and so, Vladimir Ilyich, I wish to conclude this message by reminding you of a lesson you taught me when we played chess together. You said I should never display my full strength to my opponent at one time. I have told you in this letter of some of the things I have learned about you and about your organisation. I have not told you of some of the others. These are things you will have to discover for yourself when we next meet, an event to which I keenly look forward. Of course, it may be that your ignorance of my knowledge means that you may be prevented from meeting me. Accidents will happen, and even in the most trusted of circles, there are those who will clamour for their thirty pieces of silver. With regards, your former chess partner, Brian

Finch-Malloy. You see, I was right about Michelov. Dispose of him immediately. And what do you make of the rest of this shit?"

"This has set back our chance of revolution by several years."

"At the least," exploded Lenin. "We are going to have to develop a completely new strategy. If I understand what he is saying, it appears that Kolinski knew too damned much about what was going on, and has told them everything he knows. It seems that all our comrades in Russia will soon be in Siberia. This damned Englishman has set back the whole revolution and made us start again from the beginning. Get out and deal with Michelov before it's too late, damn you!" Zinoviev quickly hastened to obey.

Lenin sat at his desk, still holding the letter. He read through the last page again, his lips moving silently. He stopped reading, flung down the paper, rose to his feet abruptly, and swept out of the room, slamming the door behind him. The black chess piece teetered on the edge of his desk before falling to the floor.

Gold on the Tracks

I hope you have enjoyed reading Red Wheels Turning. *As well as this book and* Beneath Gray Skies, *there will be more adventures involving Brian Finch-Malloy. The next one in the series (provisionally called* Gold on the Tracks*) will also be set in an alternative history Russia, with psychotic warlords, complex shifts in the political scenery, wealth beyond measure, and Brian attempting to save the day. Here is a brief extract:*

"COME IN AND sit down," said a thin, delicate voice. "I think we need to talk. You, I understand, are Fanny Kaplan, alias Fanya Kaplan, alias Dora Kaplan?" She nodded. "Not your real name, of course, but then how many of us use our real names these days?"

She groped for a chair and sat facing the direction from which the voice came. "Excuse me?" she asked. There was only a slight tremor in her voice.

"Oh, pardon me. I am, as you might already have guessed, Felix Dzerzhinsky, the head of the Extraordinary Commission for Combating Counterrevolution and Sabotage—the Cheka. Some tea?"

She nodded, hardly able to believe what was happening. She had

had no doubt that by this time she would have been beaten nearly senseless, trying desperately not to name comrades and colleagues as the blackjacks thudded on her body. Instead, she was sitting in a comfortable chair, being invited to drink tea with the feared and hated head of Lenin's arm of terror. This needed even more courage for her to accept than the blackjacks would have done. Her headache pounded in her skull. The samovar bubbled and the tea glasses clinked. There must be a third person in the room, she realized. A cup was pressed into her hand.

Dzerzhinsky's voice, but not addressed to her. "You may leave us." A click of heels and after a few seconds, the sound of the door opening and closing.

Dzerzhinsky's voice again, sounding as though he were smiling. "Comrade Lenin is dead. Twenty minutes ago."

She gasped. "Did I … ?"

A chuckle. His face was just starting to come into focus, and she could make out a rather delicate face with a high forehead and a heavy moustache, together with a wisp of beard. The face of a somewhat demonic saint. Or a saintly demon. "No, my dear. You did not. We know that you didn't. You know that you didn't. With all due respect, my dear Miss Kaplan, with your eyesight and lack of experience with a pistol, I wouldn't expect you to be able to hit an elephant at five meters, let alone a middle-aged politician at fifteen."

"You don't sound very upset about his death," said Fanny. Funnily enough, she had little fear of the feared head Chekist now that the conversation had started.

"Oh, really, please. Let's be realistic. Lenin's death is the best possible thing that could have happened to the Revolution."

Fanny stared at him. "I thought…"

An improbable giggle. "Never mind what you thought, my dear. Things are not always what they seem. Shall we simply say that the leadership of the Bolshevik Party is not always the united monolithic front that our late beloved Vladimir Ilyich would have had us believe." His tone was mocking.

"But you're not a Menshevik? Or an SR?"

"Oh no, certainly not. Of course, there are those who were close to VI who were not always Bolsheviks. I need hardly mention names, I think, to someone of your sophistication and intelligence. But please don't misunderstand me. I personally, as a good Bolshevik, would never dream of espousing whatever principles moved you to take that fatal shot."

"But you said I didn't kill him?" She was confused.

"Of course you didn't. That's why you will be executed. So that no-one knows that you didn't kill him." His cheery good nature remained. "Not now, three days from now. The Council of People's Commissars will be informed at regular intervals of the progress of your interrogations." He seemed to be waiting for a sign of fear, and she steeled herself once again not to display anything in front of this monster of terror. A silence. "Well?"

"What do you want me to say? Do you want me to betray all my comrades now? Or would you rather I waited till the Chekists start to break my body and rape me?"

Dzerzhinsky's seeming good humour didn't seem to have evaporated in the least. "Please, you misunderstand me. You have no need to betray your comrades. We know who they are." He pulled out his watch. "And in some cases, by now, who they were," he added meaningfully. "We have no need to interrogate you. All we require you to do is to stay peacefully in your cell, eat the three good meals that will be provided for you each day, and at the end of three days, walk quietly out into the yard at the back of this building. Before that time, we expect you to write your confession of how you plotted Lenin's death. If I may make a suggestion, I would suggest that you write that you acted alone, and you have no knowledge of any other parties to the plot. Of course, we could write all this confession ourselves, but

I think it will sound better coming from you." He paused. "You have no questions?"

She sat silently, considering what she had just been told and working out the implications. So Bronstein, or Trotsky as he now called himself, had engineered Lenin's death, with the help of the comrades she had trusted. She really couldn't have expected anything else from any of the Bolsheviks, whose treachery towards anyone who trusted them, whether friend or foe, was legendary. "May I ask you just one question?"

"Of course."

"My comrades. Did they know of your involvement and that of Trotsky in Lenin's death?" She held her head high, forcing her unfocussing eyes to stare into his face, though the light made her head throb.

He shook his head. "No, they believed they were working for your beloved anti-Bolsheviks. Congratulations, by the way, on your keen intelligence as it relates to the inner workings of the Council. My agent in your little circle, who is now dead, and you will never know his or her name, I am afraid, had no wish to shatter all your illusions. Please do not imagine that any one of your true comrades betrayed you. You must look higher than that for your Judas. Any more questions?" He sounded more like a kindly college professor helping a student with problems than he did the head of the secret police. "No? Then I must bid you good night. It's been a pleasure to have met you. I won't be seeing you again – alive, that is – so it's good-bye, rather than *au revoir*." He must have pressed a hidden buzzer, as the door opened behind her without any audible command having been given.

"Take her back," Dzerzhinsky said. "And treat her well. Proper food, and she must have access to paper and pen. Good-bye, my dear," as she was led out of the room. "Sleep well."

❧

www.ingramcontent.com/pod-product-compliance
Lightning Source LLC
Chambersburg PA
CBHW050522190726
48284CB00003B/905